The
Jigsaw Man

Leigh Goodison

This is a work of fiction. Names, characters, places, and incidents are products of the author's imagination or are used fictitiously and are not to be construed as real. Any resemblance to actual events, locales, organizations, or persons, living or dead, is entirely coincidental.

SHEFFIELD PUBLICATIONS

The text for this book was set in Garamond.

Printed and bound in the United States of America.

10 9 8 7 6 5 4 3

Leigh Goodison

The Jigsaw Man / Leigh Goodison / 2nd edition

Summary:
What if you woke up one morning looking
like a completely different person?

[1. Medical thriller-Fic. 2. Psychological thriller-Fic. 3. Suspense-Fic.]

I. Title

St. Augustus Chronicles [Fic]

ISBN-13: 978-1-945136-01-6 (Sheffield Publications)

Cover design and Copyright: SelfPubBookCovers.com/JTLDes1gn5

For David and Sid

LEIGH GOODISON

The
Jigsaw Man

Leigh Goodison

LEIGH GOODISON

ONE

1986

Under normal circumstances, an unfamiliar car parked in Peter Volk's driveway might have alarmed him. But the Portland detective, already preoccupied with the impending legal separation from his wife, attributed it to a leftover guest from a party given by the teenagers next door. Although *her* friends usually drove battered old Jeeps, not expensive foreign sports cars. In the foreseeable future, whoever was visiting in this cul-de-sac of austere, pre WWII homes would no longer be his concern. He was here to pick up a few of his belongings, nothing more.

As he stepped along the inlaid granite slabs that wove a path toward the entrance of his two-story brick home, he noticed that the grass was overgrown and the sickly flower beds held more weeds than plants. His wife had never been much of a homemaker, even less of a mother. He knew he had a fight on his hands when it came to a single father gaining custody. But it was a fight he was willing to take on for the sake of his son.

A waft of marijuana, mingling tantalizingly with the scent of roses, stopped him for a second as his first instinct was to follow the source and issue a stern warning. Then as he reached the top step he realized that the marijuana was coming from his own house. His mood surged from irritation to anger. Peter unlocked the front door and pressed it gently back into its frame to close it. He hesitated for a moment, apprehensively running his hand over the stubble of his gray crew cut. Wanting at all costs to avoid an unpleasant confrontation, he called out a greeting to Alicia to make her aware of his presence. There was no answer. At this late hour of the morning the television was usually on, but there was none of the typical commotion of cartoons slicing into the silence. His wife and five-year-old son must have gone out shopping. He let out a sigh of relief, grateful at being able to avoid the inevitable confrontation.

He worked his way toward the master bedroom, kicking aside Alicia's crumpled bathrobe and panties that lay in his path. She'd been an exotic dancer before they were married; he supposed it was second nature for her to toss her clothes where she pleased. And he was reasonably certain that this floor wasn't the only place they'd landed during the tumultuous five-year span of their marriage.

He paused at the door of the master bedroom, which was slightly ajar, listening for any sound. Though he could hear nothing, his twenty years with the Portland Police told him something wasn't right; his instincts making him wary. For a moment he had an overwhelming urge to leave. Come back at another time when she was home, even though he dreaded the awkwardness. Then he told himself he was being irrational. His tiny walk-up apartment was clear across town and it was about time he had more than a handful of clothing changes.

He gave the door a slow push with one hand. As it arced open, shadows from the ceiling fan windmilled a rhythmic pattern across the floor, the soft whir from the motor momentarily halting him in his tracks. Then he barged into the room and collided with his divorce attorney, who wore only a pair of boxer shorts, and a startled expression on his handsome face.

For a second it seemed perfectly natural for Reg Forbes to be at his house. But as his mind riffled through the possibilities for an appropriate explanation for Reg's state of undress, he discarded them as improbable. His lawyer had no place being here when he was not. And where, during all this, was Alicia?

"Wait," Reg began, the urgent whine in his voice making him sound pathetic, like a child caught in a forbidden act. He grabbed Peter's arm in an attempt to hold him back.

Peter shook away Reg's grasp and pushed past him into the bedroom. His wife lay naked upon the bed amidst twisted sheets, her back toward him. The glistening long blonde hair she so coveted, tangled with knots from apparent post coital bliss. She rolled over and stretched lazily.

"Reg?" she murmured, "who are you talking to? Come back to bed." Her words were met with a silence so pervasive that her attention jerked sharply toward Reg. But it was her husband who stared back at her with aching, accusing eyes.

In those first interminable moments no one spoke. Alicia did not recoil in shock or cover herself as Peter expected. Instead she jumped out of bed, breasts bouncing. Then she laughed at them standing there with their mouths hanging open like a pair of prepubescent boys, as if she enjoyed being the cause of it all.

"Peter, I can explain," Reg stuttered, though it seemed for once he was unusually devoid of words.

Peter ignored him, instead moving further into the room. He stopped with his back to his dresser, his eyes never leaving his wife. He couldn't tell if he was more upset or hurt. He'd suspected her of infidelity, but not with his attorney, who was handling his divorce. No doubt there were many more and Forbes was just one of a series of men, like himself, who had been seduced by the woman.

But as he stared at Alicia, his pain and rage grew so acute he scarcely comprehended his hand sliding across the top of the dresser. A carved bone letter opener, a gift from a former partner, lay beside a notepad and pen. Peter's fingers found the letter opener, curling around the base.

Alicia saw the movement and her expression slid from mockery to horror. She took two running steps toward Forbes, but Peter caught her mid-stride. His hand flashed forward, plunging the letter opener into her chest until it reached the base. He released his grip, the weapon taking on a life of its own as it quivered in her chest. Alicia crumpled and fell to the floor.

Taking advantage of the diversion, Reg dropped to a squat, fumbling for his trousers. When he leapt up, a .357 Magnum wavered in his hand.

Peter laughed.

"Too late, asshole," he said, and his adrenaline surged. He grabbed Reg's wrist, turned the pistol against him, and squeezed. The lawyer hit the floor with a heavy thud.

Peter stared down at each of the bodies in turn, his breath coming in short, ragged bursts. He swallowed hard to steady his pulse rate. It had taken less than five minutes to walk through the door and eliminate two lives. Although he could feel dagger-like pains rising up through his chest and tightening around his heart, he forced himself to remain calm. He had to protect himself.

Peter walked over to where Alicia lay bleeding, grabbed the letter opener and yanked it out, dropping it to the floor. He touched his fingers to the pulse in her neck, but it appeared that she was already gone. With the tips of two fingers he lowered her lids to avoid what seemed an accusatory stare. He straightened up and glanced around the room, his brain racing through the details he needed to set in place a probable scenario.

He stepped across Alicia's body toward Forbes, not noticing that when he did so he inadvertently kicked the letter opener across the hardwood floor. He pried the Magnum from the lawyer's stiffening fingers then squatted alongside Alicia's body. He watched her for a few moments, savoring the uncustomary quiet, somewhat surprised at feeling nothing at all. Then he knelt and pressed the barrel of the pistol against the puncture wound in her chest. He closed his eyes and fired a single shot into the wound.

Peter reached across her body and grabbed a handful of tissues. After wiping the handle of the pistol clean, he thrust it into the lawyer's outstretched hand. He stepped back and surveyed the bodies. Though his heart pounded painfully in his chest, his rational detective's instincts calculated how the crime scene would appear to investigators. Two bodies; two gunshot wounds; one weapon. He'd let the prosecutor work out a motive. Then he remembered the letter opener.

He stared across the room, trying to recall what he'd done with it and remembered he'd dropped it at Alicia's side. But when he checked around her body he discovered the letter opener was no longer there. As he frantically searched the room, he realized he was running out of time to get out of the house and establish an alibi. Someone might have heard the shots. *Where the fuck was the letter opener?*

Somewhere in the distance came the wail of a siren. And then another. Knowing it would mean a life sentence if he was discovered at the house, he gave the room a cursory once over and stumbled toward the front door.

He jerked the door open and stepped outside. Then just as he was about to turn the key in the lock he heard a sound that chilled him as no death gurgle had ever done.

"Daddy?" came a whimpering cry from the doorway.

TWO

Thirty Years Later

Dr. Thea Donovan stared down at her sleeping patient, his head haloed by yards of newly removed gauze bandaging. She was so elated with the spectacular postoperative results of the reconstructive facial surgery that she scarcely noticed her aching muscles and tired eyes. She had succeeded in transforming a charred, unrecognizable mass of a face into finely chiseled features, uncannily flawless. Almost too perfect, she thought then chided herself. Hadn't her years in medical school, studying plastic and reconstructive surgery, trained her to accept nothing less than perfection?

She was looking forward to speaking with this man, sedated since his arrival ten days ago. A twelve-year veteran of the Portland Fire Department, he had received third degree burns to his face and hands while rescuing two children from a house fire. Besides his anxious mother, an entire waiting room full of well-wishers kept vigil. She had lost track of the number of callers concerned for the welfare of Malcolm Dean.

In the short time Thea spent talking with Malcolm's mother, she felt as if she had come to know him. He had received citations for bravery in his work as a firefighter and was the coach of a Little League baseball team. He was also a devoted son and all too recently, a widower who had lost his wife and young son in a car accident. If anyone deserved to recover from catastrophic injuries and have a chance for a better life it was Malcolm Dean.

She adjusted the drip on the intravenous bags, one that contained vital replacement fluids and anti-rejection medication, and the other that administered painkillers, and checked the injection site on his hand. Slowly the heavily bruised eyelids opened. She felt him looking at her and glanced down into a pair of bloodshot blue-gray eyes. Malcolm attempted a smile that seemed unnatural, more of a grimace, but she quickly attributed that to the rigid newness of the skin. Even so, it was disagreeable, and his eyes seemed to sparkle with a fever not clinical, but malevolent. Her stomach lurched under his scrutiny, her mouth tightening in a concentrated effort not to let her emotions show.

He gave a short laugh that came out as a dry, postoperative croak. "Am I that frightening to look at?"

The squeaks and wheezes from the tracheostomy, a sound that never failed to unnerve Thea, made caricatures of the words. She struggled to regain her composure, allowing her ingrained professionalism to take over.

"On the contrary," she said, forcing a smile. "I think the surgery turned out remarkably well. Maybe even better than we anticipated."

Immediately she regretted her candor, for the man's granite-hard eyes did not soften. He continued to stare at her until she was compelled to look away. As a diversion from the awkwardness of the moment, Thea rang for a nurse.

Several moments later a nurse appeared in the doorway, wheeling a cart laden with a tray of sterile medical instruments. The nurse left the cart at the foot of the bed then retrieved the patient's medical chart. She stood behind the doctor, awaiting her report.

Thea straightened her back and adjusted the stethoscope to her ears.

"Lie back and don't speak," she ordered. She began performing the examination in almost ritualistic fashion, perfunctorily relating blood pressure readings, temperature, and postoperative findings to the nurse who jotted them upon Malcolm's chart. Then she leaned closer to inspect the Reflesh. Her discomfiture at the patient's demeanor vanished as she admired her work.

During the eight-hour surgery it had been necessary to rebuild Malcom Dean's crushed cheek and jaw with new facial bones made from synthetic material using a 3D printer. Before surgery, the prep team had shaved away his burned hair, which now revealed the reddened outline where the Reflesh ended and natural skin began. It was almost like sculpture with an unusual medium, constructing the framework then covering the form with the synthetic skin created by using the patient's own DNA. But there was an unanticipated translucence to the finished product that gave him the appearance of a living waxwork.

"How does it look?" He was frowning now.

"You're wrinkling my handiwork." She laughed but Malcolm did not. He seemed offended. Deftly she avoided his question by changing the subject. "Your postoperative signs are excellent. The tracheostomy will be removed tomorrow and you should be able to be discharged in a few days. But in the meantime, your mother has been waiting a long time to visit you. Shall I ask her to come in?"

Malcolm stared at her, narrowing his eyes. "I want to see what my face looks like first."

Thea hesitated, glancing around the room for a hand-held mirror, but there was none. "As soon as you're able to stand on your own you'll be able to see the results when you go into the bathroom. I'll ask the nursing staff later if they can locate a mirror."

But her deferral of his request had the opposite effect of her intent and only seemed to make him think she was hiding something from him.

"Why can't I have a mirror now? Until I know what I look like, I don't want to see anyone." He paused for a few moments, looking introspective. "Actually, I'd prefer it if no one saw me right now."

Though surprised at his reluctance to allow his mother in, she managed to conceal it. Unpredictability was common after anesthesia and extensive reconstructive surgery. Preparing the patient for the shock at their change in appearance was all part of the process. But was this postoperative trauma or something deeper? He'd been evaluated by a neurosurgical team before she'd been called in, with no unusual findings. Despite all the injuries to his face, his brain scans had come back normal. Fortunately it was routine for a staff psychiatrist to work with burn patients in cases of major readjustment. She would have to watch him closely over the next few days to find out if he would need one.

"It's your mother, Malcolm," Thea coaxed. "She's been here almost the entire time you've been in hospital. She even slept the first few nights in the waiting room. Won't you let her come in?"

He tightened his lips and turned his head away. Thea took this as acceptance and motioned for the nurse to call Mrs. Dean from the waiting room. She pulled a straight-backed hospital chair, tucked in the corner of the tiny private ward, closer to the bed. Then she sat on the chair nearest the I.V. pole and covertly observed Malcolm as his mother entered the room.

But suddenly it wasn't Malcolm who concerned her. Thea cringed, unprepared for the shock on Meredith Dean's face. Before she could speak, Meredith crossed the room, grabbed her by the arm and dragged her off the chair into the hallway.

"What have you done to him?" she hissed.

* * * * *

Several months earlier, Thea had attended a seminar on computerized medicine in one of the glass monoliths of the Portland Convention Center. As a plastic and reconstructive surgeon, it was a necessary part of her continuing education to seek out information on the latest medical technology and updates on patient care. Erik Sorenson, a computer program designer, had been a featured guest speaker. Though his privately owned company covered almost every aspect of computer programs for industrial and business applications, his own medical background was in the computerized development of prosthetic and automated mechanical limbs.

After Sorenson ended his presentation and the applause died down, a line of attendees waited to speak to him. He was still answering questions as he packed away his laptop and presentation materials so the next speaker could take his place. Not interested in the remaining sessions, Thea stood, squeezed past the horde and headed toward the exit, ideas for new surgical techniques swirling in her head.

"Wait!"

Startled, Thea whirled around to see Erik Sorenson motioning to her from the podium. When the remaining crowd noticed his haste in trying to get her attention, they began to dissipate and move away. Thea stood waiting patiently, her curiosity piqued as she pondered what his interest in her might be.

Erik finally reached her, freed up his right hand and held it out to her. She shook it briefly, though still perplexed.

"If I'm not mistaken, you're Dr. Thea Donovan. The reconstructive surgeon?"

She nodded and watched as his eyes dropped to the identification tag pinned to her jacket that gave her name, profession and city, as if to verify her identity. As they'd never met in person, how he'd known who she was before he called out to her, she couldn't say.

He cast several furtive glances around them before he continued, sounding a little embarrassed. "Please don't take this the wrong way. I'm aware of the research you've been doing and have a proposition I'd like to discuss with you over coffee."

She looked at him with a combination of curiosity and caution. He was not handsome in a conventional way, with fine-boned, aquiline features. In direct contrast to his youthful appearance, his collar-length, straight sandy hair had a pure white streak in front. Whether it was artificially bleached or natural, Thea could not tell. Though he was just Thea's height as she stood before him in low heels, his gauntness and the pin-striped black cotton shirt and tan Dockers he wore made him appear taller.

Thea demurred. She'd attended the seminar to learn what final steps would be needed to ready the experimental surgery she'd been working on for patient use, but she wasn't ready to divulge details. Unable to trust anyone to assist with her research since the death of her mentor, Dr. Stanton, she'd forged on alone. There had been no one with whom she could share new triumphs or results, no one with whom she could brainstorm when she ran into a blockade. She sighed, knowing it was a gamble, but she realized she had to trust someone, sometime, at some stage.

"I've read articles about the developments you've done with medical computer programming. But my research is not at a stage where I'm ready to share or collaborate. I need to keep the extent of my progress under wraps, so to speak, until it's ready to be tested."

"You're right to be cautious," he replied. "But from what I've heard of your project, I know you could use help. The entire process would have to be prepared through a computer program, which, if I'm not mistaken, goes beyond your capabilities."

He gave a quick questioning tilt to his head. Thea nodded slowly, still trying to decide whether it was a good idea to hear what he had to say or leave before she inadvertently revealed too much. She waited while Erik shook hands with a few of his colleagues and bid other participants goodbye. Then they walked out together to the corridor and stepped into the elevator. She pressed the button for the main floor and glanced over at Erik.

"All right," she said, "I'll hear you out. Before we discuss anything, though, I need your word that whatever I tell you will remain confidential, just between the two of us."

"Agreed," he said.

As they entered the nearly deserted coffee shop on the ground level, Erik muttered, "Two coffees, please," to the passing server. Thea headed toward a table near the back. Erik took a seat opposite her, his hazel eyes watchful as he waited for her to speak. Thea clasped her hands on the table in front of her, and glanced around once more to make certain they were not overheard.

"What are you afraid of, industrial spies?" Erik asked with a laugh.

"When you hear what I have to say, you'll believe industrial spies could be feasible."

His smile vanished. He seemed as if he was just about to say something when the waitress appeared with the coffee and a frown that seemed to say 'we're closing soon'. Erik picked up six packets of sugar, tore off the tops and dumped them into his coffee. He stirred twice then took a sip. Thea stared at him with something close to awe. He grinned.

"Never gotten rid of my sweet tooth. Tell me more about your project."

"Several years ago when I was still a resident at the University of British Columbia Hospital, I was fortunate to have Dr. Oliver Stanton as one of my preceptors." She looked up at Erik, expecting to see a flash of recognition at the name but he just stared blankly back at her.

"He was a leader in cranial-facial surgery in Canada. Cranial-facial surgery is a technique developed to correct skull deformities, usually congenital, by strategically breaking the skull and refitting it like pieces of a puzzle to create a more cosmetically acceptable result."

Because Erik's expression had become dubious, she hastened to clarify the concept for him.

"I'm oversimplifying, of course," she went on. "There are many other steps to this. The procedure involves the skill of neurosurgeons, plastic surgeons, ophthalmologists, and occasionally even psychiatrists. But the result was that a patient who previously had severe deformities could now lead a normal life.

"After we had improved cranial-facial surgery, we began treating patients who had suffered facial injuries from car accidents. But even though the bone structure was repaired, the remaining scar tissue was often disfiguring. There were also the burn patients to consider. So Dr. Stanton moved on to artificial skin research."

She stopped for a moment to sip her rapidly cooling coffee. Erik sat silent, but motioned to the impatient waitress for a refill.

"Are you following?" Thea asked.

"Yes. It sounds fascinating. Go on."

"You probably know that in the past, a major difficulty in treating burn victims was where to obtain enough skin to graft over the burns. Like many other researchers, Dr. Stanton and I were working together on a new idea for a synthetic skin. To prevent rejection we used the patient's own DNA to clone their skin cells. Eventually we were ready to try our final experiment: grafting it onto living tissue.

"Unfortunately, Dr. Stanton suffered a massive stroke and died before it could be tested. I had to go on as best I could. It's taken me several years but I believe I now have the skin, which we named Reflesh, ready for transplant."

"And that's where I might be able to help, right?" Erik interrupted. He ripped open another packet of sugar, poured it into his palm and tossed it into his mouth.

Thea watched him, feeling as nauseated as if she'd eaten it herself.

"Yes," she replied, "I would need you to develop a computer program that will process the artificial skin into a 'mask' that would be graftable onto a patient's face. Once the bone structure is intact, a veneer of skin could be grafted into place with laser surgery. The thickness of the skin will depend on the extent of the injuries needed to be covered."

Erik took a pen out of his shirt pocket and began drawing on a napkin. Thea sat quietly, watching him and waiting for a response, wondering if she had chosen the wrong man in which to confide. After a moment he stopped sketching and slid the napkin over to her, using his pen as a pointer. He had drawn a roughly three dimensional graph outline of a human face.

"First we need the patient's CAT scan. Sensors placed on

strategic points of the skull will give us precise measurements to gauge a mask made from skin. A previous photograph or maybe even a detailed sketch of the patient can be scanned into the computer to give it the patient's original features. Once we process the information there should be no problem in forming blueprints for a skin mold."

Thea gazed at Erik with respect. Although he appeared to have immediately gathered the concept, she knew refining the procedures could take years. They would have to learn and create together, but would they be compatible in such a close liaison? Only time would tell. She did not consider herself a risk-taker but she knew she would have to take some eventually to achieve her goal.

She tried to convince herself that the timing was right in collaborating with Erik. If she hesitated now she might miss the opportunity because there were already researchers working on similar projects. Though it was unlike her to seek notoriety in this way, she felt Dr. Stanton would have wanted her to proceed. Besides, this Erik Sorenson intrigued her. He had the background and the brains to provide the missing piece of the puzzle to her project.

"You've outlined what I visualized, but would never have been able to achieve on my own. I hope we can complement each other's work as well in the future."

Erik shook his head in wonderment, his eyes lighting up with excitement. "This procedure has unlimited possibilities. Do you know what it could mean in terms of money-making potential? Women and men will be lining up at our door, clutching photos of their favorite celebrity or old photos of themselves, waiting for the face of their youth to be grafted back." He stared at the ceiling as if fantasizing about the future.

Thea felt a small pang of forewarning. "A beautification process for the wealthy was not what I had in mind," she said then winced. Her voice sounded harsh even to her. *How could he even consider exploiting the Reflesh product?*

"I want it to be new hope," she went on. "Maybe the last

hope for those patients who otherwise would lead the life of a social outcast; a life of being stared at, shunned, and ridiculed. Not a race of perfect, wrinkle-free clones with aged bodies." She stood up quickly. The impatient waitress moved in to take their cups.

Erik raised his hands as if in surrender and shook his head. "Don't get so upset. I didn't mean to cheapen your ideals. This is your project; we'll do things your way." He smiled in an ingratiating way at the still scowling Thea, who felt her mood beginning to soften.

"If you agree to pursue this project with me on an integrity basis and not as a fountain of youth, get-rich-quick scheme, we can work together. If not, this conversation never happened."

Erik stood and dropped a ten dollar bill on the table.

"I apologize. I didn't know what your ultimate goals were. Of course I'll do my bit for the humanitarian benefit of it. Eventually, though, if and when the traumatic injuries lessen we could teach this as a cosmetic procedure. That, at least, would help defray the cost of the surgery and future research." He turned and helped himself to a handful of sugar packets, ignoring a glare from the waitress.

"It's probably none of my business," Thea said, "but your dentist must love you."

Erik looked her straight in the eyes, without smiling. "You're right," he replied. "It's none of your business."

Thea stared back at him for an awkward moment and then broke into a short, rueful laugh.

"Call me tomorrow." She produced a business card and passed it to him. "We'll discuss our partnership in more detail and then have a contract drawn up. I'll make arrangements to have you brought on staff at St. Augustus Hospital where I'm conducting the research. But I want to be working in complete privacy on this until we get a patent application on file."

She held out her hand and Erik extended his. They shook on the deal and walked away to their cars. A surge of excitement passed through her now that the early basis for their partnership was in place. She congratulated herself on having registered for his seminar, never dreaming he'd be interested in collaborating. Even so, she couldn't help wondering how he seemed to have already known who she was when he approached her. Her research had been kept under complete confidentiality until she had shared it tonight.

THREE

Over the next few months Thea and Erik worked hundreds of late evenings together, first on the program itself, then on designing the copying machine that would manufacture a three dimensional skin mold. When they'd finally created an acceptable mask from the face of a donated cadaver, she was ready to begin their first experimental surgery.

"Do you want to assist me, or would you be more comfortable just observing?" she asked Erik. A successful transplant, even on a corpse, would determine if their project was getting close to being used on live patients.

"Probably neither," Erik replied, appearing paler than usual. "I've been known to faint at the sight of blood."

"Good news for you," Thea said with a laugh. "The guy's dead. There won't be any blood." Then she regretted her glibness because Erik's expression had morphed from reticence to alarm. She squeezed his arm.

"Hey, it's not necessary. I've worked by myself for so long that it's second nature now. I keep forgetting that not everyone has the stomach for this sort of thing." But Erik surprised her when he shook his head.

"No, it's okay. I just have a huge aversion to being around dead and dying people. But I think it's important that I assist you and see how it's done. We're in this together."

Although Thea felt a moment of misgiving, wondering if she'd be picking him off the floor before the procedure was through, she led him to the scrub area to don surgical garb and mask.

"Here," she said, handing him a jar of Vicks VapoRub. "Rub a bit of this under your nose, it'll help mask unpleasant smells. If you feel nauseated, or as if you're about to pass out, force yourself to grin. It's an old trick I learned from doing an elective in pathology. It actually works."

He nodded, following her into the operating room where the corpse of a recently deceased man lay on the steel table, covered with a light sheet. Though the bone structure was intact, the skin looked as if it had been removed with a vegetable peeler. Erik wavered, clutching the end of the table for support.

"You okay?" Thea said, not looking at Erik, or waiting for an answer. The Reflesh version of the dead man's new face lay in a saline bath on the instrument table, ready to be applied.

"Get on the other side of the table," Thea ordered, no longer concerned about how Erik was feeling, "and help me place the Reflesh on this poor guy's face, then I'll get you to help with the laser."

Erik followed her instructions and as they worked together, seemed to lose his discomfort. After several hours they had the Reflesh grafted onto the patient and were able to view the results. She pulled down her face mask and patted Erik gently on the back.

"What do you think?"

Though he let his mask remain on, he shook his head in wonderment. "It's incredible. I can't believe you've done it."

"*We've* done it," she corrected him. "I think you missed your calling. You have a surgeon's hands."

Erik gave a short laugh. "But not the bedside manner."

Together they moved away from the operating table and headed back to the scrub room, buoyed with the results of their first trial.

After that Erik assisted Thea on all the experimental surgeries she performed. Although he was initially still queasy and unsure of himself, it wasn't long before he was perfecting their techniques on his own without her help, though with her supervision.

Eventually they had the Reflesh operation running to their mutual satisfaction. After receiving FDA approval, the skin was in the last stages of preliminary testing for live transplant. The quality of the artificial skin was superb and almost as lifelike as natural flesh. Thea began using it to graft small localized burn areas on patients. Then she created a new ear for a man who'd had his torn off in a car crash. To her delight, there were no cases of rejection.

Because it was colorless, matching the complexion tones of the recipients would not be a problem as it had been with traditional skin grafts using tissue from other areas of the patient's body. As the patient's circulation improved, the Reflesh took on the natural skin tone color. But Reflesh lacked the ability to regenerate skin cells and its delicacy gave it potential for infection. As the patients she'd treated thus far had just minor burns, it was impossible to tell if the new tissue would continue to live and grow on patients with injuries so devastating that they would require the full Reflesh mask. And of course, the cadavers they'd used for testing could not provide this information.

Now they were ready to present the complete computer-assisted facial graft procedure to the hospital. It seemed to Thea that she spent nearly as much time convincing the hospital's Board of Directors of the viability of the project as she had in developing it. After several weeks of appearing before barrages of medical panels and board meetings, she finally had approval to go through on a trial basis with the "Reflesh Procedure," as they christened it. It was time to apply their techniques to their first patient. Ten days later in the early morning hours, Malcolm Dean was brought into Emergency.

Thea, at home sound asleep after spending a long, grueling day at her clinic, turned over to discover the source of the persistent ringing in her ear. Though aware she was the only plastic surgeon on call that night for Emergency, she opened her eyes grudgingly. The dim glow from the hanging lamp she always left on at night cast looming shadows across the bedroom's dark mahogany paneled walls.

She glanced at the glowing red numbers of the digital clock and saw it was 3:15 a.m. With a start she realized that the ringing came from the phone. She grabbed it quickly, sighing with relief at the silence.

"Dr. Donovan," she said, mumbling the words. She closed her eyes and with one hand pulled the comforter up to cover her shoulders.

"St. Augustus Emergency." The curt reply on the other end was the Emergency physician working the undesirable graveyard shift. "A patient was just brought in with third degree burns to his face. Fortunately the rest of his body escaped unscathed because of protective clothing—he's a Portland firefighter—but he's not going to be posing for beefcake calendars for a while."

Thea sat up quickly, her professional life taking over.

"Is he stabilized?"

"Yes. The pulmonary and cardiology guys are finished with him. The neurological team had CAT Scans done of his skull and despite the severity of his head injuries they don't see any indications of brain damage. I don't know if you can do anything with him right now because there's a lot of edema, but you'd better have a look at him as soon as you can."

Thea suppressed a groan, mentally calculating how long it would take to reach the hospital at this time of night. "I should be there in half an hour. I'm on my way."

She hung up the phone and swung her legs over the edge of the bed, digging her toes deep into the fleece of the sheepskin rug. To be needed in Emergency did not make getting out of bed at this ungodly hour any more desirable.

She struggled into her clothes, not caring what she wore. There wasn't much time. Third degree, full-thickness burns to the face meant that the skin was necrotic. If she was to evaluate this patient for the Reflesh Procedure she'd need Erik's assistance with the program. Could she reach him in time? But Erik Sorenson, true to form, appeared to have been still awake, no doubt hard at work on another project.

"Don't you ever sleep?"

"Only when I have to." She could almost see him smile over the telephone. "What's up?"

"I think we've got a live one." She sighed. "At least for now because he sounds pretty serious and might not make it. If he doesn't die from damage to his lungs due to smoke inhalation, he'll be faced with years of painful skin grafting. It looks as though this new procedure is his only alternative."

"All right," said Erik. "I'll meet you at the hospital."

Thea hung up the phone, thankful for Erik's reliability. Without his brilliant mind this project would still be in embryonic stages. She was fortunate to have found him when she did or the Reflesh project might never have happened.

She glanced at the open bedroom window and noticed water dripping onto the sill. Quickly she slammed it shut. Then out of habit, she grabbed her medical bag and threw in a change of clothes, just in case. No matter how many years they'd been in practice, a surgeon never knew how long they'd be stuck in the operating room.

As she stepped through the adjoining garage door and slid behind the wheel of her Mercedes convertible, she was relieved to discover that, despite yesterday's sunshine, she'd had enough sense to leave the top up. She pressed the automatic garage door opener and the door lifted, jerking and screeching, as she placed the car in reverse and carefully backed down the driveway. Deep in contemplation of the Reflesh Procedure's surgical premier, she scarcely noticed Portland's spring drizzle cascading down the windshield like rivulets of tears.

* * * * * *

Thea stared at Meredith, perplexed. She had spent considerable time explaining the nature of this experimental operation to Malcolm's mother. She liked the look of silver-haired lady who, even after days waiting for her son, still looked as fresh as if she'd stepped out of a salon, dressed in tailored white slacks and a navy blazer from Nordstrom's. But more important, Thea recognized that Meredith Dean had the formidable, tenacious mothering skills of a she-bear, and was the polar opposite of the woman who had given birth to her.

Her own mother, at sixteen pregnant and addicted to drugs, had abandoned Thea at birth, leaving her with strict Catholic grandparents. Determined not to make another mistake in raising a child, they were overprotective and stifling, resulting in her becoming shy and introverted. As a teen she had buried herself in her studies, a model student with almost no social life. Tall and angular, she excelled in athletics, and her choice of loose-fitting, almost baggy clothing, seemed purposely chosen to hide her femininity.

Seldom relying on a personal stylist, she trimmed her light brown hair to shoulder length, allowing it to bounce freely around her squareish jaw line. With large, dark-lashed doe eyes, she generally eschewed the overkill of cosmetics. Her lifelong desire had been to please her grandparents and be as little like her mother as possible, and in that she succeeded.

Now Thea searched Meredith's face, trying to put herself in the woman's position, how she would feel if it were her child who had undergone such a drastic change in appearance.

"I know the skin is unlined, but that will come back over time. It's not that different from a facelift, where the skin is tight at first. Right now there's just a matter of healing and adjustment."

"Adjustment! He looks like a bloody mannequin," Meredith almost shouted. "Not a bit like himself."

"What do you mean? The computer didn't err in duplicating the photograph and transferring it to the skin mask. We checked and double checked everything." For the surgery, Malcolm's mother had provided Thea with a semi-profile shot of him, the most recent photo she had.

Meredith opened her wallet and removed a small snapshot. With tears threatening to spill onto her cheeks, she handed it to Thea. The photograph was of Malcolm and a small boy who looked just like him. Even in the tiny photo, she could easily discern a handsome, dark haired man with a lopsided grin, a bent nose, and somewhat irregular features.

Thea stared at the photo for several moments digesting this new bit of information. A cold sliver of ice seemed to crawl up her back, causing her to shiver. It was scarcely possible. They had anticipated and corrected all the problems with the sebaceous glands, sweat glands, and nerve supply to the face. Every obstacle had been foreseen. Or so they thought.

The fact remained. They had made one incalculable error. Malcolm in profile was not Malcolm when viewed head-on; anteriorly. She should have realized that rarely is one half of the face the mirror image of the other. When the computer automatically filled in the missing area of the face in the profile shot, it created a bizarre, human scion.

* * * * *

"Why couldn't we talk at the hospital?" Erik had just arrived at Thea's home in Portland Heights, panting as if he was out of breath. "I damned near got sideswiped on that godawful, twisting road. This better be good."

Thea gave him a solemn look and waved a hand toward a large brocade sofa. "You'd better sit. It's not good. In fact it's very bad."

She left the room and marched into the kitchen. When she returned she was carrying a bottle of brandy and two empty snifters. She handed Erik a glass. He held it while she poured from the bottle. Then she sat on a matching loveseat opposite him and filled hers.

"We've fucked up royally," she said.

Erik swallowed hard and set his glass on the *T.V. Guide* lying on the coffee table. "Mind clarifying that?"

"Did you notice anything odd about the surgical results on our first patient? Anything unusual about his appearance?"

Erik shrugged and took another mouthful of brandy, rolling it around on his tongue. "Nothing other than if I looked like he does now I'd be beating the women off with a stick. Not too hard to take, if you ask me."

"What if I told you that he bears little or no resemblance to the man he was before the fire? I saw another picture of him. By comparison he now looks like a freak, or at least his mother thinks so."

"Why?" He contemplated for a moment. "Because he doesn't resemble her anymore? Let him grow into his face. It's true the Reflesh tissue is a little rigid at first, but normal character lines will begin forming soon enough every time he smiles or frowns. It's the ultimate face-lift." He stood up, walked over to Thea and sat beside her. He reached behind her head and began massaging her neck. "I really don't see the problem."

Thea shook his hand away, irritated. "There's something sinister about the outcome, I'm just not sure what."

Erik shrugged and leaned back against the sofa. "Get Steiner to talk with him tomorrow, straighten the guy's head out a bit. If nothing else, we can always correct our mistake using a better photograph."

"Steiner *might* be able to help," Thea said, referring to St. Augustus's staff psychiatrist, Sheldon Steiner, "but you have to remember, a falling beam shattered Malcolm's cheek and jaw bones. I had to rebuild damned near the whole side of his skull before we applied the Reflesh, so now his bone structure is different."

She paused to take a drink. "If we'd had previous skull x-rays to go by it wouldn't be a problem, we could just reform the bone using those as a reference. But we don't. So he'll never look quite the same no matter how we smash and rearrange the bones."

"Then maybe *you* should take two Aspirin and call Steiner in the morning. The guy looks better than before, right? So what's the worst that could happen?"

"I'll get sued," moaned Thea. "Or lose my license. Or get deported."

To her annoyance he chuckled, and their eyes met and held. She felt her mood lighten. It seemed odd that it was only then that Thea realized how attractive Erik could be outside the sterile environment of the hospital. They'd been thrown together for months, how could she have missed it? Erik's eyes softened, making Thea wonder if he might be feeling the same way.

She stared at him for a moment seeing him through new eyes—alcohol blurred eyes—as a man rather than just a coworker. A flash of warmth rushed over her chest and up her neck. She glanced away, embarrassed. Then, in spite of her halfhearted motion to cover her glass, he leaned forward and refilled it, though she noted that he hadn't poured another for himself.

Loosen up, she thought, it's been too long. He watched as she drank the brandy in one long swallow then took the glass from her hand. He shifted his weight and leaned closer so that their shoulders touched. With a barely perceptible motion he placed his hand under her hair, caressing her neck. When Thea didn't object, his other hand slid along the inside of her thigh.

Thea closed her eyes and exhaled heavily. Erik moved nearer still, nuzzling along her throat, his tongue doing intricate things that made her feel as if she were melting into the sofa. She put her arms around him, pulling him on top of her. She felt him growing hard against her thigh and she could not stop herself from pressing closer to him.

He fumbled with the buttons on her shirt and unhooked her bra. Slowly he slid her shirt back over her shoulders and let it drop around her waist. He hesitated for a moment until Thea realized he was looking at the crescent-shaped birthmark on her shoulder. He traced it with his fingers but the physical imperfection of it made her feel self-conscious and uncomfortable. Then he said something that at any other time would have disturbed her.

"That would be easy to remember if anyone had to identify your body," he said. Failing to see any humor in it, she nipped him lightly on the neck.

He lowered his lips to her breasts and when Thea thought she would scream from wanting him, he slid her skirt up and thrust down hard. She gasped, not from pain, but a combination of release and ecstasy. During the heat and passion of the moment she felt as though she had never wanted anyone more than this.

But when they separated, damp and exhausted, she gazed

at his profile beside her on the sofa and realized that she didn't know him at all. And she realized something else. Erik had not experienced the same release. She felt a momentary flush of shame at letting her guard down and losing the barrier that separated her personal and professional life. She couldn't help wondering how this evening's development would affect their working relationship. Or their personal one, for that matter.

FOUR

Sheldon Steiner, Chief of Psychiatry at St. Augustus, had read Malcolm Dean's postoperative chart several times, each time trying another way to psychoanalyze this guinea pig of Dr. Thea Donovan's. His vehement disapproval of the new surgery was no secret to any of the staff at St. Augustus, but the undercurrent of friction between he and Thea lay deeper than just professional conflicts.

A former chain-smoker now in his early sixties, Sheldon Steiner personified what Thea thought of as a gray man—gray hair, pallid, grayish skin and a somber, humorless gray personality. Sensing his hostility toward her, Thea had attempted to locate another psychiatrist to examine Malcolm. But Dr. Steiner's tenure made it nearly impossible to replace him.

Now, as he entered Malcolm's ward, Dr. Steiner had to struggle to keep the shock from his face. He took a moment to assess the situation. The bed sheets, slashed by some razor-sharp object, hung in strings and tatters. Food smeared on the walls patterned it like bizarre wallpaper; windows and mirrors splattered to coordinate. Pages ripped from magazines lay about the room like fallen autumn leaves.

Though the man in the hospital bed appeared no different from patients he had counseled before, he did not fit the standard mold that most of Steiner's burn patients fell into, and it wasn't only because he was extraordinarily handsome. There was a strange uncanniness to his appearance, something that Steiner had never encountered before. Perhaps it was that this man looked more like a department store mannequin than any live person he had ever seen.

Still, Dr. Steiner marveled at the quality of Thea Donovan's work and gave her credit for talent. There was no doubt even in his mind that this surgical technique would make history. But more important was the benefit to patients and surgeons everywhere.

For a moment Dr. Steiner experienced a pang of jealousy. It wasn't that he wanted the project to fail, though he did feel that it ought to be delayed. In his opinion, the Reflesh alone needed far more testing and research. But there was something else more important to Dr. Steiner. At stake was a bequest from a former patient of the hospital, a grant to the Department with the most outstanding or promising research.

Dr. Steiner had been working on the research and rehabilitation of patients suffering from post-traumatic stress disorder, or PTSD. He felt the grant should rightfully be his. The research took long hours, with funding scarce. This grant would enable him to hire assistants to interview and counsel the victims and perform the tedious studies and documentation for which he lacked the time. Though he realized that this Reflesh program would one day be a winner, he believed his research—healing from within—was just as important.

With this in mind, he surveyed Malcolm's room, feeling empathy for the patient though little remorse for his thoughts about his colleague. Obviously the man had experienced a complete psychotic break to have done all this damage to the room. He wondered if any of the cleaning or nursing staff were aware, or if they were just avoiding contact with the patient at all costs.

A note on Malcolm's chart had him tentatively scheduled for discharge early next week. Dr. Steiner's findings after interviewing Malcolm would have a substantial bearing on whether or not he should be released, especially if he didn't feel that Malcolm could function independently. Judging from what he could see, it would be unlikely he'd recommend releasing the patient. In fact, it was highly probable that this patient suffered from PTSD, as well.

Steiner gave Malcolm a lukewarm smile, the best he could muster under the circumstances. Like a predator scrutinizing his prey, the man had not moved or taken his eyes off Steiner since he entered the room. He wore a hospital gown stained and smeared with food and other substances Dr. Steiner chose not to identify. A sour pungency filled the air.

"Hello, Malcolm. I'm Dr. Steiner," he said. "We'll be having several chats together before your release next week. If you have any concerns, problems or questions, we can discuss them. I'm at your disposal."

Malcolm stared at him. "I don't need a shrink."

"No, you may not," Dr. Steiner replied, "but it's my job to assess if you're having trouble adjusting to any radical changes from the surgery."

"I'd say my face is pretty fucking radical, wouldn't you?" Malcolm exploded. "Do you know what I looked like before?"

Dr. Steiner suddenly found himself at a loss because he had never even seen a photo of Malcolm. He had read a note on the chart that intimated Malcolm's appearance had changed considerably. He had attributed this to the burns and disfigurement.

Suddenly Steiner realized that Dr. Donovan had gotten more than she intended; obviously this patient had deep psychological issues. Possibly he was even irreversibly psychotic. The question was, did he have these tendencies before the surgery, or was this a manifestation due to shock and trauma of the Reflesh Procedure results? He managed to suppress his glee that the answers to these questions might be valuable tools to thwart Thea Donovan's progress.

He noticed that a pair of bandage scissors left by a careless employee lay on the floor beside the bed. No doubt they'd been used by the patient to alter the drapes and bedding in the room. Steiner covered them with his foot and gently punted them safely out of the way under the bed. Crossing his arms, he pressed the chart close to his chest then sat gingerly on a chair less defiled than the others.

"I understand the trauma you've been through," he said. "You've experienced a series of losses that would be the breaking point for anyone." He paused. "Were you under the care of a psychiatrist after the loss of your wife and son?"

Malcolm glared at Dr. Steiner. "I don't wish to discuss my family with you. Their deaths have no bearing on what's happened to me."

Steiner gave no outward sign of surprise. He expected denial in patients experiencing severe emotional problems.

"Your chart says that you had a young son who died in the accident with your wife." This time he saw Malcolm flinch.

"You really go for the jugular, don't you?"

"We have to deal with your problems, not just dance around them," he said. "It would be very easy to treat you with kid gloves. Make everything pretty the way Dr. Donovan has recreated your face, but we can't afford to do that. From what I understand, you're the kind of person who would appreciate honesty."

"Touché. But I don't feel recreated." Malcolm raised his chin in defiance, staring at the doctor.

"In the fraction of a moment," he said, snapping his fingers, "the best part of my life was destroyed. Then, as if that wasn't enough, I was turned into some kind of sideshow freak by a doctor trying to boost her career." He turned away from Dr. Steiner, as if lost in his thoughts. "Living with disfiguring burns would have been better than this."

Steiner didn't know how he should respond to that comment. As a fireman, he knew Malcolm Dean would have seen the worst. It was hard to believe that severe burns would have been preferable to adjusting to a new face. Or was there more to his distress than that?

Though Malcolm appeared reluctantly cooperative throughout the rest of their interview, Dr. Steiner was acutely aware of a veiled hostility, a smoldering hatred he couldn't identify as contempt for him alone. Perhaps it was contempt for everyone who came in contact with him. In any event, Malcolm Dean would require more sessions, more talks and perhaps anti-psychotic medications.

He made a notation on the file for Dr. Donovan's viewing: *Patient is experiencing symptoms of a psychotic break, with schizo-*

phrenic tendencies. Strongly advise AGAINST patient's discharge until further evaluation.' He stood up to leave, unaware that even at that angle, Malcolm was able to read everything he wrote.

* * * * * *

Malcolm was awake when Thea performed surgical rounds the next morning. He made no comment when she greeted him, though he kept his eyes fastened on her as she approached. His shaved hair had started to grow back in dark curling patches, though whether it would fill in completely it was too early to say. Thea reached for his wrist and took his pulse. When she'd finished he let his hand drop limply back on the covers.

"You've met Dr. Steiner?" she said, more as a statement than a question because she knew he had. Malcolm nodded.

"I understand there wasn't an immediate bond between the two of you." She smiled wryly, hoping this would bring him out of his lethargy. "I spoke with him this morning and we both agreed that I should perform corrective surgery with a new Reflesh mask. He also wants to keep you under observation a little longer."

This brought an unexpected response.

"No!" His face twisted in a way that suggested he was fighting to control his anger. "No," he said again, this time in a hoarse whisper. "Keep him out of here and away from me. I won't agree to go through surgery again."

Her heart ached for him. Was he truly psychotic, or was he just attempting some kind of façade to throw them off? If it was a false veneer he'd thrown up to protect his emotions, eventually it would crack and the real Malcolm could emerge. But who was the real Malcolm? And he couldn't remain here forever. Eventually he would have to be released from hospital, or sent to a psychiatric facility with the means to treat his psychoses. Unless he had further surgery, or his mother had him committed, Thea could not hold him. Without looking at him again, she left the room.

FIVE

It was apparent that Dr. Steiner had prepared his report with deliberate precision. Because it would be unprofessional to malign Thea before the twelve-member hospital Medical Board, she watched as he attacked the Reflesh Procedure itself. His PowerPoint presentation showed photo after photo of Malcolm's preop and postoperative appearance; the disarray of his room after he had viewed his new face for the first time; and his inconsistent behavior and apparent radical change in personality.

"To summarize," Steiner intoned, staring pointedly at Thea from across the Board room table, "I believe that without further extensive research and testing, Reflesh surgeries are a risk both to patients and the hospital. In fact, it's questionable if our insurers would allow them to continue if they knew the facts. Malcom Dean is a potential time bomb, a danger to himself and the public. As Chief of Psychiatry I strongly recommend you suspend any additional surgeries, limiting Dr. Donovan to performing research on donated cadavers until the Board is able to reassess the project."

Thea glanced surreptitiously at the Board, equally represented by all medical and surgical departments, male and female. Steiner had been so convincing that the Board, for the most part, appeared ready to go with any recommendations he made. There was one Board member who held out, Sarah Lawson, Chief of Radiology, and a longtime adversary of Dr. Steiner's.

"I believe Dr. Donovan should be allowed to say something in defense of her program," she said, sending a humorless smile to Steiner, and a friendly nod toward Thea.

"Agreed," replied Dr. Stone, Chairman of the Board. "Dr. Donovan, are you prepared to uphold your project here today?"

Thea nodded and stood, making her way to the front of the room where she plugged a thumb drive into the computer on the podium.

Like Steiner, Thea presented Malcolm's gruesome pre-operative and extraordinary postoperative photos. But she had a different plan.

"St. Augustus is a research and teaching hospital," she explained. "The pioneering nature of our programs has brought it to the forefront, ahead of many other facilities, for grants and endowments. Not so long ago you all approved the Reflesh Procedure for surgical use. Nothing has changed. It's still in experimental stages, yes, which is why we inadvertently overlooked the problem with the photograph that was used. But we've passed the point where testing on cadavers is useful. Only live patients will be able to tell us how beneficial it will be in the long term."

She paused for several minutes to collect her thoughts.

"The only problem with this first surgery was the photograph. The Reflesh itself was not at fault. The Procedure was not at fault. We're in the process of trying to convince Mr. Dean to let us redo the surgery using a different photograph, one that he would approve beforehand. We believe this will eliminate the problem and allow the patient to go on to live a normal, productive life."

She took her seat, trembling as she awaited questions or rebuttals. Not only was the fate of the Reflesh Procedure in their hands, so too was Malcolm's future. And hers, for that matter. She busied herself with her file, not daring to make eye contact with any of them.

Finally Dr. Stone spoke. "I believe we've heard enough from both sides. Dr. Donovan, would you please step outside while we vote?"

Thea nodded and left the room, painfully aware of Steiner's glare burning into her back. She took a seat on a chair outside the Board room and forced herself to take slow breaths. After what she and Steiner had shared with the Board she had no idea which way the vote would turn. But she was only in the corridor for less than five minutes before the Secretary brought her back in.

"We've agreed not to suspend further surgeries at this point," Dr. Stone said. "If the patient agrees, you have permission to perform remedial surgery. However, even without surgical intervention, you have our approval to release Malcolm Dean on condition that you personally follow up on his progress with impromptu visits to verify his mental health. He must also continue to see a psychiatrist until the Board meets again and we can re-evaluate his condition. If he refuses to see Dr. Steiner, we have a new psychiatrist, Dr. Rand Morrissey, who would be willing to consult with him."

For a few minutes, Thea was speechless. Finally she said, "Thank you, Dr. Stone." She glanced around at the rest of the Board, avoiding Steiner's angry stare, and repeated her thanks. Then she left the room while the Board moved onto other hospital business, acutely aware that she had made a dangerous enemy in Sheldon Steiner.

On the day Malcolm Dean was to be released from hospital, Thea ventured into his ward to check his healing progress. The Reflesh had adhered to his facial structure as if it was his original skin. The translucence had regressed to an opaque flesh color that matched his own, and there were signs of tiny lines around his eyes and the corner of his mouth. Smile lines, she thought, hopeful that was the case. Over the past few days his demeanor had changed from the anger they'd seen postoperatively, to a reluctant, disgruntled acquiescence.

"How are you feeling now about the results of the surgery?" she asked. Despite no longer displaying the irrational rage he'd shown during his initial outbursts, she still was never quite certain how he would react to her questions.

"I'm all right. I just want to get the hell out of here and put everything behind me."

Thea leaned against his bedside table. The hospital staff hadn't yet retrieved his breakfast, which appeared to have been only picked over. "You are aware I'm committed to following up with you for a while?"

He sighed and looked out the window, frowning. "I'll go along with that only as long as I have to."

To break the awkwardness of the moment she leaned over and picked up the chart from the end of his bed. She heard a rustling behind her and the close of a door. When she turned, she realized he'd left her to go into the ward's tiny bathroom. She shrugged, unable to think of anything else to discuss with him now. He'd agreed to allow Thea to follow up with routine visits to study the Reflesh. If he consented to further psychiatric evaluations, he would see Dr. Steiner, or if Steiner was unavailable, Dr. Morrissey. But to Thea's disappointment, Malcolm adamantly refused to go through with more reconstructive surgery, despite her assurances that there should be no further postoperative problems.

Two weeks later, Thea made the first of her follow up visits, only to find a distressed Meredith Dean, but no Malcolm. Malcolm had conceded to moving in with his mother until he'd sufficiently recovered, physically and mentally, to return to work. And having Meredith to watch over and mother him until he was well was an added bonus.

Meredith's house was in Oregon City, the historic old town that had seen four generations of Deans. Thea found the address with little difficulty—meticulous flower beds and blossoming trees graced the front of a wood-framed, daffodil colored house. Even without the identifying name plate on the door, she would have guessed this to be Meredith's home.

Meredith showed her to an obese sofa and as Thea sat she couldn't help noticing that the photographs in the room made it a veritable shrine to Malcolm. There were other photos, too: Malcolm with a lovely young woman and a boy of about two years of age. Thea blinked rapidly, realizing immediately who they were and the sadness that must have fallen over this house at their deaths.

"Malcolm disappeared three days ago," Meredith said, her voice shaking. "I'm terribly worried. He's still so different from how he was before the accident. He stares into the mirror for hours, talking to himself and pulling at his face as if trying to somehow change it back. I know I should have called you or his psychiatrist, but I kept hoping that in his own home he would eventually become the old Malcolm again."

Thea felt ill. What could she do? If Malcolm refused to have any further sessions with Dr. Steiner or another psychiatrist, whether because of personal dislike or strictly antisocial behavior, it was beyond her control. All they could do was obtain a court order declaring him incompetent. If, in fact, he was. But clearly Malcolm needed additional counseling. For now that would have to come from her if she was to continue to vindicate and salvage the Reflesh Procedure. Not to mention, salvage the life of her first patient.

"Has he kept his appointments with Dr. Steiner?"

Meredith shook her head. "He did once. After that he refused to see him though he wouldn't tell me why specifically. He says there's nothing wrong with him on the inside, it's the outside that's the problem."

Thea considered this, feeling the burden of guilt pass over her. Despite having managed to convince the hospital Board otherwise, she realized now that she and Erik hadn't been nearly as prepared for their first patient as they thought they'd been. They should have done more studies on postoperative plastic surgery cases where the patient could no longer identify with their pre-surgery self. In her years of practice, she'd never encountered anything like this. There was really no way they could have predicted it either.

"I'll do what I can. Can you think of anywhere he may have gone? Does he have a girlfriend?"

"He has no one except me since my daughter-in-law and grandson died six months ago. Should I call the police?"

"Oh no," Thea cautioned. "Please not yet. He's probably gone away to think for a while. He's still got a lot of adjusting to do. We can't expect him to recover overnight."

"You wouldn't say that if you'd seen him recently," said Meredith. "He's not the man he was, neither physically nor emotionally. He needs help." Meredith's voice dropped. "He's made threats."

"What threats?" Thea demanded, suddenly wary.

"Oh, not against you, dear," Meredith reassured her. "He did say some terrible things about Dr. Steiner, though. But I don't think he meant anything by them."

Thea felt a weight on her shoulders that bore no resemblance to the long hours and sleepless nights she had experienced as a medical student. Or the months she and Erik had worked on the Reflesh Procedure. All she had worked for had come crashing down on her.

"You sound as if you believe his personality has changed as much as his appearance. I'm certain that it's just postoperative trauma or a delayed reaction to the accident."

"*I'm* not!" Meredith slammed her fist on the table. "Maybe it would have been better if Malcolm had remained burned and disfigured," she went on. "I believe he could have adjusted to it better."

Thea felt her heart sink with despair. "Please don't say that. I'll find Malcolm and get him the help he needs." But she said the words with a conviction she herself did not fully believe. The truth was that she did not know if she could help him. She would have to find him first.

* * * * * *

Several days following Thea's visit to Meredith Dean's home, Erik Sorenson stopped at the hospital lab to retrieve Thea's postoperative notes on Malcolm's progress. After Thea had met with Meredith, she and Erik had discussed the idea of performing new surgery on Malcolm. To do this they would first create a new Reflesh mask, then take a photo of it to show Malcolm and try to persuade him to allow further surgery. But as Erik attempted to slip his key into the laboratory door lock, it swung open on its own accord.

Odd, he thought, he always double-checked the locks before leaving. He knew Thea was at least as careful, if not more so, than he. In addition, none of the cleaning personnel had access to this room without being accompanied by either one of them. Whoever was inside was not authorized to be there.

He let the door remain open, noticing that no lights were on and all within was quiet. He padded softly along the inside wall to the right, past the filing cabinets and the microscopes, all the while keeping the Reflesh machine in his line of vision. He noticed a shadowy figure move behind the machine and toward the computer. Erik leaned over, stretched out his right arm and with one deft movement flicked on the lights. A startled, angry Sheldon Steiner glared across the room at him.

"Want to explain what you're doing here?" Erik asked. "You don't have clearance to use this room."

"I have a legitimate access to Dr. Donovan's patients. And I don't have to remind you, I am also on the Board of Directors of this hospital and report to the Medical Ethics Committee. If you two are committing any medical infractions, I'm obligated to disclose them. I have enough legal clout to have this whole operation shut down permanently."

"Well, I watch enough cop shows on television to inform you that you're trespassing. I'm sure there are a few additional charges regarding spying or patient confidentiality. You'd better get the hell out of here before I call Security."

"You little weasel," Dr. Steiner sneered. "While Dr. Donovan is the flavor of the month you've got yourself a pretty cushy position. But I'm just as entitled to the research grant as she is. It probably wouldn't take much digging to uncover something on one of you. When I finish with her she won't be qualified to empty bed pans."

"So that's what this is about," said Erik. "It has nothing to do with patient welfare or what's best for the hospital. It's all about that fucking grant you've been lusting after."

Sheldon began edging toward the door. "Just tell your partner to watch her step. If I even see either of you in a 'No

Parking' Zone, I'll have everything you've worked for taken away."

Erik scanned the room, trying to discern if Sheldon had tampered with anything. Fortunately the lab appeared untouched.

"Until you've got something concrete, keep your nose out of here." Erik paused for a moment then smiled in a cold, all-knowing way. "Instead of running like a crybaby to the Board of Directors, you might want to contact the Housekeeping Department," he said. "I've heard there's a surprising amount of dirt in the Psychiatry Department."

SIX

Caryn ended her shift at a downtown 24-hour convenience store at midnight. She loathed working nights and had promised herself when she could find a better job she would quit this one. It was hardly worth the minimum wage she earned for putting up with creepy nocturnal customers.

On the sidewalk outside the store she shivered, zipping her windbreaker to discourage the pelting rain from saturating her clothes. She flipped the hood over her long blonde hair, which was already drenched. She'd phoned her boyfriend for a ride a half-hour earlier. Now she wondered if she could count on him to pick her up.

Opening her purse, she took out a cigarette, lit it and dragged deeply. After five minutes had passed she tossed the cigarette to the pavement and let the rain put it out. Fifteen minutes later, with still no sign of her boyfriend, she tightened her lips and mentally dumped him. Then she stepped defiantly into the darkness of the parking lot toward home.

She'd walked only two blocks when a passing car slowed then pulled alongside her. The driver leaned over and threw open the passenger door. It made her slightly uneasy that she could see her reflection in the dark wet paint better than she could the man behind the tinted windows. But he sounded sincere, concerned at her walking alone, bedraggled and soaked. Though she knew the rules, there was no sign of her boyfriend and she yearned for sleep. It would be all right just this once, she reasoned.

"15 Parkside Lane," she told him. She glanced around, taking in the unaccustomed luxury of the expensive foreign vehicle. "This is a really nice car." He didn't answer, but just nodded and shifted the car into gear without looking at her.

They drove for several minutes with only the scudding scrape of the windshield wipers breaking the silence. She stole a glimpse of the silent driver and noticed with dismay that though it was a cool night, perspiration streamed down his forehead.

"Are you all right?" she asked, alarmed at first then regretted her words when he didn't reply. She glanced out the window and found she could not recognize any familiar landmarks. He had ignored her directions.

"Do you know how to get to Parkside Lane?" she asked, trying to keep the terror from her voice. "That was Exit 224. We should have turned off a few miles earlier."

But instead of responding he continued to stare at the interminable stretch of road, peering straight ahead as if he was having difficulty seeing through the heavy rain. He must have a good reason for taking this route, Caryn thought, trying not to imagine the worst.

But Caryn knew the city well. She also knew that her home was nowhere near the route they were taking.

Forcing her voice to remain calm against her rising panic she said, "If you drop me off at the next exit I can find a ride home from there." Her heart pounded in her ears as she realized that they had passed the last of the city's street lights. Other than the rain, the only thing she could see was the illuminated dash of the car and its reticent driver.

Now, despite her protests they were getting farther and farther from the city limits. Her terror began to escalate until she was faint with dread. And when he turned the car down a narrow dirt road, miles from nowhere, her final thoughts were that no one would think of looking for her here.

* * * * * *

Thea set the book she had been reading on the night table and stared across her bedroom. Despite the two lamps blazing near the wall, the shadow on the mahogany paneling remained. She stood, walked over to the tallest lamp and rearranged it so that the beam shone down over the darkest spot of the wall. Then she stepped back for another look. The workmanship could have been better, she thought, for there was a visible gap beneath the paneling and the floor where a section of baseboard was missing. Oddly enough, the shadow lingered. It wasn't a stain in the wood. There was no way to explain it.

She went back, moved the lamp to its original position and crossed to the other side of the room, hoping a different perspective might make the shadow disappear. But it remained, much like the shadow that covered her professional life now that her project was in question. Momentarily she forgot the shadow on the wall.

Her thoughts reverted to Malcolm. Where on earth could he be if even his mother did not know? It was premature to call the police, yet Dr. Steiner felt Malcolm was dangerous. How could he make that assumption on so little evidence? Was it really possible that his personality had changed that radically from just the after-effects of the surgery? She was still pondering this when the phone rang.

It was Meredith again. The combination of dealing with Sheldon Steiner, the hospital Board and now Meredith, was giving Thea an unnecessary stress test. She reluctantly had to inform Meredith that she had not heard from Malcolm. Winding the phone cord around her fingers, her thoughts wandered as she gazed around the room.

"Perhaps you should go through his personal things," Thea suggested. "There may be some clue to his whereabouts, a phone number or address perhaps. Does he have a computer you can access to check his email?"

"He does. But if it's protected by a password I wouldn't know how to get into it."

"There are computer experts who can hack into personal computers and emails," Thea said. "In fact, I probably know of one. But if Malcolm still hasn't contacted you by morning I think we should file a Missing Person report. Under the circumstances it's the next logical thing to do."

"You may be right," Meredith replied. "I want to respect his privacy, but knowing that he may be in danger makes it impossible. I'll visit the Police Department in the morning." After thanking Thea for her help, she hung up.

Thea breathed a sigh of relief. There was little she could do to help anyone at this point, not even herself. According to Steiner, it wasn't Malcolm who was in danger, but the unsuspecting public. Pressing her fingers tightly against her temples she massaged them until the pounding slowed then stopped. She glanced at the clock on her desk, noticing the portrait of herself accepting an award from Dr. Stanton at UBC. Memories of her resolution to immigrate to the U.S. flowed back. A disastrous love affair had first prompted the move, but then her career took precedence and an irresistible offer finalized the decision.

After the death of Dr. Stanton, the opportunity to continue her research had come from the Research Department at St. Augustus Hospital in Portland, Oregon. It was Thea's love of tradition that prompted her to choose a home in an older part of the city. She had been intrigued and entertained by the realtor's knowledge of the houses, many with memorable events that had helped to shape the new clay that today was a cosmopolitan city.

She had been thrilled at finding this house, which was new on the market for the first time in decades. Listed at a price far below other homes in the posh area of Portland, she'd had to outbid several other potential buyers. The traditional mahogany paneling and cherry wood floors polished to a high shine gave it an old world feeling. It reminded her of her grandparents' manor house where she had grown up in the gorgeous Dundarave neighborhood of Vancouver. Only at a fraction of the cost.

But recently she had begun to wonder if she had made a bad decision in buying the house. On the bright spring morning she'd viewed it with the Realtor it had seemed perfect. Now she wasn't so sure. It wasn't that she heard thumps at night or saw floating images in the darkness. There was just this constant, pervasive sense of gloom. It was not a happy house. Not at all. And living alone didn't make it easier.

She glanced back to the wall she had been staring at while talking with Meredith. In that corner of the room hung an antique, Bowery-style saloon lamp, an original fixture of the house. Although Thea had never liked it, she had to admit it amplified the ambience of the house.

The lamp hung from a heavy cord strung through a small pulley, enabling it to be raised or lowered to redirect the light in the room. Thinking that lowering it might change or remove the shadow, she walked over to the corner and untethered the end of the cord giving it enough slack until the lamp slowly began to descend. Suddenly there was the screech of metal grinding on metal. Startled, she dropped the cord. The lamp plummeted with the finality of a hangman's noose.

She glanced over to the wall. The complete panel of mahogany had slid away, revealing a closet-sized opening. Heart pounding, she stepped cautiously toward the gaping maw and peered inside. Cumulus billows of dust and cobwebs lay on the floor. Although it must have once been a hiding place for valuables, there were no shelves. And it was not completely empty. At the bottom of the aperture lay what appeared to be a dead mouse.

She shuddered and gave the corpse a gentle poke with her toe. As the dust balls fell away she saw that it wasn't a mouse at all, but a letter opener. She picked it up and blew away the dust. It had a 6" long blade and was made of scrimshaw. The sharp, pointed end was stained and appeared to be rusted. She tried wiping it clean, but the discoloration remained.

Swathing the opener in a tissue, she dropped it into the desk drawer beside her arm chair. Then she raised the lamp again, watching as the panel screeched back into place. Inexplicably, the shadow had disappeared. But her disquiet remained. Of one thing she was certain: the Realtor had been completely unaware of this feature of the house.

That night seemed interminable as she fought the demons that kept her from sleeping. She lay unmoving and deathlike on the bed, eyes closed tightly as if in pain. Eventually she drifted off to a restless, nightmarish sleep. And for the first time in years she dreamed of Anna, an unfortunate young classmate from her past who had inadvertently directed her future.

The next morning was a Sunday. With no inpatients and no hospital rounds to make, her presence at the hospital was unnecessary. Despite the oblique shafts of sunlight streaming through the windows, she could not bring herself to get out of bed. She grabbed a book from her night table and lying in bed, read and reread the same lines over as her concentration kept shifting. She threw the book down and thought of turning on the television, then abandoned the idea. Was it too early to call Erik?

But when she summoned enough courage to call him, a cheerful, 'Come on over' inflated her spirits. Today, unlike most days, she carefully applied mauve eye shadow to highlight her large brown eyes then added mascara, finishing with a light peach lip gloss. She took more time than usual choosing her clothes, slim-fitting jeans and a long winter-white cable knit sweater. She took a last look in the cheval mirror and smiled at her reflection. This would be her first visit to Erik's apartment.

Erik's pale eyebrows raised slightly when he opened the door and saw her changed appearance, but he didn't appear displeased. He wore a tea-towel tucked between corduroy slacks and a blue-checked flannel shirt. He motioned her to a black leather sofa and returned to the kitchen from where the pleasant aroma of bacon and perked coffee welcomed her.

After he left, Thea had a look around the room. It was strange that he would have all the curtains drawn at this hour of the morning. Her forehead puckered slightly. Weird, she thought. With the exception of several pieces of Erté glass, every furnishing and ornament in the apartment was either black or white. Very art deco, she mused, but to her taste the overtones were too stark to be inviting.

Erik returned with two mugs of coffee and placed them on the smoked glass table. He caught the bewilderment she attempted to hide.

"How do you like it?" he asked.

Thea hesitated a moment, searching for a complimentary response.

"It's very...dark."

Erik laughed. "That's probably the most flattering comment anyone has made, if not the safest," he said. "Do you want to tell me what's bothering you?"

"Why do you think something is wrong?"

He stared thoughtfully at his mug of coffee.

"Is it about the other night?" he asked.

Thea blushed and couldn't raise her eyes to meet Erik's. She actually hadn't thought about their night together, or Erik's apparent inability to complete their lovemaking. But he seemed to want to explain. He reached over and cupped her chin gently in his hand. "There's nothing wrong with me, except sometimes I work too many hours. And I don't get enough sleep."

She pulled away from his grasp, walked over to the shrouded windows and pulled on the drawstring. For a second the glaring sunlight forced her to shut her eyes. When she opened them, she was speechless. The overwhelming grandeur of Mt. Hood eclipsed the window frame. On the same horizon miles away, Mount St. Helens, which had erupted many years before, lay deflated and temporarily spent.

Erik put his arm around her shoulder and pulled her close.

"Spectacular, isn't it?"

"Why do you cover it up?"

Almost in a whisper he said, "It makes me claustrophobic." He smiled at her, a little ruefully, she thought.

This time Thea met his gaze with a hunger in her eyes so strong that for a moment it surprised them both. In cocooning herself in work, she had not permitted herself to become lonely, not allowed herself to need the warmth of another person. She knew that she did not love Erik yet, but an embryo of hope grew in her mind. He was different today from that evening in her apartment, less aggressive and single-minded. Perhaps he felt more at ease in his own surroundings.

In a wordless, yet mutual decision, Thea found herself led into Erik's bedroom. She had not expected to be astounded again, yet his bedroom was just as great an enigma as the man. The room was clean and tidy, though black vertical blinds nearly obscured an oversized black comforter that had fallen off the bed onto the floor. Only a crimson lamp glowed in the darkness, throwing blood-like shadows across the bed.

SEVEN

Thea awoke to the thump of a newspaper landing on the granite steps outside. She scrambled out of bed and quickly wrapped her terrycloth robe around her as she dashed to the door. It would only take a few moments for the paper to become rain-sodden. As she leaned outside, though, she saw that the morning had arrived with as much splendor and aplomb as yesterday. The sun was shining.

She smiled to herself, wondering if her mood had affected the weather or vice versa. Yesterday at Erik's had been wonderful. She couldn't deny it, even to herself. He had been warm and loving and she had discovered leaving him afterward to be a difficult thing. But away from him she couldn't explain a certain sense of relief. She told herself it must be from living alone so long, this need for solitude.

With the coffee gurgling in the machine and the toast browning, she set the paper on the kitchen table and scanned the headlines. A local girl had disappeared after leaving work the night before. It was small comfort that they had not yet recovered a body. Thea shivered, but not from cold. She could scarcely imagine what the family of the missing young woman must be enduring. Maybe she would still be found unhurt, she thought. Knowing it was unlikely, positive thinking kept her from dwelling on something over which she had no control.

The next story was about a rash of fires deliberately set, according to fire investigators. Although no injuries were reported, a witness claimed to have seen a man running from the scene of the largest, a clubhouse for underprivileged children. She skipped a few sections to the weather page, noticing a prediction for the sunny days to end. Folding the paper, she resolved not to dampen her spirits with any more of the printed gloom. After all, in an hour or so she'd be at work. And so would Erik.

Last week she had scheduled a young patient for the Re-flesh Procedure, a heartbreaking case of neurofibromatosis—Elephant Man syndrome. Now she was finally able to do something to help. But as the girl had had the fibromatas almost since birth, there were no suitable photographs to emulate. A computerized drawing would have to give the child her new identity. And once again, she was reminded of Anna.

Anna was an unfortunate little girl she had known when they were both in grade school. She had been born with fibrous tumors covering her face and neck. The freak of the school, the other students taunted, tormented and called her 'Ugly Anna'. Though Thea had never taken part in the teasing, neither had she attempted to intervene. And Anna, in a child's cruel world where physical perfection is the key to survival, had no friends.

One day after school, Thea had gone to play at a friend's house in an unfamiliar neighborhood. Afterward it was a long-er walk to her home than she had expected and for some reason the streets appeared never ending. After walking for blocks and blocks, the rows of houses with neatly trimmed lawns and flower beds had given way to seedy, unkempt shacks with abandoned cars in the front yards. Before too long she realized she was lost.

By now her grandparents would be frantic at her absence and she dreaded the scolding and punishment she would receive for being late. She glanced from house to house, praying for a familiar landmark, anything to point her in the direction of home. She stopped beside an old house with peeling paint and a falling down wooden fence. Three grubby children, play-ing hopscotch on a crudely drawn outline on the sidewalk, stared curiously at her pretty cleanliness.

One older girl boldly walked up to her.

"Are you lost?" she asked.

Thea shook her head in mute embarrassment, too shy to

admit it, too afraid to ask a stranger for help. The girl shrugged, walked away and went back to her game of hopscotch.

Hot tears filled Thea's eyes as she stumbled forward, trying to appear as though she knew where she was going. Then she saw a tiny, old house that was different from the rest. It had a pristine yard and a freshly painted exterior that reminded her of a petunia growing among weeds. And playing in the front yard was Anna.

Thea just stood there on the street, so grateful to see a familiar face, yet not daring to ask for help from a girl whom she had never attempted to protect from harassment. She need not have worried. Anna had the soul of an angel. She walked over to Thea, took her hand and led her into the doll-like house.

To her shame, Thea could not bring herself to look at Anna's deformed face, but she explained to Anna's mother that she was lost. Anna's mother made sympathetic noises, offered her lemonade and cookies. Then, in a rusty, battered Ford, she drove Thea home to her grandparent's neighborhood of brick mansions. Later Thea realized she had learned more about life in that day than almost any other. Ultimately, it was because of Anna that she became a plastic surgeon.

She was leaving the doctor's lounge after the operation and on her way to a scheduled press conference about the surgery, when Erik caught up to her.

"That was incredible," he said, breathless from running. "I'm proud of you—well, proud of us both. We gave her those new features."

Thea stopped and turned, smiling at him with tired relief.

"It's like we're starting over," she said. "Especially after that Malcolm Dean fiasco. This is the way it should be. That little girl can lead a normal life now. I just wish we could find Malcolm and make things right for him."

Erik shrugged. "That's his decision, Thea. He's no longer your responsibility." He took her hand in his. Though she didn't know why, Thea felt a knot of apprehension form in her stomach.

"He's still my responsibility," Thea said, gently removing her hand. "I have to follow up with his care and that's been impossible because no one knows where he is."

"Malcolm is an adult who had reconstructive facial surgery. Don't forget, he also suffered an enormous loss when his wife and son died. Sure it's going to take him a while to adjust but apart from the commitment you made to the Board, I don't think he needs our intervention anymore."

Thea shook her head. "I don't agree," she said, and started moving away but Erik caught her arm and stopped her.

"We make a great team," he said. "I wish you'd consider us moving in together."

Startled, she shook her head and took a light approach. "What would your parents say? We'd be living in sin." Actually it was something *her* grandparents would have said. Up until their deaths she had called them every Sunday and managed to keep her personal life out of their grasp to avoid the inevitable recriminations.

"They wouldn't care," Erik replied with a laugh. "After Dad retired from the Merchant Marines he bought a fishing boat. He and mom are somewhere in the San Juan Islands pulling more fish out of the ocean than they can eat. I don't think they worry too much about who their little boy is sleeping with. And I never share personal stuff with my brother, but even so, he wouldn't care."

Thea tried to smile back but it was a subject too serious for her to laugh away. "There is a lot we don't know about each other. I don't think I'd want to move into your apartment and I don't think you'd like living in my house any better." She hesitated. "We've been moving pretty fast lately. Maybe we should take things slower for a while, at least until I get this Malcolm Dean issue settled."

Erik's face tightened. Inwardly, Thea cursed herself. She hadn't wanted to hurt him. In fact, she enjoyed spending time with him and she couldn't deny they were sexually compatible, but she wasn't ready for that much commitment yet. She heard him sigh and with both of them lost in their thoughts he fell into step with her. They made their way toward the press conference that had been arranged for a follow-up report on this latest surgery. But scarcely had they stepped through the doors of the hospital when a clamor from outside cut off further discussion of their burgeoning relationship. A sea of reporters, complete with microphones, camera crew, and a news van descended upon them prematurely.

"Dr. Donovan," one tall, male reporter shouted. "Have you created another Frankenstein? Or was this operation a success?"

Thea straightened her shoulders and took a deep breath. She had known this would come eventually and braced herself for their questions. She glanced around for Erik. To her astonishment, she saw him back quietly out the door and disappear, without any of the reporters being the wiser.

For a moment she froze, unsure of herself without her partner for back up. Then she took a deep breath and turned to face her inquisitors and their barrage of questions.

"How is the patient?"

"Is she conscious?"

"Can we talk to her?"

Thea raised her hand in an endeavor to maintain silence.

"I'll answer any questions I can but, please, one at a time." She nodded to a perky young woman standing nearest her.

"Is it true that the patient has Elephant Man syndrome?" she asked.

"Had," corrected Thea. Her eyes roved the crowd for a reaction. "The correct term would be, had neurofibromatosis. We expect the patient to make a full recovery with minimal scarring. Her appearance will be as acceptable as most of yours." She smiled mischievously and winked at them.

"How about before and after pictures, Doctor?" an older man asked.

Thea shook her head. "Sorry. You know I can't do that

without the consent of the patient's family."

"Ask her about Malcolm Dean," a familiar voice from behind her suggested.

Thea whirled around and came face to face with Sheldon Steiner. Their eyes locked in a cold stare. He gave her a poisonous smile. Then, ignoring the curious glances from the group of reporters, he stalked off in the opposite direction.

Thea gaped after him, astounded at his uncharacteristic lack of professionalism. Still in shock, she turned back to the reporters.

"Yes, tell us about Malcolm Dean," shouted a man in a loud checked shirt. "Is he to be rescheduled for the same surgery?"

Thea gnawed her lower lip, thinking rapidly. "I have consults to take care of," she said, careful not to meet any eyes. "Due to HIPAA regulations and doctor/patient confidentiality, I'll issue a statement this afternoon that will give you all the information I'm at liberty to discuss."

She turned on her heel and walked hurriedly away, leaving several reporters scribbling rapidly in notebooks, no doubt reminders to investigate the apparent animosity between Plastic Surgery and Psychiatry.

Thea's press conference would have made the headline in the morning *Oregonian* were it not upstaged by Sheldon's version of the Reflesh Procedure. She could scarcely believe what she was reading, so denigrating were his words—if they were his—and she felt they probably were. He'd reiterated for the press what he'd presented to St. Augustus' hospital Board, only amplified and exaggerated for sensationalism.

She was studying the article for a second time when Erik stormed into her office. He threw a copy of the paper on her desk.

"I've already seen it," Thea said, wearily waving her hand across her desk.

"This will ruin us," Erik shouted. "He tainted the whole procedure with inaccuracy and innuendo. Why?" He began walking back and forth across the room, rubbing his forehead.

Thea knew why. Steiner's avid dislike of her stemmed from an early encounter when she had criticized the dosage of antipsychotic medication he prescribed for a mutual patient, a known addict. Though a newcomer to the hospital, she had filed a complaint to the Medical Ethics Committee. Steiner had taken it personally. In his defense, she now realized, she probably would have felt the same if she had been one named in the complaint.

The allegations had been duly investigated then dismissed as a misunderstanding, most likely due to Steiner's tenure and Thea's lack thereof, but not before they cautioned Sheldon against future infractions. If she had only taken the time to discuss the patient with him first, the situation might have been avoided. Now it was too late.

"Correction," she said to Erik. "*I'm* ruined, not you. You still have a career to fall back on. Mine is pretty much screwed. *Why did he do it?* It's irrelevant now, but that article is too damaging to be just jealousy." Or spite, she thought.

Erik stopped his relentless pacing and leaned over the front of her desk, his hands gripping the corners.

"Why don't you sue for libel?"

Thea groaned. "That would effectively nail down the coffin lid. I can't sue another doctor in the same hospital. Even if I won, no one would ever speak or refer a patient to me again. They might even find a way to revoke my privileges. If that happened there wouldn't be a hospital in the country that would hire me."

Erik pounded the desk with his fist, making her jump.

"Well, *I* can do something," he growled. Thea shrank back in alarm at the intensity of anger on his face. "I'll find out what his angle is because there's nothing he can do to me."

"Be careful," Thea warned. "He's been here a long time. He's powerful and he has a lot of allies. You could get hurt."

"So could he." Erik stalked toward the door. He opened it, turned and forced a grim smile. "Don't worry about me," he said. "I'm a survivor."

EIGHT

Early the next day, after Thea had checked on her young new post-op patient and completed her morning rounds, she phoned Meredith to enquire about Malcolm. Although Meredith sounded strained and anxious, she claimed she had nothing new to report. Then she suggested Thea help her sort through Malcolm's personal belongings for clues to his whereabouts. Thea hesitated. She was reluctant to intrude further into Malcolm's personal life. But it was inexplicably difficult for her to say no to Meredith. So once again she found herself heading southeast toward Oregon City.

She parked beneath the cathedral of trees in front of the picket fence surrounding the Dean home. Opening the miniature gate, she stepped lightly up the flagstone path to the front door and saw a large golden retriever calmly watching her from the front porch. He hadn't been there on her previous visit. Just seconds before the dog had the opportunity to bark, Meredith opened the door.

"Lie down, Sport," she ordered, explaining, "I just picked him up from the kennel. He's Malcolm's." She smiled at Thea and enveloped her in a rib cracking hug. Thea responded with a kiss to Meredith's cheek. Then Meredith led her inside the house and a warm breath of hot cinnamon rushed out to greet her. Thea smiled to herself, thankful she had skipped breakfast.

"I'm so glad you came," Meredith said as she removed her apron and pulled out a wooden chair with a padded strawberry-print cushioned seat at the kitchen table for Thea. She set a mounded plate of cinnamon rolls and two coffee mugs each bearing the sentiment, 'World's Greatest Mom', on the table, filling both from a French brew coffeepot before she sat opposite Thea.

Meredith leaned forward on her elbows, eyes glistening. "I didn't want to tell you over the phone," she said. "The police were here this morning asking questions about Malcolm."

"Did you file a Missing Person report like I suggested?" asked Thea.

"No, I didn't," Meredith said, sounding guilty, "even though I still haven't heard from him. The police wanted to know if I knew his whereabouts the last two nights. I lied and told them he was here with me, but they said he was seen at the clubhouse beside the playing field where he coached Little League. It burned down last night and they think Malcolm did it."

Thea stared at her in shocked silence. Was it possible that Malcolm, a fireman with commendations, would deliberately set fires? How little she knew of him! She took a long swallow of her coffee and set it back down.

"Let's get started on his room," she said to Meredith. "If the police have any evidence at all, we need to locate him and clear his name before they issue a warrant for his arrest."

Meredith nodded in a forlorn way, stood up and pushed back her chair. Thea followed her up the stairs as she led the way to Malcolm's room.

As Thea stood in the doorway gazing around Malcolm's bedroom she forgot for a moment that he was an adult. Football pennants from his high school years hung on the walls. On a child-sized dresser, tiny trophies from T-ball and swim meets shared space. An assortment of toy fire trucks and stuffed dogs and bears lined a bookshelf above a large collection of Hardy Boy mysteries. Off to one side was a single captain's bed.

"Is *this* where he sleeps?" she asked in amazement.

Meredith nodded, unaware that Thea considered it a very odd room for a grown man. Then Thea remembered that Malcolm had another home once, a home with a wife and a son. No doubt this room had remained the same since his childhood and when he moved back, Meredith had lacked either the heart or the strength to change it.

"You take those drawers," Meredith pointed to the left side of the room. "And I'll start over here."

"Okay," Thea replied as she began sorting through the cluttered cabinet. There was little or no evidence to suggest that a grown man had opened the drawers recently, much less used them. Then she found a small box filled with pencil stubs, broken crayons and other childish treasures. Among them, only a book of matches spoke of the Malcolm of today. She glanced over to Meredith.

"Does Malcolm smoke?" she asked. Meredith shook her head, sneezed twice and went back to her exploration. Thea placed the matches in her jacket pocket to examine later.

After searching and analyzing the contents of the drawers and closets, she turned to the bookcase. As a child she had been an avid mystery reader. She pulled out a volume of the Hardy Boys *A Figure in Hiding*, a book she especially enjoyed, and noticed a manila file folder hidden from view behind the books. She removed several more volumes to get it free. 'Unsolved' was written in pencil on the file.

Setting the file aside she placed all the books except *A Figure in Hiding* back on the shelf. Alongside the books, several photographs of Malcolm at various ages stared back at her with the now familiar crooked grin. Unsettled at seeing the real Malcolm, Thea turned away. She picked up the file and book and glanced over to Meredith.

"Did you find anything yet?" Thea asked. Meredith shook her head, stood and dug her fists in her lower back as she straightened up. She gazed with interest at the file in Thea's hand.

"What's that?" she asked, leaning over to see the label.

Thea shrugged. "I thought you might know."

"I've never seen it before," said Meredith. "Let's take it downstairs and have a look."

While Meredith poured fresh coffee Thea opened the file. Inside she found yellowed newspaper clippings with what appeared to be the date of the articles' publication handwritten in the top corners. The articles were about murders ranging over a period of thirty years. Having only moved to the United States recently, and being too young to remember most of them, none of the incidents held any significance to Thea. Meredith walked up behind her and peered over Thea's shoulder.

Thea looked up at her. "Whose handwriting is this?"

Meredith reached for her reading glasses and picked up several clippings. After examining them she placed them in the open file.

"That's my husband David's writing," she said. "It resembles Malcolm's a lot, but I'd know it anywhere." She smiled almost shyly. "He wrote me love letters when we first started dating, so many years ago."

"Do you think this was your husband's file or Malcolm's?"

"It's hard to say. Given the age of the articles and the writing on them, most likely my husband's. What are the clippings about?"

"They're all unsolved murder cases," Thea said. She waited, anticipating Meredith's surprise. But Meredith took her off guard by laughing.

"Either David shared those cases with Malcolm before he died, or Malcolm saved them from his father's things afterward. Malcolm was in his early 20's when David passed away. I let him take whatever he wanted of his father's personal belongings, but I threw a lot of stuff out."

Thea raised her eyebrows. "Was this a hobby of his?"

"I don't know if you'd call it a hobby, more like part of his profession. Unlike Malcolm who's a fireman, David was a police officer. Although it happened before we were married, one of these cases in particular riveted him because he was the second person on the scene. The wife of another police officer was murdered by her lover who then committed suicide."

"I wonder why he put it in an unsolved file. And if he was the second, who was the first on the scene?"

"David never told me any details, but it's probably in the article," said Meredith.

Thea sifted through the clippings and came to one dated 1986, headlined, "Portland Detective's Wife Victim in Murder/Suicide." She read it aloud to Meredith.

"Alicia Volk, wife of Portland Detective Peter Volk, was found murdered in her home this morning along with prominent divorce attorney, Reg Forbes. It was Detective Volk who discovered the bodies. Each appeared to have died from a single gunshot wound.

"It is believed that Mr. Forbes may have shot Mrs. Volk after an argument then turned the gun on himself. Mrs. Volk is survived by her husband, Peter and two sons. Mr. Forbes is survived by his wife, Jean, who is expecting their first child."

Thea glanced up at Meredith. "It doesn't say anything about them being lovers."

Meredith laughed dryly. "You'd hardly expect them to print a story like that in those days. It's not unusual for newspapers to protect people in positions of power. Maybe the reporters were hushed up by the killer's law firm as there would be no end of a scandal. Not to mention the additional trauma to his poor pregnant widow."

Thea rapidly scanned the rest of the newspaper clippings. Finally, she came to a carbon copy of the Coroner's report on Alicia Volk. Wondering briefly why David Dean would have kept a copy, she scanned the contents. A gunshot wound from a .357 Magnum pistol, registered to Reginald Forbes, was listed as the cause of death. A puncture wound found close to the same location as the gunshot was noted, though the Coroner indicated it did not appear to have been life threatening. Apart from several notations about marijuana being found in her blood stream and her general state of health, there were no further details.

She closed the file and took a deep breath. Was this collection just a hobby Malcolm's father had shared with him, or was Malcolm involved in solving old mysteries? Were he and his father mixed up in it somehow? She felt it was inappropriate to ask Meredith these questions but one thing still baffled her.

"It still doesn't explain why David placed it with the un-solved crimes."

Meredith shrugged, raising her hands to the back of her head to secure a few strands of hair behind her ears. She slid into a chair across from Thea and absently fingered the old clippings before looking up.

"I really have no idea. He never shared his work or any of that stuff with me. For all I know, the last time he looked at it might have been so long ago that he forgot it was there. Or it could have been misfiled. Unfortunately, neither David nor Malcolm are around to solve the puzzle."

And how convenient is that? thought Thea.

NINE

That night Thea had trouble falling asleep as visions of the disastrous press conference and Steiner's deception clouded her mind. Because she wasn't on-call for Emergency, she took the phone off the hook to avoid being disturbed. She stared at the ceiling thinking about the events earlier that day at the Deans' home. With Meredith's permission she had taken the 'Unsolved' file and the book from Malcolm's shelf. Hoping to read herself to sleep she pulled it out, smiling at the irony of the title.

She read for about an hour, enjoying the simplistic formula of the writing that took her back to her childhood days as an avid reader. After a while the reading succeeded in dulling the edges of her frazzled nerves and she gratefully accepted the sleepiness that washed over her. Vowing to finish the chapter, she turned the page. A small newspaper clipping, probably used for a bookmark, slipped from between the pages and fell onto the sheets.

Though yellow with age and similar to the articles in the file Thea found earlier in the day, it bore no date. There was just a small notation that read, "Detective Peter Volk was placed on permanent leave from the Portland Police Department today after failing a routine psychiatric evaluation following the death of his wife, whom he had discovered murdered in their home. He has voluntarily committed himself to a private sanitarium where, according to what little information the doctors would release, he will remain indefinitely."

Thea reached over and placed the tiny clipping in the unsolved file with the others. Why were Malcolm and his father so interested in the Volk/Forbes murder? Could Peter have had more to do with his wife's death than just discovering the bodies? And what had been David Dean's role? She wondered if there was anyone who remembered the case. It occurred to her that while Alicia's sons were possibly still alive, Peter was probably dead now. Even if he was still living, his sanity would be another matter.

* * * * * *

Thea arrived at the hospital the next morning to discover chaos had taken over. The unmistakable smell of burned rubber emanated from the laboratory housing the Reflesh machine. The corridor outside the lab swarmed with security guards, police, hospital personnel, and Erik. He rushed over when he saw her, a mixture of frustration and fury on his face.

"Where the hell have you been? I've been trying to reach you all morning."

Thea's mouth fell open in surprise. "I took the landline off the hook last night and turned off my cell phone so I could get some sleep. I must have forgotten to turn them back on. What's going on here?"

Erik threw his hands up then let them fall helplessly at his sides. "Someone sabotaged the machine last night. It's so messed up, I'm not sure if we can work with it again. It seems there's no evidence of a break and enter so it had to be someone with hospital access."

Thea frowned and hastened to the door to enter the lab, Erik close on her heels. A security guard held her back until she displayed her hospital I.D. Once inside, she raced over to the Reflesh machine. Erik had not exaggerated. Remnants of the machine lay bent and covered in melted rubber. Thea pulled a scrap of it free.

"This is surgical glove material," she said, sounding puzzled. "But the machine appears to be only structurally damaged. The internal workings should be operational. If you can get a tech guy to come in and repair it, we should be able to have it functioning in about a week." She paused and turned to

Erik. "You found it like this?"

Erik nodded, his eyes narrowing in anger. "I have someone who should be able to fix it and get us back up to speed. Got any ideas who would want to terminate this project?" he asked, sarcasm heavy in his voice.

Thea caught his meaning and shook her head. "I can't believe Dr. Steiner would do this. This looks like the work of an amateur. It's too juvenile to be anything but random vandalism."

"Believe what you want," said Erik. "But it wasn't a forced entry. And there's something else I should have told you about Sheldon," he hesitated for a moment then stiffened when he saw Sheldon Steiner standing in the doorway. Thea turned to follow Erik's gaze, contemplatively studying Dr. Steiner as he crossed the room.

"What happened here?" he asked, glancing at each of them. "It looks like a war zone."

"It could be that, if you stay in this room any longer," Erik said, insinuation heavy in his voice. Thea placed a restraining hand on his arm.

She took a deep breath, forcing herself to be diplomatic. "Do you know anything about this?"

Sheldon cocked his head to one side and gave her a disagreeable glare. "Obviously less than you think. I warned you Malcolm Dean was dangerous."

"You think Malcolm tried to destroy the lab?" Thea said in disbelief.

"He is familiar with the layout of the hospital and the lab. He's disappeared and no one seems to know, or even admit, where he is. Not to mention, he made comments to me that could be construed as threats."

Erik gave a short laugh. "I seem to remember you doing the same."

Sheldon's face flushed an angry red. "Are you implying that I did this?"

"It's no secret you want to kill this project. Especially given that stunt you pulled with the newspaper story," Erik said, his voice rising louder than Sheldon's. Several heads turned to observe the action, pens poised above notebooks. Thea noticed the sudden interest of the onlookers and glared at each of them.

"We're getting nowhere with this attitude," she said, keeping her voice low. "Let's leave the investigation to the professionals." She stalked out, leaving the two men watching her in troubled silence. Erik looked at Sheldon.

"I know what you're thinking," said Sheldon. "But you're wrong. Malcolm Dean has deep-rooted psychological problems that, left untreated, may manifest into irreversibly destructive behavior."

Erik watched him, not saying a word.

Sheldon began to fidget under Erik's scrutiny. "While I have my reservations about the validity of your project, there's no reason for you or Thea to believe that I want it canceled. We have our own interests and for the benefit of our patients should stop working at cross purposes. Can't we call a truce?" He held out his hand in an offer of good will.

Erik's eyes dropped to Sheldon's outstretched hand, then back up to his face. Ignoring the overture of friendship, he turned and walked away. Sheldon slipped his hand self-consciously into his pocket and surveyed the damage again. He sighed heavily. Then he too walked out of the room, leaving the investigative team to discover what they could.

Thea had left instructions with Gwen, her secretary, to hold all phone calls not related to patient care. She was glad of the foresight because it kept Gwen busy bringing in messages, most of them from Erik. But Thea could not bring herself to deal with him right now.

In addition, Sheldon's allegations about Malcolm distressed her. If he broke doctor/patient confidentiality and told the police about Malcolm's erratic behavior, their suspicions about his involvement in the arson would be substantiated. Not to mention wanting to implicate him in the destruction of the Reflesh lab. Evidence was piling up against Malcolm and there was no doubt in Thea's mind that a warrant would be issued for his arrest. And soon.

Thea spent the afternoon dictating medical reports and reading research articles. She was nearly asleep when Gwen poked her head through the doorway and asked if she would be required to work overtime. Thea glanced at her watch, startled at the late hour.

"Go home," she said, stifling a yawn. "I'm just about finished here for the day, anyhow. I'll lock the office."

Gwen inclined her chin and backed out of the room, closing the door gently behind her. After she'd gone, Thea spent another hour on her paperwork then decided to call it quits until the morning. She grabbed her purse and a couple of medical journals to keep her company for the evening. Out of habit she locked her desk drawers then locked the outer office doors. There was no harm in taking precautions.

She strode rapidly through the nearly deserted hospital corridors, nodding to the occasional familiar faces she passed, several of whom had witnessed the altercation between Sheldon and herself. It seemed to her that their gazes lingered on her longer and more inquisitively than usual, but she immediately dismissed this thought as overactive imagination.

She paused outside the Reflesh laboratory door and double checked to make sure it was locked. Then she said goodnight to the security guard and turned to leave the hospital through the rear entrance electronic doors. As they closed noiselessly behind her, she noticed Sheldon Steiner near the Emergency entrance of the staff parking lot, heading toward a lone Lexus parked there. For a moment Thea hesitated. She needed to make peace with this man if they were to continue on staff at the same hospital, and it was apparent she would have to make the first gesture. She began to trot toward him.

"Dr. Steiner," she called out, still running. Sheldon had his hand on the door handle now and did not appear to hear her.

"Dr. Steiner," she repeated, slightly out of breath, "wait up a minute, I need to talk to you."

Just as Steiner was about to open the door of his Lexus, he stopped, apparently having finally heard her. Simultaneously, he opened the car door and turned. As the door swung open, a ball of heat and metal fragments exploded into the air. Thea watched in horror as the Lexus appeared to turn inside out. Sheldon's body flew across the lot like a discarded toy, the roar of flames muting the impact of his body striking the pavement.

Ignoring the heat from the burning vehicle, Thea raced to his side and dropped to her knees. She felt for his pulse and found it rapidly weakening. A large piece of flying metal had struck him in the chest, exposing his vital organs. Suddenly Emergency room staff seemed to emerge from nowhere, pushing her out of the way. In vain they tried stemming the blood that flowed from his arteries like red wine. He opened his eyes just once and stared at Thea. There was a question in them that she could not answer. Or maybe she was reading more into it than that and it was just the last moments of his life leaving his body.

She stood up and stepped back, letting the trauma team cope with Steiner's injuries. But she knew from experience that his wounds were too critical for him to survive. A heavy numbness consumed her mind and body as she stood watching the ineffectual efforts of her coworkers. In the periphery she heard a wail of sirens from either firetrucks or police cars or ambulances; she could not tell the difference and at this point it didn't really matter. Then a comforting arm slipped around her shoulder and squeezed hard, pulling her close.

It was Erik. Turning blindly toward him, she buried her face in his shoulder and began to sob. He led her back to the hospital, unnoticed by the horde of bystanders, still hypnotized by the chaotic inferno before them. Then suddenly she was sitting in a chair in her office, unable to recall how she got there. Erik opened her credenza and brought out two small glasses and the bottle of Remy Martin he had given her as a celebration gift for the partnership. He poured a shot for each of them and handed her a glass. Thea shook her head.

"Drink it," Erik insisted. Obediently she tossed it back in one gulp, spluttering and coughing as it burned its way down her throat.

"Good girl," he said.

Thea wiped her mouth with the back of her hand. She glanced up at Erik with anguish twisting her face. "What happened out there?" she whispered hoarsely.

Erik sat in the chair opposite her desk. His head turned slowly from side to side. He studied her as circumspectly as if she were a microscopic specimen on a glass slide.

"I got there when everyone else did, after the fact. You were the closest person to him. Didn't you see anything?"

"I was trying to catch him, running over to declare a truce. He heard me too late and when he opened the door the car exploded. It seemed as if he was trying to tell me something," Thea stated in a flat voice, "and then I watched him die." She stared unseeing into the glass as she rolled it back and forth between her fingers.

"You couldn't have known the car was going to explode," Erik said, frowning. "If you'd gotten to him seconds earlier you'd have been injured or killed too."

Shaking, Thea took another swallow of the drink. "I hadn't thought of that. It all happened so fast. There was no warning at all." She shook her head, numb with shock. "What kind of person is capable of killing a doctor who only cared about helping people? We may not have been friends, but I wouldn't wish that on my worst enemy."

Erik put his arms around her again. "That's what the investigators will have to determine, I guess." He planted a soft kiss on her forehead and got up to refill the glasses.

Just then there was a loud banging on the door. The glass dropped from Thea's fingers and shattered across the floor.

They stared at each other for a few seconds, alarm on each of their faces. "Who is it?" Erik finally called out.

"Portland Police," came a loud voice from outside the office. "We'd like to talk to Dr. Donovan."

Erik moved across the room to the door and opened it to

see two uniformed officers. He stepped back, allowing them to enter.

One officer turned to him and said, "We'd like to speak to her alone, please."

Erik glanced quickly over to Thea and raised his eyebrows. As if to reassure her, he said, "I'll be just outside if you need me." Thea nodded in mute acquiescence.

Half an hour later when the police officers left, Erik immediately returned to Thea's office. She sat with her face cradled in her hands, elbows propped up on the desk, her face twisted as if she was about to cry.

"What did they want?"

"They wanted to know my whereabouts just before the explosion. I had to tell them I was in my office alone. No witnesses, of course."

Erik frowned, looked as if he were about to make a comment, then changed his mind. For a few moments he was silent. Finally he said, "Maybe you should talk to an attorney."

"I hate lawyers," she said.

Erik shrugged. "Lawyers are like laxatives. You go through life trying to avoid them, but eventually you need one just to get rid of the shit."

Thea snorted in a humorless laugh. "Maybe you're right. If the police keep questioning me, I should be aware of my legal options."

Erik's lips had formed a tight line that attempted to impersonate a smile but failed. He walked up behind Thea's chair, placed his hands on her shoulders and gave her a squeeze.

"It looks like Steiner might have been right about Malcolm Dean," he said. Thea spun around, the action ripping his hands off her shoulders.

"What are you talking about?" she gasped, incredulous. "You can't believe Malcolm was responsible for Sheldon's death?"

Erik shrugged in a noncommittal way and began heading toward the door. He opened it, pausing in the doorway.

"First the botched surgery to his face, then the damage to

the Reflesh machine, and now Steiner. Steiner suspected him of sabotaging the lab. So, I guess you'd have to ask yourself, who else had more motives?" he said. Then he slipped quietly out, closing the door behind him.

TEN

With the Reflesh machine down for repair, Thea canceled all upcoming surgeries until after the investigation into Sheldon's death. While the police were only doing their job in casting suspicion on her actions, given her tumultuous relationship with Steiner, they cautioned her that she, too, may be in danger. She wondered where their concerns lay. They had not mentioned Malcolm and she had not volunteered any information about him. Did they, like Erik, suspect Malcolm killed Sheldon Steiner?

Making the most of the free time on her hands, she couldn't help reflecting on the clippings in David Dean's file. She resolved to spend the day looking for Peter Volk, dead or alive. And with Erik busy working on other projects that were separate from their mutual interests, she was grateful for the break. Too many outside opinions were clouding her judgment. She needed the objectivity of solitude.

After making several telephone calls to local cemeteries, she learned that there was a listing for a Peter Volk at the Eternal Sunset Cemetery she passed each morning on her drive to work. Once there, she retrieved a map of the layout of the grounds from the cemetery office. It was difficult to follow, and no one was available to help her locate a grave. But to Thea a graveyard was a quiet, calming place with little chance of interruption and if nothing else, a walk in the fresh air would do her good.

It wasn't long before she realized that it was an interminable, time-consuming exercise. She encountered many headstones with names she immediately recognized as early settlers of the city. The streets and parks that bore the names of these former citizens and to which she had never given any thought suddenly had historical significance. It was an education. But she also acknowledged the futility of searching for a grave that might not exist.

Finally in exasperation she turned and began walking across the soft greenness, between the grim monuments, vases of wilted flowers, and helium balloons long spent. She paused for a moment and looked back across the cemetery with its view of Mt. Hood. Death had never been Thea's enemy and as she took in the tranquil beauty she thought that this would not be such a bad place to spend eternity.

Then she glanced down at a grave near her feet that bore no headstone, only a bronze plate. To her amazement she saw that upon it was engraved, *Alicia Volk, beloved wife of Peter.* Beside Alicia's grave was another plate with Peter Volk's name and date of birth. The date of death was not yet recorded. Then she realized that the office had misunderstood her. His name had shown up in their records because it had been listed for a prepurchased gravesite; he wasn't necessarily interred here. Could it be possible that Peter was still alive? Thea let out a long gasp of relief and excitement. For the first time she felt a small surge of hope.

She recalled that the clipping of Peter committing himself to a sanitarium had not shown a date. The building would have to be a private hospital at least thirty years old. If he was still there and not released, that is. Or dead and buried somewhere else. She drove until she found a library and sat at one of the free computers to do an internet search. She checked all the variations of nursing homes, sanitariums, and mental hospitals, noting down numbers and addresses. Then she went outside to use her cell phone and called several listings without success. On her last call she got lucky. A gruff-sounding staff member of a small, private clinic in northeast Portland confirmed that Peter Volk had been a longtime patient.

Although the clinic was in an older, rough area on the outskirts of the city, it appeared clean and well maintained. The ward clerk at the reception desk looked like she'd just graduated from high school. She confided to Thea that she'd only been on the job for a week. Thea smiled at her enthusiasm, secretly thankful for her inexperience. It was unlikely she'd question a visit from a doctor.

"I'm Dr. Thea Donovan. I'm here to see Peter Volk."

A confused frown crossed the clerk's brow then she brightened.

"Oh, you mean Jigsaw," she said with a laugh. "Sure. Follow me." She made a notation on a clipboard and handed it to Thea to sign in. Then she emerged from behind the desk and led Thea down the long corridor.

"Jigsaw?" asked Thea, curious.

"Yes, that's what everyone here calls him. I'm not sure why but it must be because he likes puzzles. He's always got unfinished ones where he sits in the rec room."

The clerk stopped before a door with a sign that read, 'Recreation Room'. She reached into her pocket, produced a key and unlocked the door, relocking it behind them once they were inside. As Thea stepped into the center of the Spartan room she saw approximately fifteen patients dressed in regular street clothing. Some watched TV while others read or played checkers. Only one man sat far off in the corner by himself. There was a small table beside him. An unfinished jigsaw puzzle covered the surface.

"That's him over there," said the girl, pointing to the solitary man. "Visitors have a half-hour. If you want to leave sooner, just push the buzzer and someone will come and let you out." She indicated a small button near the door. Thea nodded.

"Thank you," she said. "I don't think it will take long."

After the clerk left, Thea silently observed former Portland Detective, Peter Volk. For a second she felt a flicker of recognition, but just as suddenly, it vanished. She was certain she would have remembered this man had she met him. He had high, craggy cheekbones framed by sparse, light gray hair that only reached halfway up his scalp. Long legs stuck out stiffly from the depths of an upholstered chair that easily supported the rest of his emaciated body. His lifeless hazel eyes stared straight ahead and as Thea approached, he did not give any indication that he could see her.

Thea pulled a chair from a neighboring table and sat opposite Peter.

"Are you Peter Volk?" she asked quietly. Peter remained motionless, continuing to stare straight ahead as if he could not hear her. Although psychiatry was not her area of specialty, Thea recognized the signs of catatonia and wondered if she could reach behind the wall he had built.

A chubby, bespectacled young man came up behind Thea and startled her when he spoke.

"You wo-wo-wo-won't g-g-g-get any any anything out of him," he said, his head bobbing comically toward Peter. "He never t-t-talks to any anyone. He n-n-never s-s-s-says any any anything 'cept jigsaw."

Thea turned toward him and smiled in a friendly, reassuring way. "Jigsaw? Why is that?"

The man cocked his head to one side, thinking for a few moments. "D-d-d-don't know," he finally admitted. Then he turned and walked away as quickly as he arrived.

She picked up a piece of the puzzle beside Peter, searched for its correct location and pressed it together.

"Do you like jigsaw puzzles, Peter?"

He neither looked at her nor made a reply. She decided to try another tactic to break through his mental barrier.

"Do you remember your wife, Alicia?" This time she noticed a perceptible comprehension cross his face. She tried again. "What about your former attorney, Reg Forbes? Do you remember anything about him?" she asked.

Then she stopped, for Peter was now rocking slowly back and forth, muttering something inaudible under his breath. Thea glanced around the room for assistance but to her consternation remembered she had been left completely unassisted. And the room was locked. She turned back to Peter, determined to try again before he became unreachable.

"Can you tell me anything about the murders?"

The rocking motion increased in momentum. He began chanting incoherent syllables that made a chugging sound resembling the word 'jigsaw'. Thea leaned back in alarm. Peter's movements became more and more frantic. She stood up and placed her hands on his shoulders to calm him, but he shook her off as easily as if she were a fly. Arms flailing, he hit the small table, scattering the jigsaw puzzle pieces across the floor. Out of the corner of her eye Thea saw the young man who had spoken to her push the call buzzer. In moments an enormous white-coated orderly was at her side.

"What happened here?" he demanded. He produced a syringe from his pocket, rolled back Peter's sleeve and injected the needle. After a few seconds Peter became less agitated. Then suddenly he was sitting in his original position, staring straight ahead as if nothing had happened.

Thea masked a small pang of guilt. She lifted her chin and said, "I'm a doctor. I asked some questions that seemed disturbing but I didn't mean to alarm him."

The orderly straightened up beside the now calm Peter and glared at her.

"This patient has restricted visitors. Who gave you permission to see him?" he said in a terse way Thea found abrasive for his station.

Then she realized the young ward clerk had, in oversight, allowed her to visit Peter and if she had encountered a more experienced staff member, they would not have permitted her to visit him alone. Feeling fortunate at her timing she decided to try to protect the innocent young woman.

"It was my mistake," she said, backing toward the door. "I'll sign myself out." Then she was outside the ward and walking down the hallway toward the main door. Out of the corner of her eye she caught a worried glance from the young clerk but it was too late now. She was on her own.

Back at her house she found a succession of messages on her voice mail. While they played back, she reached into the fridge for a can of Coke and sat at the kitchen table to write down the messages. The first three were from Erik, wondering where she had been all afternoon. There was a call from a woman sounding like Meredith, but to Thea's annoyance left no name or phone number, expecting her to recognize the voice. The last message was from a homicide detective with the city police, requesting that she return his call when possible.

Thea sighed, took a long swallow of Coke and belched softly. What did the police want now? She was beginning to wonder if she were under suspicion. She felt a cold chill envelop her body. Did the police suspect her of withholding information and have her under surveillance without her knowledge? Maybe Erik had been right about calling a lawyer.

She returned Erik's call but this time it was he who wasn't home. After leaving a message on his answering machine she called his cell phone and had to leave a message there as well. Then she called the police department and asked for the detective who had left his name and number on her voice mail, Stan Peltzer. What could they do to her anyway, she wondered, she had nothing to hide. Still, she could not assuage the uneasiness that squirmed in her stomach.

ELEVEN

On the telephone at least, Detective Stan Peltzer sounded like a congenial man who managed to assuage Thea's fears despite the seriousness of the situation. Although he would not go into details, he insisted Thea come to his office for questioning. By implying that any reluctance on her part might be misconstrued by the police, he gave her little choice. Still, her spirits lifted only slightly after she had hung up the phone. It was always preferable to be summoned rather than apprehended.

Although she had nothing to be concerned about, having never been on the inquisition side of the law, Thea entered the detective's office with trepidation. The small, cheaply furnished office held a couple of mismatched chairs and a desk with a scarred leather recliner behind it. The room was too hot and smelled as if a window hadn't been opened in a long time. At Peltzer's gesture she perched nervously on the edge of one of the chairs and waited, her perspiring hands tightly clasped. But Detective Peltzer, a stout, balding man with a bulbous nose and conversational attitude, soon put her at ease. Once he'd provided Thea with a cup of coffee that resembled her last oil change, it was time to get down to business.

Detective Peltzer took a seat in his chair and leaned across the desk over a file he scanned briefly before looking up at Thea.

"In the statement you gave to the police after Dr. Steiner's death, you said that you had been working in your office alone, just prior to the explosion, is that right?"

"My secretary, Gwen, was in the office with me until late in the afternoon. I wanted to finish up some paperwork so I told her she could leave."

"Do you normally work in the office that late?"

Thea shook her head. "If I have patients to see, I do. More often I do my surgical notes in between rounds or post-surgical visits."

Peltzer glanced down at the file and turned over a few papers. "Do you and Dr. Steiner generally work the same hours?"

"I really don't know what Dr. Steiner's hours are." She paused, suddenly uncomfortable and glanced toward the window. "Were. He'd been asked to do routine consults on a couple of my cases, but we had very little contact other than conferring about his recommendations. Or, if he continued to see a patient of mine on a long term basis, he'd correspond with me by email about the patient's progress."

Peltzer was silent for several moments. "We've spoken to a few of the hospital Board and other staff members who mentioned that you've had several run-ins with Dr. Steiner recently. Would you tell me what those were about?"

Thea wiped her sweaty palms on her slacks and tucked her hands under her legs to stop them from shaking. "We disagreed on the treatment of a patient. Dr. Steiner advised against his release, recommending the patient stay in the hospital for further psychiatric counseling and evaluation. He thought the patient was a danger to himself and possibly others."

"And you thought the patient was fine for release?"

Thea hesitated. "It's complicated. The plastic surgery didn't go as expected and I wanted to do a follow-up surgery. The patient began demonstrating psychotic behavior and refused further surgery. I felt that until he changed his mind there was nothing we could do to help him other than counsel him as an outpatient."

"And this patient is Malcolm Dean, correct?"

"Yes," Thea whispered.

"I'm sorry. I didn't hear what you said."

"Yes, it was Malcolm Dean."

"And how did Mr. Dean get along with Dr. Steiner?"

Thea thought about this, trying to form her words in such

a way that they wouldn't set Malcolm up as a potential killer.

"He didn't seem to like him very much, but then he didn't appear to like anyone after the surgery. I think both Dr. Steiner and I believe he suffered from PTSD. Mr. Dean's wife and son died not long ago and with the burns and post-surgical trauma, it possibly pushed him over the edge."

"Can you think of anyone else who might have had an issue with Dr. Steiner?"

Thea shook her head. "Not that I'm aware of. Dr. Steiner and I had our differences but we respected each other's work. His death will be a huge loss to the Psychiatry Department at St. Augustus. And to his patients, of course."

"Hmmm," said Peltzer. He scribbled some notes on a yellow pad. Finally he looked up, rubbing a finger absently along the bridge of his nose. "You were both competing for a large research grant, is that right? A grant that would only go to one department."

"That's right," Thea said. "But there are other ways and areas that funding can come from. It wasn't as if a strong research program would be in danger of being discontinued due to lack of money."

"You consider your program a strong one?"

"I do," Thea replied.

"What about Dr. Steiner's research?"

Thea struggled with a surge of annoyance for a moment then replied heatedly, "Dr. Steiner's research had merit. But it's completely different from mine. My research is surgical. His was in psychiatry. I don't see how anyone could lump them together."

Peltzer's eyebrows raised at her vehemence but he made no comment. After making a few more notes, he glanced up at Thea and gave her a brief smile. "Thank you, Doctor," he said. "You've been a big help."

While Thea couldn't see how, she was relieved that he seemed satisfied with her responses. She was just about to ask if she were free to leave when, to her amazement, the interrogation took a new direction.

"In layman terms, what is Reflesh?" he asked, leaning back in his chair.

Startled, Thea glanced at him, wondering where he had heard about Reflesh. Patiently she explained, in much the same way she outlined it for Erik what seemed like so long ago, the Reflesh and its capacity for rebuilding the human face. After a while, Stan Peltzer nodded as if he comprehended, which from his expression Thea was not certain he did. Then he stood up, motioning her toward the door.

"I'd like you to come down to Forensics and have a look at something," he said. "It may have a connection to your patient."

She followed him as he led her through a labyrinth of anonymous offices and finally stopped at a locked door. He brought out a set of keys, unlocked the door and walked over to a table with a row of microscopes. A tall, thin man in a lab coat stood beside the largest.

"This is Dr. Andrews, our Forensic Pathologist," he said. Thea nodded recognition. They had met once or twice in the past.

"We've had trouble identifying the tissue found under the fingernails of a young woman who was found murdered," Dr. Andrews explained. "I remembered reading an article about you and your artificial skin research. We need you to confirm whether this tissue is Reflesh." He stepped back from the microscope to allow her to examine the specimen.

Thea leaned over and squinted into the microscope. Although there was foreign matter mixed in with the tiny scrap of Reflesh on the slide, she had spent too many long years hovered over a microscope creating it to be in doubt about its authenticity.

"It's Reflesh, all right," she said, looking at each of them in turn. "You said you discovered it under a fingernail?" Stan Peltzer and Dr. Andrews glanced at each other.

"It's part of another murder investigation," said Peltzer. "You understand this is confidential and not to go beyond this room?" Thea nodded.

"How many patients have undergone the Reflesh procedure?" He paused. "More specifically, how many men?"

Thea swallowed hard. Now she understood their line of questioning.

"I've done surgery on several women," she said, her gaze wandering across the room, not settling on either of them, "but just one man."

"Malcolm Dean?" asked Peltzer, sounding almost smug.

"Malcolm Dean," Thea whispered.

* * * * * *

Not having been in touch with Erik because they'd been playing phone-tag for several days, Thea was curious as to how the repairs were coming along on the sabotaged Reflesh machine. It had to be in perfect working order before she'd be able to perform surgery on a patient she had scheduled for the following week. She blamed herself for not following up on its status, but prayed Erik had found someone reputable to repair it as he'd said he would.

Although she didn't have any current inpatients to check on, she still had paperwork to do and realized it was about time she'd made an appearance at the lab to check on the repair progress. She slipped into casual grey workout pants, t-shirt and hoodie, and pinned her hair into a ponytail. Then she headed to St. Augustus to complete any preoperative admission forms needed for next week's upcoming surgery.

As she entered the hospital, no one appeared to recognize her in the uncustomary casual attire, for which she was grateful. She had to admit she was becoming more and more anti-social as time went on and people recognized her from her recent notoriety. Fame wasn't something she courted. In fact, as of late she'd come to resent it.

She reached the door to the Reflesh lab and found the hospital staff, perhaps assuming that further sabotage was no longer a danger, had ceased providing a security guard at the door. Feeling unsettled at the possibly premature move on the hospital's part, she glanced up and down the corridor for any onlookers. But she was all alone.

Removing the lab key from her hoodie pocket, she was just about to insert it in the lock when the door swayed opened on its own. Startled, the keys fell from her hand. She knelt quickly and snatched them from the floor, then pushed the door slowly ajar. Why would Erik be working today? she wondered, then realized he might be going over repairs with the tech person. As the door swung soundlessly inward she saw a tall, well-built man with a full head of gleaming blonde hair leaning over the Reflesh machine.

"Who are you, and how did you get access to this lab?" she demanded.

The man whirled around, startled, then flashed an easy smile. "You must be Thea," he said.

Thea frowned. The man bore a strong resemblance to Erik, but it definitely wasn't Erik. Despite having the same blonde hair and hazel eyes, he was at least a head taller and had a heavier build that spoke of regular workouts.

"Okay, so you know *my* name. Now who the hell are you?"

The man smiled again and approached her, holding out his hand, which was covered in Reflesh material. He saw her glance at it and hurriedly wiped it on a rag near the machine. He held his hand out again. She took it and gave it one shake, not feeling at all friendly about this man who for all appearances was trespassing.

"I'm Drew Sorenson," he said. "Erik's my brother. We're co-owners in our computer programing firm. We work together sometimes, although I tend to lean more toward the industrial and engineering portion of the business, while he prefers to work with surgical applications."

Thea felt her attitude soften a bit. She moved over to the Reflesh machine and saw that it had been disassembled, with new plastic-wrapped parts lying alongside the damaged pieces.

"Are you the tech he was talking about bringing in to repair our damaged machine?"

Drew nodded. He glanced at the machine. "It'll probably take another day or so but I have all the replacement parts now."

He smiled again and for several minutes only an awkward silence filled the room. It was an uncomfortable way for her to meet the repair technician, but even stranger to meet Erik's brother. She was at a loss as to whether she should stay and make certain he was on the level, or leave and let him finish the repairs.

Finally Thea said, "This room is a high security area with limited access to anyone other than Erik and me without express permission. Please make certain it's locked when you leave."

Although Drew appeared somewhat dismayed at her abrupt rudeness, he nodded and watched her until she'd closed the door behind her. And as Thea stood outside the lab door pondering over the unusual meeting she couldn't get rid of the overwhelming sense of doom that swept over her like a dark mood.

* * * * * *

When Thea returned home she found she was right in her assumption that the unidentified female caller on her voice mail had been Meredith. Since that one call there had been several more from the distraught sounding woman. Thea sighed, wondering how much she could tell Meredith without compromising the investigations of either murder. She was just about to pick up the phone to call her, when it rang.

"Dr. Donovan. It's too late," Meredith wailed into the receiver. "Two officers were just here. They searched our garage and took some of Malcolm's things away in plastic bags. Then they produced a warrant for his arrest." Thea could hear her crying softly at the other end.

Thea hesitated. "What are they charging him with?"

"He's under suspicion of murder, conspiracy, arson, and a whole bunch of other charges I've never even heard of." She

88

let out a loud sob. "Malcolm couldn't do those things. He always helped people."

The old Malcolm perhaps, thought Thea, but no one knows just what the new Malcolm is capable of doing.

"Has he contacted you? They might not be able to find him if they can't trace him through you."

"No, he hasn't," said Meredith, sounding just a little bit brighter. "But they warned me that if I were hiding him, I'd be in big trouble and could possibly be charged with withholding evidence."

"You're not in any danger of that," said Thea. "I'll talk to the police and see what I can do to help." But her words held more conviction than she felt. After all, she too was probably a suspect. If not directly, then as an accessory.

After she finished with Meredith, Thea made a call to Stan Peltzer. She had a feeling the detective would be straight with her and respect her professional interest in Malcolm's welfare. She got right to the point.

"I just spoke with Malcolm Dean's mother who told me the police were at her house with a search warrant and a whole grocery list of charges against him. You'd better have more evidence than an angry patient and Reflesh under a victim's fingernails to support such charges." she blurted, too upset to realize how threatening her tone had become.

"It's part of an ongoing investigation and I can't tell you very much or it could jeopardize our case. You were here earlier, you know about some of it. Details haven't been made public but we've obtained evidence from the explosion that killed Dr. Steiner and it points directly to Malcolm Dean."

"What sort of evidence?" Thea asked, feeling a sense of doom fall over her.

"It was an incendiary device used by the Fire Department for training purposes that caused the explosion, an item to which only inside personnel, such as Mr. Dean, would have access. We found similar items in his garage." Peltzer waited for Thea to comment and when she did not, he went on, "I'm sorry about your patient, but the case against him looks pretty grim."

Scarcely hearing her own voice, Thea grudgingly thanked him for his time and hung up the phone. It was over for Malcolm. She felt no relief that she was no longer a suspect in Steiner's death. Her error during surgery appeared to have produced a killing machine and in attempting to recreate one life she was inadvertently responsible for the loss of two others.

TWELVE

Erik's persistence in reaching Thea finally ended in victory. Now he was on his way over she found herself scrambling to tidy the house she had neglected these past few days. A week's worth of newspapers lay scattered about, keeping company with discarded wrinkled clothing. The house plants that initially survived her apathetic care were now beginning to wilt and yellow. Feeling guilty, she oversoaked them, vowing in future to buy silk plants.

After wiping an accumulation of dust off the counter surfaces with the side of her sleeve, she noticed Malcolm's file and the book she had taken from his bedroom. She carefully tucked them out of sight in an empty drawer. If Erik saw them he might ask questions about Malcolm and she wouldn't be able to lie about her visits to Meredith and discussions with Detective Peltzer. Or the warrant for Malcolm's arrest. Although she had nothing to hide, for some reason it made her uncomfortable discussing Malcolm with him.

She answered the doorbell feeling confused at the mixture of emotions that haunted her at seeing Erik. When they lightly embraced, Thea did not experience the rush of joy that should have been present when greeting a lover. She wondered briefly at this, but she had questions that needed answering.

"When were you going to tell me about your brother?" she blurted, without preamble.

Erik reeled back. "Whoa!" He gave a short laugh. "I'm pretty sure I mentioned him to you before."

Thea tilted her head, eyes narrowed. "You didn't tell me he was your partner in your computing firm. Nor did you tell me he was the person who was going to repair the Reflesh machine. Don't you think that's something that I, your other partner, should have been made aware of before I embarrassed myself?"

Erik threw up his hands in resignation and frowned. "I'm sorry I didn't clear it with you first. After all we've been through together I didn't think I needed to. I thought you trusted me enough."

She didn't reply, moving instead into the kitchen to fix coffee and divert an argument.

"Thea?" he called. "Are you okay with this?"

She responded by returning to the doorway. "Yes, I'm okay with it. I just have no idea of what your brother's credentials or background are. That much, at least, you could have shared with me before you brought him in on the project. You know how cautious I am bringing outsiders into the fold. Not to mention, it's me who has hospital privileges at St. Augustus. I'm the one who should have been consulted about hiring him because ultimately I'm the one who would have to vouch for him."

Erik had the grace to look contrite. "You're right. I'm sorry. If it's any consolation, Drew is one of the few people in the world I'd trust to do the job." He paused and moved across the room, busying himself by examining a painting on the wall, as if trying to decide what else might be safe to share with her.

"Drew is my best friend. After you, of course," he added hastily. "He's always been there for me, even when we were little. Sometimes he's a bit over protective, but that's what big brothers are for, right?"

Thea stared at him. "I wouldn't know. I don't have a big brother."

Erik shrugged. "Look, I'll get you his CV and a bunch of references from other jobs we've done together."

"It's not necessary," she said, turning back to the kitchen to retrieve coffee for them both. "If you say he's the right guy for the job then that's enough for me." She set a cup of coffee and a plate of store bought cookies in front of him, then sat down beside him on the sofa. Together they sipped their coffee in brooding silence.

But Erik wanted to share his own predicament and momentarily she put the issue with his brother from her mind.

"In other news," he said caustically, "the police have been hounding me, asking about Malcolm Dean." His statement came out in a way that seemed to question whether they had subjected her to the same interrogations. She nodded in empathy.

"I don't think I'm under any doctor/patient confidentiality and it may be unprofessional," he went on, "but I told them Malcolm is extremely disturbed and from what I'd observed might have something to do with Steiner's death." Thea's reaction startled him.

"You did what?" she shouted. "How could you? We only saw his postoperative responses. Since his discharge from hospital we haven't been able to study him long enough to find out if he's disturbed or not." She stood up and began pacing across the room, shaking her head. "I can't believe you told them that. That was up to Dr. Steiner and we both know what happened to him."

"Lighten up," Erik chided. "You suspect it too, don't you?" He placed his arms around her waist and drew her close. Roughly, she pushed him away.

"What's wrong?" Erik persisted. "The guy is looney tunes and he needs help. He probably killed Steiner and you're defending him." He tilted his head to one side and studied her in an introspective way. "You're protecting him, aren't you? Maybe you're hiding him. Maybe you're even sleeping with him."

Thea shook her head angrily. "You're way off base, Erik. I'm not convinced about anything when it comes to Malcolm. And you have no right accusing me." She stared at him through narrowed eyes. "You haven't told anyone *your* whereabouts when Steiner died." Realizing she was being unfair, she stopped. Then she saw that her words had a far greater impact than she could have foreseen.

Erik's face hardened to the point that it looked as if you

could break rocks on it. Though he made no threat, his silent fury frightened her. And because in that moment he bore no resemblance to the Erik with whom she shared everything she held dear, it was more terrifying than any physical action he might have taken. For the first time she realized that intimacy and time spent together does not necessarily mean that you truly know someone.

"I'm sorry," she said, voice shaking. "I didn't mean that. This day didn't get off on a very good start. I think you'd better leave before we say something we'll regret later."

"For your information, and if you had even bothered to ask you would have already known, but I was leading an all-day training session in St. Augustus' IT Department. That's why I was on the scene so fast and at your side after the explosion. There were at least a dozen hospital employees who can verify that I was in their department the entire day."

She walked over to the door, held it open, then stepped aside for him to pass. Erik stared coldly at her, with such an unfiltered anger in his eyes Thea wondered if it was really her he was seeing. Then without even saying goodbye he walked out, slamming the door behind him.

Thea let out a long sigh, feeling like she'd been holding her breath during their entire altercation. She listened at the door just in case Erik decided to come back. When it became apparent he wasn't, she locked the deadbolt and sat on the living room sofa. Erik's accusations and his reaction to her heated remarks had left her aching and hollow inside. Then she remembered why she had always been so obdurate in avoiding relationships. It had begun with Chris.

Thea met Dr. Chris Jacoby during her first year internship at the University of British Columbia. She was taking an elective in gynecology and although he was not her preceptor, he was on the obstetrical/gynecological staff. With the crushing time burden allotted to medical students, especially in an obstetrical ward, they were often in contact.

Oddly enough, she had not been attracted to Chris the first time they met. He was tanned and fair-haired, well-muscled. Only two years out of medical school, he was the brash, 'I know I'm devastating' type that she usually avoided if possible.

"He's a womanizer," warned the nurses, not generally friendly, nor looking out for the welfare of young, attractive, female doctors who so often were their competition. "Steer clear of him." But after several months of Chris's teasing and innuendo (which nowadays she realized would be considered sexual harassment) she gave in to pressure and they began dating.

At first they were covert about their relationship. It was improper for a staff physician to date a medical student and in any event, there was scarcely time for sleep, let alone a social life. But hospitals are like small towns with their gossip and it wasn't too long before others noticed that at social functions a certain two doctors had no time to talk with anyone else.

After it became common knowledge that they were seeing each other, Thea did not object too strenuously when Chris suggested they move in together. Although Thea was still living with her grandparents, her heavy schedule kept her coming and going at all hours and the strain was beginning to show on them all. She did not inform her straight-laced grandparents of her intended living arrangements, nor did they come to visit her once she'd found an apartment with Chris and they retired to a seniors' residence.

If Thea found it unusual that she actually saw Chris less after they began living together, she did not mention it. By now she had moved on to a new elective in Radiology and was busily embroiled in her studies. The current baby boom trend kept Chris away for long hours and most nights he slept at the hospital. At least that's what he told her.

It would have been a normal evening for most young couples. Thea had changed into an old shirt of Chris's and it hung just above her knees. She cooked dinner and for the first time in weeks they had time to eat together and talk. After dessert, they settled down on the sofa to drink tea and watch television like an old married couple. Then came a buzz from the apartment intercom. Chris sat up quickly.

"Don't answer it," he said. Thea laughed.

"Of course I'll answer it, silly."

She jumped up and kissed him on the top of his head. But when she pushed the intercom button whoever had rung was no longer there. She shrugged and started to turn when there was a loud knock at the door. She smiled tentatively at Chris. The tan on his face had drained to a ghost-white. A tiny tremor of apprehension began to grow inside her.

She walked to the door and slipped on the safety chain. Then she opened the door just a crack.

"Yes?" she said.

"Is Chris there?" A woman's voice from the other side of the door nearly spat the words at her. Out of shock more than anything Thea opened the door. A very pretty, very pregnant, furious young woman stood before her. Then, just as surprisingly, the woman burst into tears and ran away before either Chris or Thea could say anything.

Thea, on the verge of tears herself, turned to Chris for a chance to explain that this was not what it seemed, that the whole event was a bizarre soap-opera. But the guilt in his eyes told the whole story. There was no fight, no screaming or re-criminations as Chris packed what little he owned in the apartment.

Thea held back the anguish until he left, then proceeded to smash and destroy everything in the apartment that reminded her of Chris. In the end, he became her major reason for deciding to leave the country. She never wanted even an inadvertent encounter with him again.

But just before Thea left Canada for the U.S., she was eating dinner out alone and noticed Chris, his new wife and their infant son near the back of the restaurant. Though their gazes met and Thea was certain he recognized her, Chris glanced quickly away and became overly attentive in feeding his son. Thea hastily requested the check and nearly laughed aloud when she read it.

The waitress had erred in the spelling of her drink, referring to it as a 'gyn and tonic'. As Thea shot one last glance toward the perfect little family she thought wryly, of all the gyn joints in all the towns in all the world, I had to walk into his.

The intricacies and nuances of personal relationships always seemed to elude her, she thought. How different would her life have been if she'd grown up with a father to guide her, instead of an aging, uncompromising grandfather. Then again, maybe she would have made the same choices. And now there was Erik.

THIRTEEN

Thea overslept the next morning and it was the doorbell's Westminster chimes that finally woke her. She decided to stay in bed, covering her head with the sheets to muffle the persistent ringing. If it was Erik, she did not want to see him today. If it was someone else, they could leave a message in her mailbox or on her voice mail. Today she was willing to take a chance at missing something important.

After she was certain that whoever was at the door had gone, she crawled out of bed, got dressed and cautiously opened the front door. There was no one in sight. She reached into the mailbox. Her searching fingers contacted a hard object she had difficulty removing. Although it was too early for her regular mail delivery, someone had left a brown paper-wrapped parcel small enough to fit in the mailbox. She tucked the parcel under her arm and quickly closed the door. Then she went back to the kitchen to open it.

There was no address either to or from anyone on the brown paper, nor was there any postage. So whoever had left it had hand delivered it. She peeled away the paper carefully with two fingers, setting it aside for later if it should need to be dusted for prints. After the wrapping had fallen away a hard covered book was revealed. Its title was *Historical Oregon Homes*, a compilation of Oregon houses on the Historical Register. A small piece of white paper serving as a bookmark, jutted from somewhere near the center. Thea opened to the marker and scanned the page. A photograph of a house identical to hers seemed to leap off the page. Though the house looked the same, the tiny, dwarfed trees in the picture scarcely resembled the present mature landscaping.

Thea stared at the picture in amazement. Then she began to read the paragraph beneath the photo.

"One of Portland's oldest historical homes, built in 1921, achieved notoriety not as much through its ageless beauty as from a murder/suicide that took place in 1986. Upon returning home from work one day, the owner discovered his wife had been murdered by her lover, who had then committed suicide.

"Although many rumors abounded, it was ultimately considered an open and shut case. It is believed the couple's five-year-old son witnessed the murder but was so traumatized he could never testify. The owner sold the house a short time later.

"Over the years the house changed hands often and was used as rental property. Through neglect and lack of repair it became rundown. Eventually it was purchased by a local architect who did the necessary renovations and had it placed on the Historic Register."

Thea finished reading and sat back, dumbfounded. Who had left the book? Could it have been her realtor, a young woman named Lauren, or someone else? The bookmark was just a piece of white bond without notation. Still pondering over the mystery, she set the book down on the table and headed for the shower.

As she lathered shampoo into her hair, Thea thought back over the murder story. It was so similar to the clipping in Malcolm's file, she realized now that her house must have once belonged to Peter Volk. And it was the house where he had discovered his wife and attorney murdered.

An enormous wave of vertigo swept over her. She gripped the shower door and took slow, deep breaths. What an eerie feeling it was, knowing now that two people had died in her home. She quickly rinsed off the soap and stepped out of the shower, shivering from shock as much as cold.

After dressing in jeans and a sweatshirt at record speed, she considered her alternatives. Going to work did not appeal to her. And with what she now suspected about her house, there was no question of staying in it today. Though she knew

compiling data on her Reflesh surgeries to date would be beneficial, she dismissed this notion immediately. Her brain was not
at its sharpest. The other option was to make up with Erik.

At first she rebelled against making the first move. Erik
had started with the recriminating comments and withholding
information about his brother from her; he should be the one
to apologize. But that thought left her with a trace of doubt.
Somehow Erik did not seem like the peacemaking type. She
felt certain that unless someone else made the first overture,
Erik might well hold a grudge indefinitely. But both had too
much at stake to remain angry with the other.

Feeling that it would be easier to apologize face to face,
she decided to surprise him and go straight to his apartment.
They had never had a serious disagreement before, much less a
fight of this magnitude. Despite their differences over the tragic circumstances these last few days, she felt a sudden tingle of
excitement. Making up might be an enjoyable experience.

After lowering the convertible top of the Mercedes, she
set off for Erik's apartment, ten minutes away. As she drove,
her enthusiasm increased, and when she was within a few
blocks of Erik's home she was singing to the tune on the radio.
She slowed then stopped for a red light. Out of her peripheral
vision she noticed a sleek foreign car entering the intersection
to make a left turn. Her stomach did a quick flip. The man at
the wheel looked just like Erik!

The sunlight glinting on the car's darkened windows
slightly obscured the driver, making her uncertain that it really
was Erik. But then she saw that the car had a passenger—a
blonde, female passenger.

"The bastard!" she hissed.

But a moment later she told herself she was being ridiculous. It might not be him, after all. She had no idea what sort
of vehicle he drove. When they went out together they had
always used her car. But the memory of her previous disastrous
romance was still too painful. So at the next parking lot she
made a U-turn and drove toward home.

She knew that she lacked any claim to Erik's affections.

Other than on a professional level they had not made any commitments to each other or agreed not to see anyone else. But sharing a bed was not something Thea took lightly. For her, that meant an unspoken fidelity. She was unable to decide what hurt the most, the shock at seeing him with someone else or the anger that he did not feel the same way she did. If it was him, of course.

The main problem, she thought, was that she didn't have any female friends with whom to share things. She was aware that being shy gave her an aloofness that might be interpreted by some as arrogance. With the exception of hospital employees, women outside the medical profession had the erroneous notion that they would not have anything to talk about with a female surgeon. More often than not she was excluded from social invitations other than hospital functions. The closest friend she had made here was the realtor who had shown her the house.

She smiled to herself, a little sad. Lauren had been friendly and helpful when she first moved to Portland; maybe she could invite her to have lunch. In addition, it might well have been Lauren who had sent her the book and this would be the perfect time to ask. She picked up the cell phone and realized that Lauren's office number was still in the phone's memory. It hadn't been that long after all.

Lauren sounded pleased to hear from Thea and they made plans to meet at a local bistro at noon. Thea's spirits lifted higher than they had been in days. She changed her jeans to slim fitting black slacks, and threw a light pink shirt over top of a white tank top. When she recognized Lauren, a tiny pale girl with a shock of wavy red hair, waiting at an outdoor table at the cafe, she went over and gave her a warm hug of welcome.

"You look awful!" Lauren said candidly when she relinquished herself from Thea's grasp. "I've read about your research in the paper lately and meant to call you but I thought you'd be too busy."

"I wish you had," Thea murmured. "But I'm guilty for not thinking of calling you sooner. Anyhow, we're here now and I need to ask you a few things."

A waiter came over, passed them handwritten menus and poured two glasses of water. Thea glanced briefly at the menu.

"Spanakopita and a Greek salad, please" she said. "Oh, and an iced tea." She handed the paper back to the waiter.

"Make it two," Lauren added. After the waiter had gone she turned back to Thea. "So what's been happening?"

"In my professional life, too much. In my personal life, too little." She laughed. "I have a knack for getting involved with men who don't want to get involved with me."

Lauren smiled. "What's new?" she said, pushing back her red curls. "I have the same problem. But I can see there's more to it than that, isn't there?"

Thea nodded, remembering what she'd wanted to talk to Lauren about in the first place. "Did you leave a book at my house this morning?" Lauren blinked.

"No, why do you think it might have been me?"

Thea shrugged. "It was called *Historical Oregon Homes* and it had an article on my house. You never told me about the murders that took place there. I thought you might have found the book and brought it over."

Lauren's face crinkled with concern. "I wouldn't have sent something like that without telling you about it first. It might scare you."

"It did," Thea admitted. "But that's not all that's been happening. Did any of the previous owners have problems with the lights?"

"Not that I know of. The last owner was an architect who did a lot of renovations but never lived on the property. Why do you ask?"

"No matter how I arranged the lamps in the bedroom, the walls had dark, gloomy shadows." She poked around her salad for a moment and took a mouthful, while Lauren waited patiently. "One day I tried pulling that old lamp cord and one of the panels moved, revealing a hiding space. I found a scrimshaw letter opener lying on the floor behind the wall."

"Cool," said Lauren, letting out a low whistle. "Any idea

who it might have belonged to?"

Thea hesitated. Then she remembered something that made her skin crawl. Was it really just an innocuous letter opener someone had left behind? Or maybe she was just letting her imagination run away with her again. She could feel Lauren's eyes on her and looked up.

"Nothing for certain," she said. "But I'll let you know if I find out."

"Tell me more about the murders." Lauren's face became guarded. "Even if it wasn't my listing, the listing agent should have known about that. It's called Disclosure, and if you don't do it when you sell the house you can get into big trouble. Even sued for it." Suddenly she stopped, shock flooding her face, and her hand flew to her mouth.

"You don't think the letter opener was part of the murder?"

Thea shook her head. She poked around at her salad for a few minutes. "From what I read, the weapon was a .357 Magnum that belonged to the lover of the woman who lived there. He shot her first then shot himself."

Lauren frowned, finished her mouthful of salad and took a sip of iced tea. "Did they ever find out what the motive was?"

"You know how it is with newspaper reporting of these things. They write the story but rarely is there follow-up about motive, or what happens to the people left behind. The only way you find that information is by attending the trial. From what I've been able to find out, though, the guy who committed the murders was the divorce lawyer of the woman's husband."

Lauren's face twisted. "That's weird. Doesn't really make any sense."

"No, it doesn't. But the District Attorney seemed to think it was an open and shut case. It was the husband, a Portland Police Detective, who found the bodies. He'd gone home from work to pick up a few of his things and found his wife and lawyer there murdered."

"Is the husband still alive?" Lauren asked, dropping her napkin on her plate as the waiter arrived. Thea stayed quiet until he'd removed the plates and glasses before replying.

"I finally found the husband living in a sanitarium here in town. He committed himself voluntarily shortly after the killings. He's in a catatonic state, though, and you couldn't get anything out of him if you plied him with wine."

Lauren gave a short laugh. "Well, that's probably for the best. Even if you're a police officer and you see these things on the job, when it comes to your own family it would be a trauma you'd never get over."

Thea was silent for several minutes, lost in thought. There was something that just didn't add up but she couldn't put her finger on it. Maybe she should have had a more substantial meal than just a salad and the appetizer, she thought. Her stomach had started to jump around as if she were coming down with the flu. Lauren didn't appear to know anything and although it was pleasant to have someone she could talk to, they didn't have enough in common to make it a long visit.

After pleading a stomach reaction to the salad, Thea said goodbye to Lauren, promising to call her in a couple of days. She wanted to get the substance on the letter opener analyzed before she mentioned it to anyone else. If it was just a letter opener and used for that purpose alone, she had nothing to worry about. But if the substance on the blade turned out to be blood, it would be another matter entirely.

When she arrived home she discovered that the postman had already been, and removed the letters from her mailbox, thrusting them into her pocket while she unlocked the front door. Still lost in thought about the letter opener and its significance, she headed straight for the desk in the living room. Gingerly she retrieved the letter opener from the drawer.

She turned the letter opener, still swathed in its tissue covering, over in her hands. She had originally thought that the stains on the blade were rust, but could they really be blood? She knew she could take it to the hospital lab and analyze it herself, but there would be other people around and she was under too much suspicion already. And there would no doubt be questions. Detective Stan Peltzer or his sidekick, Dr. Andrews would have to provide a positive identification of the material on the blade.

After retrieving the jacket she had last worn to Meredith's house, she riffled through the contents of her desk drawer. A case that had once held a Cross Pen, long since permanently borrowed by someone, was just the right size for it. She dropped the letter opener into it and as she did so noticed the intricate scrimshaw carvings on the handle. If the owner could not be identified from the blood stains, perhaps she could trace it down through an antiques dealer. Maybe it was even worth some money. But more important to her right now was to discover for what grim task it might have been used.

FOURTEEN

Stan Peltzer was not in his office when Thea arrived but she was able to talk with Dr. Andrews. He told her it would only take a few minutes to determine if it was blood on the blade but it would take several days to figure out to what or whom the blood belonged. Although ownership of the letter opener was not easy to prove, Forensics had already dusted it for prints. Thea prayed she hadn't disturbed any vital evidence.

While she was waiting, Stan Peltzer walked into the room. He gave her a cordial greeting as if she were an old friend rather than a former murder suspect, a favor that did not go unappreciated. Then he hopped up on the edge of his desk and stared inquisitively at her.

"You made everyone's day with that treat you brought in," he said, sitting on the top of the desk nearest her. "We love that kind of stuff. Helps clean out the books."

"Thanks," Thea said drily. "I do what I can. Any news on it yet?"

Detective Peltzer glanced over in the direction of the lab and shook his head. "It'll take a while longer. Listen, I know you've been out because of all the messages I've had to leave on your voice mail. I also think you've found out a few things that you haven't shared with me. Why don't we compare notes? I'll even buy supper afterward." He jumped off the desk.

"There are a few things I could tell you, although most of it is just intuition. It's yours, though. For the price of a dinner, that is."

"You're on," he said, taking her by the arm and leading her into an interrogation room. As he passed by the receptionist's desk he said, "Patti, send in a couple of deli sandwiches and some coffee."

Thea stared at him for a moment, thinking *cheapskate* then realized that they were in two different income brackets. A sandwich shared was better than something microwaved alone. She sat at the long table inside the drab, bare room and Stan Peltzer planted himself opposite her.

"Talk," he ordered.

"I think Peter Volk murdered Alicia, but to protect himself he made it look as if Reg did it. Then he made it appear as if Reg committed suicide out of remorse."

She noticed that Stan Peltzer's face had taken on a look of incredulity. So over the next two hours she told him about everything from the discovery of the letter opener, to finding out the identity of the original owner of her house through the anonymous book delivery. Although Stan was much too young to have worked on the Volk/Forbes murders, he remembered the notoriety of the case and had heard it mentioned occasionally. It surprised him to hear that Peter Volk was still alive, if you could call it living.

For reasons she rationalized were just patient confidentiality, Thea told Stan nothing about her discovery of the unsolved murders file in Malcolm's room at Meredith's house. If there was a connection between the Dean men and the Volks, it was too unclear to subject Meredith to further distress. Malcolm's secrets, whatever they were, were safe with her. And after Stan Peltzer's charade with his dinner offer today, she felt a small thrill of one-upmanship.

Once she had finished her story, Stan leaned back in his chair and studied her.

"Your theory is fascinating but not nearly enough to reopen the file. Everyone involved is dead or as good as dead. Peter Volk was one of our own, a veteran of the police department. It would take an earth shaker for Homicide to become interested. Or a witness would have to come forward."

Thea's mouth tightened in disappointment though she had suspected that this would have been his reaction. Promising to notify him of any developments, she left his office feeling emotionally exhausted.

As she stepped outside the police station to her waiting car, she felt for the keys inside her jacket pocket. The letters she had stuffed in there from her mailbox met her fingers, but the keys were missing. Then she discovered a small hole in her pocket. Wriggling her hand between the jacket and the lining, she grasped her keys. When they were finally freed, she found a piece of paper tangled in them and brought it out as well.

She unlocked her car door and slipped behind the steering wheel before she examined the paper. It was a normal post-card-sized piece cut irregularly from a larger sheet of white copy paper. It must have been stuck with the letters she had removed from the mailbox. What was not normal were the words printed on it in large, laser computer print, *"Your turn is coming."*

Thea threw open the door and stormed back into the police station. Detective Peltzer, astonished to see her so soon, appeared troubled when she gave him the innocuous note. A policewoman brought her a cup of the obligatory coffee while he took the paper away for inspection.

Although her presence there was no longer necessary, Thea did not want to leave the police station until she had some answers. She didn't have to worry. Again she found herself waiting in the interrogation room of the police department. About half an hour later Detective Peltzer entered the room carrying a small paper packet.

"Sorry it took so long. I just got word that they've managed to identify the prints on the letter opener, despite their age," he said. "Other than yours, that is." Thea attempted a smile, but didn't quite succeed.

"Fortunately we still had records of the Volk/Forbes murder and prints on file. It looks like Peter Volk was the last person to handle the letter opener." Thea sat upright in surprise then fell back. Of course they were Peter's prints, it had obviously once belonged to him.

"What about the blood," she asked. "Have they managed

to identify that yet?"

Stan sat on a chair beside her, leaned back and crossed his feet. "Yes. Turns out there were blood types recorded in the Volk/Forbes case file for us to compare them to. The blood belonged to Alicia Volk. But the prints on the gun belonged to Forbes. The prints on the letter opener, and who knows why it was in your closet, belong to Detective Volk. Of the three people involved, none of them died from stab wounds. Only two gunshot wounds. Unless Peter talks there's no way to prove anyone other than Reg Forbes might have been responsible." He handed the paper packet to her.

"The case is still closed and the letter opener doesn't change anything, so you can have it back." Thea shuddered and nearly dropped the packet, wondering if she should throw it into the nearest dumpster.

"Did you know that Peter's young son was at the crime scene?" she asked.

Peltzer nodded. "Yes, and CSD would not allow him to testify. He was so traumatized the Department was never certain he would have been able to anyhow. What's your point?"

"I don't know," Thea admitted, sounding disappointed. "Just the thought of being able to call in someone else who was there that day might answer all of our questions. But we don't know where he lives now. Or even if he goes by the same name." Then she remembered the note.

"Did you find out anything about the note in my mailbox?"

Stan shook his head and sighed heavily. "No and I don't know if we ever will. We couldn't lift any prints off it and there are millions of laser copiers with the same print. It's not like in the old days when they cut the alphabet out of magazines or used a typewriter with defective keys. It's pretty high tech these days." At the look on Thea's face his attitude softened.

"I know how you must feel. There are a lot of creeps running around right now. Watch your step. The note may be random or it may have something to do with the publicity you've been getting. Or it may be personal. My best advice is not to trust anyone. If you can think of anything else that might be relevant, no matter how trivial it seems, call me right away." He stood up, patted her on the shoulder and left the room.

Thea watched his retreating figure, feeling frustrated. How could she lead even a parody of a normal life constantly looking over her shoulder, mistrusting and suspecting everyone she met? The police seemed unconcerned with the threat she'd just received. With Sheldon Steiner's death and the recent unsolved murder of the young woman, she would have expected them to grab at any lead. She decided to take Peltzer's advice and not trust anyone. That included even the police.

FIFTEEN

When Thea got home she checked the locks on the doors and windows three times, turned on the burglar alarm and searched the internet until she found a dog breeder south of Portland that specialized in guard dogs. Scarcely thinking about it, she stuck the paper packet containing Peter's letter opener into the night table drawer in her bedroom. Then she made an appointment for the next week to 'interview' a potential guard dog. At the very least she could use the companionship.

With both the radio and the television on for the comfort of sound, she almost didn't hear the doorbell. At first she hesitated, then jumped up and peered out through the tiny security peephole. If it was a burglar and no one answered the door, they would just assume all the noise was a ruse and enter anyway.

But it wasn't a burglar. It was Erik. Throwing the door open, she flew into Erik's arms. He moved forward, pushing her with him and kicked the door shut with his foot. They fell back together on the sofa in a long, hard kiss. For several moments she clung to him as if he was a life preserver and she was in danger of drowning. But then she remembered the girl she thought she had seen him with and pulled away.

"What's the matter?" he said. "And why haven't you checked your voice mail? I've been calling you all day."

"*I've* been out," she said, accusation heavy in her voice. "Where were *you*?"

He appeared bewildered. "I've been at home, working on a proposal for some scientists who want to set up a computer program to record their research. Every time I took a break I called you."

Thea looked at him with skepticism. "You didn't come here? You never left your apartment?"

He shook his head and laughed.

"Not once," he said and made a crisscross motion across his chest. "Cross my heart and hope to die." She squeezed her eyes shut tightly.

"Don't say that," she said. "Not even in fun. Don't say that."

"Is there something I should know?" he asked, serious now at the sight of her taut, white face. She stood up and retrieved the book she'd received earlier in the day. She handed it to him.

"Someone left this here this morning," she said. "I thought it might have been you. Open it to the bookmark."

Erik opened the book, looked at the photo and glanced up.

"It's your house," he said, sounding as pleased as a little boy finding himself to be the center of attention.

"Yes, it's my house. But it belonged to someone else before that. Read on."

Erik began reading and Thea noticed a perceptible change in his expression, the color of his skin. When he looked up she thought he was going to be sick. He was silent for a long time.

"That's heavy stuff," he finally said. "Did you know any of this when you bought the house?" Thea shook her head and shrugged.

"If the listing realtors knew about it, they certainly didn't disclose it. Probably because they knew it would harm the sale. I mean, you get the home inspection and appraisal done, but it's not the kind of thing you think, 'hey, maybe I should check with the Police Department and find out if there were any murders in the house before I make an offer.'"

She took the book from him and tossed it toward the fireplace. "Anyhow, the woman who sold me the house was just as shocked."

"Forget it," Erik said flippantly, his composure regained. "That all took place a long time ago. You don't believe in ghosts, do you?"

"I don't believe in the 'wooo wooo' kind, if that's what you mean. I do believe in the ones who were wronged in life and come back to haunt people until their plight is resolved."

"Now that's just silly," Erik chided. "That's what the police and the courts are for."

He took her back in his arms and in a fluid motion, slipped one arm beneath her and the other behind her back and carried her to the bedroom. Half stumbling because of her height, he threw her down upon the bed and began tugging at his belt. Thea rolled quickly away.

"No," she said. "I'm sorry. I can't right now." She started to leave the room.

Suddenly Erik was blocking the doorway. Before she knew what was happening, he pushed her roughly back on the bed. He sat on her, pinning her down, as he struggled with his pants. Then he began biting at her neck. She pushed at his shoulders with her hands, forcing him off her and onto the floor. She jumped to her feet.

"Get out!" she shouted. "If you try that again I'll have you arrested." This time Erik appeared to regain his senses. He sat on her bed, his head in his hands.

"Oh God, Thea," he said. "I'm so sorry." He looked up at her and his face had changed again completely, as if he were another person, not the monster who had just attempted to rape her.

"Please forgive me. You know I wouldn't do anything to hurt you. Please." He remained sitting on the bed and to her relief did not attempt to touch her.

She stared at Erik wondering if they understood each other at all.

"I think you should leave. We're both under terrible stress and this has just been the crowning touch of one of the most horrid days of my life," she said, her voice shaking. "If you don't go now I'm going to start screaming and I won't stop until all the windows in this house and all the windows in all the other houses in the neighborhood are broken."

Erik took her at her word this time. When he stood up she backed away, though he made no threat toward her. He straightened his clothes as he walked toward the door. When he reached the front entrance he turned to Thea.

"I'm going to make this up to you," he promised. "I love you." Then he left.

As soon as he'd gone out the door, she ran to the window. She watched as Erik climbed into a sporty Nissan SUV, a car that bore no resemblance to the one she thought she had seen him in earlier in the day. As he started the engine and then drove away, she suddenly realized that this was the first time he had ever told her how he felt about her.

SIXTEEN

After Erik's car pulled away, Thea locked the front door again. Then she brought out a bottle of brandy and chugged about eight ounces straight from the bottle. When her head began feeling hot and fuzzy, she collapsed onto the sofa.

Suddenly she made a mad rush for the bathroom where she was violently sick. On wobbling legs she stood up, looked at herself in the mirror and was sick again.

She staggered back into the living room and lay down on the sofa, trying to make the room stop spinning. An icy cold shiver worked its way down her body. Unable to stop herself from shaking, she huddled under her jacket for warmth. As she slid her hands into the sleeves, she felt a hard lump in the lining.

Remembering the hole she found in the pocket earlier in the day, she felt around the back of the jacket until she located the object. It was the book of matches she had taken from Malcolm's bedroom.

The logo on the matches belonged to a Bed and Breakfast in Cannon Beach called The Sea Hag. Fortunately, there was an address and telephone number for the place. There were no other notations. She wondered how the matches had come to be in Malcolm's things when he was not a smoker. Not to mention, matches from a resort would not be just lying around unless someone had physically picked them up at the location. Could it be possible that The Sea Hag was a place Malcolm had visited before? Or even just recently? There was only one way to find out. Thea set the matches on the table and picked up the telephone.

The friendly sounding lady at The Sea Hag assured Thea

that no one by the name of Malcolm Dean was staying there, nor had he in the past. Then she mentioned that because it was low season they still had a couple of nice rooms overlooking the ocean. The invitation enticed Thea. Despite not locating Malcolm, in her present state of melancholy she leapt on the opportunity to leave the city and her problems. And what better place to forget her troubles than the Oregon Coast? Tonight she would pack and tomorrow she would be on her way to Cannon Beach.

The next day started out hot and humid, not the best day for nursing a brandy hangover. But the cool sea air at the ocean would be soothing. Thea was thankful she would be without interruption from the telephone, police or Erik. She quickly packed a couple of days' worth of clothes, throwing in a windbreaker and sandals, and a small backpack. As she entered the garage and threw her bag and backpack in the back seat of the Mercedes, she decided to leave the convertible roof down. It would be simple enough to replace if there was any hint of showers. And once out of downtown traffic, she began to enjoy the twisting, woodsy drive toward the coast.

Just a little more than two hours later, she maneuvered the Mercedes onto the exit and into the tiny resort town of Cannon Beach, frequently stopping and starting as tourists raced between cars without looking, hands clasping bags of saltwater taffy, kites, and T-shirts. Although she had to drive along the entire main street of town until she reached the end, she had no difficulty at all locating The Sea Hag. It was just across from the beach, on a cliff overlooking the ocean. A sea-bitten, gray building with turrets and twisting staircases, it looked as if it were built from driftwood.

She parked the Mercedes, raised the convertible top in case of unpredictable coastal rains, and clicked the locks. Then she headed toward The Sea Hag's entrance door with the façade of a mermaid embracing an octopus carved into the ancient driftwood. A similarly carved desk greeted her. With no one in sight she rang a small bell on the counter. Within a minute a woman with waist length, flowing grey hair that belied her youthful face appeared. She gave Thea a welcoming smile.

"I'm Andree. Do you have a reservation?"

"Yes," Thea replied. "I called yesterday."

"You're fortunate to have gotten in," Andree said. "We're usually completely booked up most of the year." While she took care of the sign-in details, and running Thea's credit card for payment, Thea had the opportunity to look around her. Driftwood sculptures were stuffed in every corner of the room, their natural wood shapes lending inspiration to the artwork they would become.

"I'll take you to your room now, if you're ready." Before Thea could protest Andree had grabbed her overnight bag, hoisting it in front of her as they moved to a twisting staircase around the corner from the desk. As they headed up the stairs Thea commented on the beauty of the sculptures.

"My husband, Steve, and I are both artists. He's a sculptor and did all the bas relief you see on the woodwork. I paint. We moved out here to live the artist lifestyle, creating by the beach, then we ended up retiring. We could never see the point in leaving such a beautiful place."

"Nor would I," Thea agreed.

Andree stopped before another carved door, this one Thea recognized as a façade of Cthulhu, the Lovecraftian Mythos. Andree slung Thea's small case onto a chair and smiled.

"There's a phone with a line to the front desk if you find you need anything. Most of the shops are within walking distance."

Thea glanced around her room, a little alcove on the third floor overlooking the ocean. "Thank you, this is perfect."

After Andree had gone, Thea unpacked her clothes and a paperback she'd brought, then curled up on the calico upholstered window seat to read until she fell asleep.

She was just dozing off when a knock upon the door startled her awake. She stood up, wincing at the cramps in her legs from lying in the same position for so long and caught a glimpse of her rumpled, sleepy face in the bathroom mirror as she opened the door. It was Andree who had knocked, and now stood outside her door.

"Hope I didn't disturb you," she apologized. "If you're interested, we do a family style dinner each evening that's included in the price of the room. We always have fresh seafood and wonderful veggies from the local farmer's market. Dinner will be served downstairs in a few minutes."

Thrilled that she didn't have to go out to eat, Thea thanked her and hurriedly went to the bathroom to freshen up. Despite her rumpled appearance, sleep had brought color to her cheeks and a sparkle to her dark eyes. She changed her clothes, putting on a leaf green shirt dress with a copper belt and matching earrings. Feeling attractive and confident, she descended the stairs to meet the rest of The Sea Hag's guests.

The dining room had oak plank flooring and the hand-plastered walls were adorned with brass sextants and other sea-going artifacts. Dim, oil-burning lamps set in wall brackets filled the room with an amber glow, sending off the heady scent of an old farmhouse. Six place settings were set at one of the two round tables; two place settings at the other. The table with the two settings was empty but the other already had five people seated at it. Smiling hesitantly at the seated guests who appeared to be couples, Thea took a chair at the other table so as not to intrude on their evening. Then Andree rang a brass bell and glanced toward Thea's table.

"Our other guest won't be with us tonight so dinner will be served right away. Thea, let's move your chair over here, I think there's enough room. No point in you sitting there alone by yourself."

Thea smiled shyly and dragged her chair to the other table while the others made space for her. Andree waited until she sat down then said, "While you're waiting I'd like each of you to tell the people at your table your name and something about yourself."

Thea's heart fell. The last thing she wanted was for anyone to recognize her or ask questions. Going against everything she held sacred in life, she rapidly formed a lie in her mind and memorized it, hoping she would not be discovered.

Including Andree's husband, Steve, the group of people consisted of John, an insurance salesman and his wife, Nancy, a homemaker; Frank, who owned a Cadillac dealership and his second wife, Carla, a lawyer. Although they did not appear too interested, Thea informed them that she had been a dancer before knee surgery ended her career and now taught classical ballet. The fib was far enough removed from any of their interests for them to question her.

After dinner, two of the couples wandered off to the living room for card games and television. Thea, seeking seclusion, started to head back to her room. Andree stopped her before she reached the staircase.

"Is everything all right?" she asked, sounding concerned. "I noticed you scarcely spoke at dinner."

"I'm fine," Thea said. "I'm not really up to being in other peoples' company right now."

Andree nodded in understanding. "We often have visitors come here just to get away from their problems." She patted Thea's arm. "You'll have as much quiet as you need. But if you want to talk, just holler." Thea smiled and thanked her, then went upstairs.

The next morning, unable to face a group of happy couples, Thea decided to skip the family style breakfast. She put on a maillot swimsuit then covered it with warmups. Grabbing a towel and her backpack, she made her way to the kitchen where Andree was in consultation with the cook, planning the supper menu.

Thea leaned through the door. "Could I ask a favor?" she said. Andree glanced up from her work.

"Ask away."

"What are the chances of getting a small picnic lunch to put in a backpack?"

Andree gave a short laugh and winked at the cook. "What are her chances, Inge?"

Inge's chubby face split in a friendly smile. "Pretty goot," she said. "Just for one, miss?" Thea nodded. Inge clucked her tongue in mock disappointment. "Too bad," she said. "But I'll fix someting real nice for yous. It vill be ready soon."

"Thank you," said Thea, sitting at the kitchen table to wait.

The kitchen was meticulous, very European with white enameled cabinets and black and white tiled floor. She was about to go over and examine a collection of porcelain knick-knacks when Inge handed her a large paper sack. Wrapping the towel around the lunch bag, she slipped them both into her backpack. Then, giving them both profuse thanks, she set off on her unplanned adventure.

SEVENTEEN

Thea parked her car in a lot just off the promenade of downtown Cannon Beach. After a couple of hours spent perusing T-shirt shops and purchasing a bag of saltwater taffy she'd probably never eat, she headed toward the beach. Though it was now noon with the sun high overhead, the wind off the ocean was cool and she was glad she had brought a heavy windbreaker. She slipped off her shoes and dug her toes into the sun-baked, crystal white sand.

She strolled along the beach for several hours, stopping to inspect shells and large beams of driftwood on her way. The pale blue of the sky and the gently lapping waves seemed to merge on the horizon. Far off in the distance and still accessible from shore loomed the rock formations of Haystack Rock and the Needles. With the tide out for several more hours she could climb the rock, have lunch and still be back at The Sea Hag in time for supper.

A third of the way up Haystack Rock her thirst and hunger forced her to stop for a rest. She noticed she was not alone. Several other beachcombers, mostly couples holding hands, were climbing the rocks but they didn't stay long. They did not even seem to notice Thea and she felt a slight pang of envy at their insular lives.

She opened her lunch and saw that Inge had prepared a bagel stuffed with chicken salad, a slice of apple pie, a banana and a thermos of coffee. Thea had never felt hungrier and eagerly polished off the entire contents of the bag. She leaned back upon the rock, the empty backpack serving as a pillow for her head, and like a sated lizard basking in the sun, fell asleep.

She awoke to find cold water lapping at her ankles. She

sat up with a start. While she was sleeping the tide had come in and separated her from the mainland. She glanced at her watch. It was nearly dusk, too early to be missed at The Sea Hag and too dark for anyone to notice her stranded on the rocks. And it would be difficult to catch the attention of a passerby this far from shore.

She stood up and waved her jacket, shouting at the top of her lungs. Then she waited. But the rhythmic lapping of the waves blocked out any other sounds. The sky had darkened ominously, with low, brooding clouds that seemed only feet above her. A spot of rain fell upon her hand. Soon another followed and then more, until a steady drizzle totally obscured the visibility of the shore. Her clothing nearly saturated, Thea began searching the slippery inclines of the rock for a shelter. Then she found a jutting overhang of rock and crawled beneath it out of the downpour.

The sky grew black and impenetrable. With sinking hopes, Thea realized she probably would have to wait until the tide went out again before she could find her way back to the mainland. But her clothes were soaked through and there was the danger of hypothermia when the coast's night temperatures dipped down.

Then she noticed a small red light bobbing in the gray dusk, too far away to tell what if it was a boat or just a stray marker. She shouted for help, hoping to pierce the muffling fog that had come up. There was no response. She yelled again until her throat began to burn. This time she heard the distant clang of a bell and the red light appeared to be coming closer.

After a few minutes a small fishing boat came into view. A man swathed into anonymity in rain gear shouted and waved to her from the bow. Although she could not hear what he was saying she understood that he could not risk getting closer to the rocks. She would have to swim to the boat.

He leaned over and tossed a white ring with a long rope fastened to the boat toward her. It bobbed comically on the water's oily surface like a single Cheerio in a bowl of black milk. Thea dove into the water and began to swim toward it.

With every stroke she took it seemed to float further and further away. Suddenly an enormous swell rose up, covering her head. Not able to tell up from down, she gave in to the cold water and lost consciousness.

* * * * * *

To the man on the boat it was as if she had disappeared into the void. Hurriedly he slipped on a lifejacket, tied a line from the boat around his waist and jumped into the water. Though he fought the current with strong, practiced strokes, he made little progress. He forced himself to keep his eyes riveted to the last place he had seen the person submerge.

Just then an object bumped his leg. Although he knew it might just be driftwood, or please god, he thought, not a shark, he began treading water, searching in the dark for a body. In a few moments he made contact; the frantic groping of a person drowning, threatening to pull him under. Though frightened himself, he grasped the body firmly under his arm and used the tow-line around his waist to inch himself toward the boat.

When he reached the boat's ladder he hoisted himself and the now limp body alongside, half dragging, half heaving it with him. With an enormous effort he threw it upon the deck of the boat and fell beside it, panting and weak.

When he caught his breath he rolled the body over, freeing a gush of water from the lungs. It surprised him to see that it was a woman and for a moment he thought he knew her. Then he realized she wasn't breathing.

He opened the neck of her jacket, checked her airways and tilted her head back. Pinching her nose closed, he breathed rapidly into her lungs—once, twice, three times—finally a fourth. She coughed twice, water sputtering from her lips. He waited for a few moments and when she began breathing on her own, he went down into the cabin in search of blankets.

Just as he returned to the top deck the woman opened her eyes. A look of incredulity crossed her face. He tried to cover her with the blanket but she shrank away from him in fear.

Mystified, he continued to stare at her, wondering why, despite the disheveled hair and streaked mascara, she looked so familiar. Then he knew.

* * * * * *

For a moment no one spoke. Finally it was Thea who broke the silence.

"Malcolm?" she whispered in disbelief. "Is it really you?"

"None other," he said, this time being successful at draping the blanket over her shoulders. He stepped down into the cabin again and held out his hand for her. "You'd better come out of the rain before you get hypothermia or catch pneumonia," he said. "Believe me, it gets cold out here."

Thea nodded, suddenly aware that she was shaking violently. She followed him into the cozy cabin that felt warm only because it was so frigid outside. Malcolm lit two gas mantles hanging on the walls. They cast a ghostly glow over the oak paneling of the cabin, allowing her to observe him.

At first she could see little difference from the Malcolm who had been her patient in hospital. He still had perfectly symmetrical bone structure and an almost ethereal beauty. But now he'd acquired a few of the character lines and crinkles around the eyes that were a natural part of his features. There was something else too, that had not been present after the operation. Four long fingernail scratches marred the side of his otherwise flawless left cheek. The scratches were open and wet, raw flesh exposed between upturned rows of gelatinous Reflesh. In the dim light it was impossible to tell how long they'd been present.

Malcolm rummaged around in the storage bin under the seat and brought out an old flannel work shirt and overalls. He handed them to Thea.

"Get into something dry," he ordered. Thea stared dubiously at the very large clothing.

"What about you?"

Malcolm held up another heavy wool shirt and pair of

pants. "Always prepared," he said, nodding in the direction of her clothing. "You go first."

Thea smiled grimly. "No, I insist. After you," she said.

Malcolm shrugged. "Suit yourself." He began peeling off the dripping layers of shirts, exposing a lean, muscular body. A thin line on his throat where the Reflesh met skin was still visible. He unbuckled his belt, staring unwaveringly at Thea as he pulled down his trousers. She glanced away hastily.

"Okay, I'm done," he said. "Your turn." Thea stood up.

"If you look in the other direction," she said.

In gentlemen's fashion Malcolm turned his head away. But when Thea let out a sudden shriek of laughter he turned to stare at her and he too, had to laugh. Despite her height, she looked like the Incredible Shrinking Woman in his large clothes. Tucking them together as best she could, she sat back down upon the seat and studied him, serious now.

"There's a lot of people looking for you," she said. "Have you been here the whole time since you were discharged from hospital?"

"Pretty much," he replied noncommittally, kicking the wet clothes into a heap near the wall. "Who wants to know?"

"Your mother for one. The police, for another." She waited for his response. Malcolm looked surprised, but not shocked or angry, as she would have thought.

"I know I should have called Mom, but I had to work things out, grow up a little, I guess," he said, staring at the floor. He looked up and gave Thea the full benefit of his steely eyes. "Why do the police want to see me?"

A hard knot of apprehension formed in Thea's stomach. Would it be dangerous to disclose what she knew of the police investigation? With no one knowing where she was, she couldn't risk unsettling him. If he was telling the truth and had been here the entire time, he might not know about Dr. Steiner's murder. It would also give him an alibi for the murder of the young woman and setting the fire at the clubhouse. She shrugged and told a lie.

"Something about filing charges against the owner of the

building in which you were injured."

For a moment Malcolm looked as though he did not believe her and she knew she'd have to be careful with what she said to him. It was crucial that she try to glean as much information about his recent activities as possible without him being aware of what she was doing. She remembered from his days in the hospital that he could be deceptive and probably would withhold explanations, if he chose to give any at all. But still, it was worth a try.

"And what are you doing here? You wouldn't know where to look for me so why did you just happen to be in the area?"

There was no reason to tell a lie about why she was in Cannon Beach. Once she'd spoken with Andree over the phone and she'd denied that a Malcolm Dean had ever stayed there, Thea hadn't given much thought to the slim possibility that she might find him here. Cannon Beach was a popular spot for city dwellers to head to on the weekend. It was coincidental, though convenient, that she'd found him. A partial truth, she decided, would work better than a well-told lie.

"I've been under a lot of stress at the hospital because of, well, for a number of reasons. I haven't really had a chance to explore the Oregon coast and it seemed like a good time and place to get away from Portland."

Though her story sounded plausible enough she had trouble looking him in the eyes while she spoke, instead making a pretense of examining the interior of the boat.

"How did you get the scratches on your face?"

Malcolm's hand flew to his cheek. He gently ran his fingers down the side of the Reflesh then let his hand fall to his lap. He paused. Was he reflecting or concocting a story?

"A few days ago I was repairing my crab traps. I had to dive to remove them and as I surfaced a nail-studded slat swung free and raked my face. The scars look a bit better now."

Thea walked over to Malcolm and stooped to examine the wound. Though she couldn't tell how long they'd been there, it was obvious the cuts would not heal without suturing or an insertion of the Reflesh to fill them. Reflesh did not heal itself. The infection potential was one of the few problems they had not been able to resolve. She straightened up and contemplated Malcolm for a minute. Maybe this was the only way.

"We need to get you back to Portland," she said. "These have to be looked after before infection sets in."

Malcolm shot her a look of incredulity.

"*No way!*" he said. "I've got too much unfinished business before I go back."

He walked over to the captain's seat and slipped behind the wheel. After studying the gauges on the dash he turned and said, "We're going to have to dock wherever we can for the night. I'll take you home in the morning."

When Thea started to protest Malcolm raised his eyebrows and cocked his head slightly.

"Unless you want to swim again, you don't have any choice." He nodded toward the bench he had converted into a bunk by folding down the back cushions. "You can bed down there."

Thea considered her options for a moment then stretched lengthwise on the bench, covering herself with the blanket. She watched Malcolm as he navigated the boat toward shore. Soon the rhythmic chugging of the boat's motor and the waves slapping on the bow had a hypnotic effect. Without realizing it, her eyes began to close and in a few moments the motion lulled her to sleep. She woke abruptly to a cold, male body snuggling against her under the blanket.

She jerked the blanket back away from him. "What are you doing?" she hissed.

Malcolm reeled back. "What do you think I'm doing? I'm trying to keep warm. Shut up and stop interpreting everything as sexual." He jerked his share of the blanket away from her and closed his eyes. Thea glared at his reclining form until he opened them again. This time he smiled at her. "As my mother used to say," he said, somewhat apologetically. "Don't rock the boat."

"Hmmph," said Thea, turning away in indignation, trying to ignore the gentle snoring that suddenly erupted behind her.

The next morning dawned cloudy but the sea was calm, the air damp and chilly. Thea glanced out the porthole window to see they were anchored several hundred feet from shore. She didn't know what had awoken her first, the gentle rocking of the boat, the smell of the fresh coffee, or the sound of it perking. But as she stretched and crawled stiffly out of her cramped sleeping quarters, she could not remember ever desiring anything more than that coffee.

Malcolm was sitting in the captain's chair with his back toward her. He turned around when she reached him and gave her a welcoming smile.

"You were good last night," he said, winking. "Not great, just good." A rush of color rose to Thea's face. He stopped teasing and said innocently, "I mean to sleep with, of course."

They both laughed and suddenly the atmosphere became less tense. Thea, though realizing she took herself and everything else too seriously, could not relax enough to forget that she was here at sea with a potential murderer. Then she stiffened, for she had momentarily forgotten the tribulations she had left behind in Portland.

"We'd better get back or the people I'm staying with will have the Coast Guard looking for me," she said.

Malcolm studied her, his brow wrinkling.

"Just where *are* you staying?"

Thea turned away from his scrutiny. It was imperative that she remain calm and in control should he show any tendency toward violence. "I've got a room at The Sea Hag in Cannon Beach."

Malcolm startled her by chortling with glee.

"You're not serious?" he said. "That's where I'm staying. Some friends of mine own it." He appeared so delighted she almost smiled.

"But when I asked if you had ever stayed there, they told me that they'd never heard of you," she said, nonplussed. At those words she clapped her hand to her mouth, realizing she had just revealed that by trying to find out if he was at The Sea Hag she had, in fact, lied to him earlier.

But Malcolm either hadn't noticed her gaff or chose to ignore it. He nodded, pleased with himself. "I told you—they're friends. If I don't want them to tell anyone where I am, they won't." Thea had to admit, that was a friend.

Then suddenly the moment vanished. Malcolm's expression changed from joviality to just barely suppressed anger. He loomed close, glaring down at her.

"Just how *did* you happen to find me?"

Thea backed away from him, putting as much distance between them as the limited space would permit. Once again she was seeing the post-operative, irrational Malcolm. Perhaps it wasn't the stress of the surgical outcome, nor was it PTSD. He'd suffered a crushed skull and head trauma in the fire. When he was admitted to hospital, the neurological team had CAT Scans done of his brain and skull fracture and found no brain damage. She knew that occasionally things get missed, or signs of damage don't appear until much later. New CAT Scans of his brain might be able to identify what was really going on inside his head. But in that instant she truly believed that this Malcolm could be capable of anything.

"It was coincidence," she said, knowing he could see right through such a blatant lie. Why hadn't he asked her before now? Malcolm stared at her with an angry sneer.

"You expect me to believe that?" he exploded. "Someone sent you and I want to know who."

Thea watched Malcolm's every movement. Who was safe from him? Was she? Was Meredith? Above all, she must protect Meredith. She took a deep breath, forcing herself to speak in a calm and rational voice. And she must be careful not to divulge too much.

"When I visited your mother a few days ago we searched for clues as to your whereabouts. I found some matches from The Sea Hag in your room. She doesn't know I took them and she doesn't know I'm here." She stopped, watching his reaction. He frowned as he appeared to consider her explanation.

When he turned away from her without speaking, her intuition told her the crisis had passed. But his instability alarmed her.

Malcolm docked the boat at the marina, not far from the parking lot where she'd left her car the previous day. As Thea drove them both back to The Sea Hag she wondered briefly if Malcolm had brought a vehicle with him. He looked fit enough to have made the three mile walk but it did not explain how he got from Portland to Cannon Beach. She did not want to provoke him further by asking.

The reception they received upon returning to The Sea Hag would have warmed anyone's heart. Thea found herself being passed from stranger to stranger, overwhelmed with hugs and good wishes. Andree was especially overjoyed to see them. She had been dialing the number of the Coast Guard just as they walked through the door. When she gave Malcolm a long, lingering kiss that didn't seem completely platonic, Thea felt an unexpected pang. Then Andree leaned back and glared at both of them.

"I didn't know you knew each other," she said.

Thea made a grumbling sort of noise and Malcolm winked at her. She shook her head, marveling at his new amicability.

"We do *now*," he said, leaving the small crowd snickering and nudging each other. He took Thea's elbow and led her toward the corner of the living room. He cupped her chin in his hands and gazed into her eyes.

"I'm not going to stick around," he said. "Please tell my mother I'm all right."

Thea studied him. "Malcolm, you *must* come back," she pleaded. "You need medical attention and . . ."

Malcolm squared his jaw, clenching his teeth.

"I can't come back. At least not yet. It's dangerous for me and it could be dangerous for you, too. I won't talk to the police either, so don't tell them you saw me. Understand?"

His tone softened. "For your safety you must remember one very important thing: Don't trust anyone."

Thea started to say something then stopped, biting back

the words that might imperil everything. Although she knew she should try· to reason with him to return to Portland it might be best for everyone if he remained here. She smiled gently at him and a look of overpowering sadness crossed Malcolm's face. Before she could speak he bent down and kissed her on the lips. Then he turned and walked out of the building, leaving Thea staring after him in dismay.

EIGHTEEN

The next morning dawned overcast and drizzly. After saying goodbye to her hosts, Andree and Steve, Thea left Cannon Beach early for the drive along the rugged coast highway to Portland, briefly stopping for gas at a roadside station. As she signed the credit card slip she noticed a dark foreign make car with tinted windows, at the station across the road. Though it looked vaguely familiar, she forgot it as she tucked her card into her wallet. Then she pulled back onto the freeway and headed north on US 101.

A couple of miles later she checked her rear view mirror and noticed the car a few lengths behind her. It had come upon her so fast she had the impression the driver wanted to pass, though he hadn't put on his signal light. Even so, she edged slightly over to the narrow shoulder. Instead of passing, the car dropped further behind.

Annoyed, Thea pulled back into the center of the lane, maintaining her speed. Idiot! If he wanted to pass, he could do it without her help. But the car sped up again, this time advancing so near to her rear bumper she feared her car would be hit. The driver was still only a silhouette in the darkened, rain-smeared windows. And the closeness of their vehicles on the narrow highway frightened her.

She glanced in her rear view mirror at his license plate. Though the car itself shone with a clean onyx-blue gleam, the muddied plate made it unreadable. She slowed again, pulling to the shoulder to allow him to pass. Again the driver dropped back. Thea's heart began to race. Whoever was in the car seemed to want to scare her. But who was it?

The car tailgated her for several more miles. Thea turned

east onto US 26 and the car, as if in bizarre choreography, made the same turn. Though Thea made no further attempts to pull over, she kept her car in cruise control, checking her mirror every few seconds. The dark car maintained its pattern of accelerating rapidly toward her, then dropping back. If the person did not mean to harm her then why were they frightening her with a cat and mouse game?

Then as she rounded a curve she came upon a small roadside diner off to the right. She braked quickly and swerved her wheels into the parking lot, sending up a spray of mud in the wet dirt road. The dark car shot past. Pressing the lock button on the key fob, she locked the Mercedes, raced into the diner and almost fell into a chair. Just another road raging asshole, she thought, her heart still pounding. After ordering a slice of homemade blackberry pie and a cup of coffee from the waiter, she slid back into her chair to relax.

Thea glanced at her hands. It had taken several minutes after she'd left the car before she was able to get them to stop shaking. Thankful she'd had an opportunity to let the driver get past and on his way, she picked up the coffee cup, took a long swallow and stared out the window into the parking lot. Then she nearly dropped the cup. The foreign car lay in the parking lot like a panther waiting to pounce. And she still could not read the license plate.

She jerked around in her chair, searching the room for the driver, but except for the server and presumably a cook, she was alone in the diner. She got up, dashed over to the unisex restroom and jerked open the door. The restroom was empty. Panicked, she stumbled back to the table and beckoned to the waiter.

"Did you see the driver of that car?" she demanded, pointing toward the parking lot. Then her hand dropped to her side in embarrassment. The foreign car had vanished.

The waiter watched her, concern in his young eyes. "Do you want me to call someone?" he asked.

Thea shook her head somberly and swallowed hard.

"No," she mumbled. "No, but thank you." Somehow in

the time she had taken to check the restroom the driver had returned and driven away. Or maybe he never left his car. Realizing the waiter thought she was a very strange woman, Thea hastily paid the bill and left. Fortunately the car was nowhere to be seen.

She got back into her vehicle, feeling more relaxed now. Maybe her imagination had exaggerated the whole incident. It was not the first time she'd been the victim of a show-off driver with a fast car. With this thought in mind she relaxed and checked her rear view mirror. The dark car was so close it completely filled the mirror.

Thea's gaze lingered on the vehicle for only a second. Suddenly a curve materialized before her. Too late to swerve, she felt the weightless sensation of the airborne Mercedes as it sailed into the void on the other side of the road. She was aware of a slowing of time, something flying into her face and then nothing.

When she began to recover her senses she realized that the car's airbag had cushioned her in the crash. Although shaken and aching, none of her bones felt as if they were broken. She wrestled with the airbag to free herself then stepped outside. She walked around the car, scrambling down into the ditch to get a look at the right side, snagging her legs on blackberry vines until tiny rivulets of blood spurted through the tears in her slacks. As she checked the vehicle for body damage she was thankful to discover only scratches from blackberry branches. She had driven into a shallow ditch and with so little impact, the tires hadn't blown out.

Thea pushed the airbag as far over to the passenger seat as she could so she would be able to drive. Then she climbed back into the car, started the engine and to prevent getting stuck, let the car idle out of the muddy ditch. Still shaking, she pulled back onto the highway and again headed toward Portland. Though the rest of the trip home passed without incident, Thea had the distinct impression that the dark car was still somewhere nearby.

* * * * * *

Thea put off the phone call to Meredith until after she had taken a shower and addressed the bloody scratches on her legs, unpacked, checked her voice mail and watered the plants. In her mind, she scripted a version of her meeting with Malcolm. She knew that the slightest hint of his whereabouts would have Meredith badgering her for more information.

But when she finally got around to calling the Dean home it was the answering machine that greeted her. Somewhat relieved, Thea left a message saying that she had found Malcolm, he was fine and would call Meredith soon. As she paused, trying to word the message as innocuously as possible, she thought she detected the sound of soft breathing on the line. Then the end-message beep of the recording machine cut her off.

She leaned outside and retrieved the two days' accumulation of mail from her mailbox. Along with the junk mail was a personal letter from the President of St. Augustus Hospital. It was an announcement for a memorial service for Sheldon Steiner, to be held at the hospital after the funeral service, which was to be held at a non-denominational funeral home. She glanced at her watch. The funeral was just about to begin.

Thea's spirits sank. With the inquest into Steiner's death she had forgotten about his funeral. She had hoped it would have taken place while she was away, although she now realized that the post mortem may have delayed it by several days. Though she lacked any desire to attend the service, she knew her absence would be more noticeable than her presence.

She searched through her closet and was about to bring out a high-necked, long-sleeved black dress she last wore for her grandparent's funeral, then realized her scratched legs might be noticed. Instead she chose loose fitting black slacks and matching jacket. Then she took out a low-brimmed, black felt hat. She tied her hair back, pulled the hat down so it covered her hair and completed the ensemble with mirrored sunglasses. Then she headed for the funeral home.

As Thea suspected, she arrived too late for the funeral service, but with enough time to follow the hearse to the cemetery. She fell into line behind the procession of cars, following as mechanically as if she were being towed along.

Thea parked the car and tiptoed between the graves as she followed the group of mourners to the gravesite. She was surprised at the number of friends and family who came to give Sheldon Steiner a last farewell, but then she had only known the professional man. She recognized his widow, veiled and shrouded in black, near the grave. She looked for Erik but could not pick him out of the crowd. Though they had not spoken since before she left Portland, she had expected him to attend. Perhaps it was only she who felt his absence.

During the final prayers and eulogy Thea glanced around the cemetery grounds. Suddenly she felt caught in a maelstrom from which she could not surface. Parked just behind the hearse was the car that had dogged her tracks from Cannon Beach.

Thea had no opportunity to react, no chance to try to catch the driver of the car because in that moment she could feel an instantaneous silence. She turned. The bereaved Mrs. Steiner stood before her, the rest of the mourners watching in anticipatory horror. Thea faced her, mouth open in surprise, uncertain of what to expect.

Mrs. Steiner slowly lifted the veil from her face, revealing a haggard, anguished visage. There was no doubt about the fury and loathing on her face.

"Murderer!" she screamed. "You're the one who's responsible for his death!" She lunged at Thea, fists flailing the air. Several people moved forward to restrain her. This time Thea did not hesitate. She turned and ran across the graves, oblivious to the dead who lay buried beneath her flying feet.

An hour later Thea sat, still trembling, in her office. In a few minutes the hospital's President would be dedicating a psychiatric rehabilitation wing in memory of Dr. Steiner's contributions. It was important she try to quell her inner turmoil and forget her humiliation because most of the people at the cemetery would be there, including Mrs. Steiner. Though Thea knew her absence would be noticed more than her presence, she dreaded even walking into the room. It was unlikely anyone would soon forget the earlier drama. As she wrestled with a multitude of emotions there was a knock at the door.

"Enter. If you're not afraid of a killer, that is," she said flatly. Erik strode into the room, looking elegant and handsome in a tailored black suit, his shoulder length blonde hair just skimming the shoulders. He sat in the chair facing her desk and studied her downcast face.

"Why weren't you at the funeral? You missed a great show," Thea said angrily. "For reasons known only to her, Mrs. Steiner seems to blame me for her husband's death." Sarcasm dripped from her words.

Erik leaned back, crossed his legs and put his feet upon her desk. "Oh, I was there. I saw the whole thing."

Thea shook her head. "I didn't see you."

He gave a dry laugh. "My disguise wasn't as obvious as yours. I stood beside the open grave." Thea did a rapid flashback in her mind and thought perhaps she did remember a man in a black suit with head bent as if in prayer, near the grave. She shrugged.

"It doesn't matter. I'm too ashamed to go to the dedication."

"Why? It wasn't your fault the crazy bat's overmedicated. You had a working relationship with Steiner, even if it was a little strained at the end. You belong there as much as anyone." Erik stood up and walked over to Thea. He grasped her elbow, raised her gently from the chair and thrust his hand through the loop in her arm.

"Come on," he said with a coaxing smile. "We'll face the inquisition together."

NINETEEN

When Thea glanced at her calendar the next morning she realized she had forgotten her resolution to find a guard dog. The trauma of the funeral the day before had left her shaken, but she was glad Erik had pressured her into attending the memorial. That it passed without further incident seemed to vindicate her of whatever outsiders suspected.

The Canine Corps, the kennel specializing in rehabilitated guard dogs, was located on an acreage near Wilsonville, south of Portland. She wondered what rehabilitated meant then decided it didn't matter. It would take one peculiar dog to surpass some of the humans she'd dealt with recently.

Though there were several signs to direct Thea to the kennel, it was possible she could have found the place if she were sightless. The sound and smell alone were enough to guide her to the location. She stepped out of her car, only to be welcomed by a pack of yapping, leaping, ecstatic dogs. She wondered if she was doing the right thing. Weren't these dogs supposed to keep her *out* of the yard?

To her relief, the owner of the kennel appeared, a tiny man scarcely larger than some of the dogs. Disproportionate to his size, he let out a shout that could have registered a three on the Richter scale. The dogs cowered, slinking away toward a large wooden shed. Thea stared at him with admiration. What authority!

"You the lady needs a guard dog?" he asked, with a thick Yorkshire accent. He held out his work-roughened hand, clasping Thea's in a deadlock grip. "The name's Hal Goodfellow."

"Dr. Thea Donovan," Thea introduced herself. She nodded toward the retreating dogs.

"Are these dogs before or after rehabilitation?" she asked, waving her hand in the dogs' direction.

"Those are me own mutts," he said, laughing. "Not worth training that lot, they're incorrigible. We keep the good dogs apart." He strode off toward an area of screened dog-runs, leaving Thea trotting to keep up to him. They stopped before a series of individual runs and kennels.

"What do you mean by rehabilitated?" She cast a dubious glance at the various breeds of dogs who stared back at her with suspicion in their round, dark eyes.

"They're usually dogs rescued from puppy mills or strays I pick up from the pound before they nuke-em. I only take the promising ones, like Ahab here." He stood before a kennel containing a dog that looked like it might be a cross between an Irish Wolfhound and a horse. Thea twisted her mouth.

"Just a bit too big," she said. The man laughed.

"All right," he said. "How about Juneau?" He stopped at the cage of a medium-sized, brown and white dog with long hair and soft, floppy ears.

"Juneau, what a pretty name," said Thea as she gazed at the dog whose large brown eyes seemed to plead with her to 'get me the hell out of here'. Thea glanced quickly away lest the dog mesmerize her into surrendering.

"She's a special dog, a one person dog. I knew her previous owner. He came to see me just before he died and asked me to find her a good home." He watched Thea walk up to the kennel, a knowing smile on his face.

"I'll leave ya to bond a bit," he said, opening the kennel for Thea to enter. She bit her lip but ventured inside just the same and squatted, waiting for the dog to move. Juneau wriggled over to Thea, licked her hand and placed her paw upon Thea's knee. Thea rolled her eyes in resignation.

"I'll take her," she said. "How much?" Hal shook his head.

"Nothin'," he said. "Only you must promise that if she doesn't work out, you bring her back here."

Thea felt tears beginning to start. "I promise." She handed the man her business card and thanked him. Then she gave Juneau a pat on the head and the dog followed, right at her heels, out of the kennel. When she opened the passenger door Juneau leaped onto the seat as if she owned the car.

After Thea drove away she realized the folly of her impulsiveness. She had none of the necessities for dog ownership, such as food or a place to sleep. Not optimistic enough that Juneau would comply and 'stay' as ordered, she tied the dog to the handrail on the front step of her house with a piece of twine, and set off to buy a collar, leash and dog food.

Thea returned twenty minutes later to discover a snarling, defensive Juneau preventing an irritated Erik from trespassing. She chuckled to herself, careful not to let Erik see her delight with the dog's capability. She patted Juneau upon the head, praised her with a murmured 'good dog' and unlocked the front door. But when Erik approached to enter, Juneau again showed her fangs and refused to let him pass.

"All right, Juneau," said Thea in desperation. "Enough." She buckled the new collar around the dog's neck and held her still, allowing Erik into the house. Then she set out a dish of food and water for her in the fenced back yard. If Juneau was this obdurate with Erik, how would she react when confronted with a genuine menace?

"Where did you get the hound from hell?" Erik muttered, flopping down on the sofa. Thea choked back a laugh as she thought of good-natured Juneau. Hound from hell, indeed!

"It seemed like a good idea at the time. Although I'm still not certain who made the final decision to take her. A word of advice: Don't go dog-hunting when you're feeling vulnerable."

Erik scowled. "No problem there. I hate dogs."

Thea stared at him in amazement. It had not occurred to her that Erik might dislike animals, yet somehow it fit with the rigidity of his life. She would have to keep Juneau out of his way if they were to continue any sort of relationship. She remembered that Malcolm Dean owned a dog. Suddenly it seemed odd that of the two of them, Malcolm would be the compassionate dog lover.

TWENTY

Thea finished seeing patients the next day realizing that for the first time ever, work had only partially occupied her mind. She had been thinking of Malcolm all day long, where he was, how he was doing, who was with him. And that kiss he had given her. Possibly it was the kiss that disturbed her more than anything. Although it hadn't been much more than a peck on the lips, the kiss was almost as blasphemous to a doctor/patient relationship as a kiss between a priest and his parishioner. Forbidden territory.

She sat at her desk, biting on the cap of her pen, concerned because her numerous calls to Meredith had gone unanswered. Under normal circumstances Meredith returned her messages promptly. She wondered if she should try phoning again and then decided to pay a visit instead. There was a hollow in her life Meredith always managed to fill.

On her drive to Oregon City, she had the distinct impression that she was being followed. It felt different from the episode with the black car. Though she repeatedly checked her mirrors, she realized that she could not readily identify any one vehicle it might be. There was just an intangible feeling that someone was watching her. Or maybe she was becoming paranoid from all the recent drama.

She parked outside Meredith's gate, walked to the front door and turned. A plain, cream-colored sedan had just pulled up halfway down the block. When the driver saw her looking his way, he held a magazine before his face, pretending to read. Had someone followed her, or were they watching Meredith's house? Then she remembered the calls she'd made where she could hear someone on the line. Again, had it been Meredith's phone or hers?

Sport, the dog, was not in his usual place on the porch, nor was Meredith at home. Thea grabbed a pen and paper from her purse and scribbled a hasty note of *'sorry I missed you. Call me when you can.'* When she opened the mailbox to place it inside, she noticed that no one had picked up the mail for several days. If Meredith planned to leave town, wouldn't she have arranged to have someone get her mail, or place it on hold? Thea felt a hard knot of worry beginning to form in her stomach. Where on earth was Meredith?

She drove home only to be greeted by an ecstatic Juneau. Her gloomy spirits lifted. What a wonderful feeling it was to have someone so devoted yet so undemanding. It occurred to her that Malcolm may have contacted his mother himself and perhaps she was with him now. She picked up the phone and dialed the number of The Sea Hag.

Though the person who picked up the phone only answered 'hello' and did not identify herself, it sounded like Andree.

"May I speak with Malcolm Dean?" Thea asked. There was a definite hesitation on the other end.

"I'm sorry. You have a wrong number," came the reply.

"Andree?" asked Thea, confused. The receiver clunked in her ear as the other party hung up the phone. She was certain she had not misdialed the number. It was one thing if Andree wanted to conceal Malcolm's whereabouts, it was another to shut her out. Then she had an idea.

She dialed the number of The Sea Hag again. It rang ten times before someone picked up the receiver, though no one spoke.

"To whom it may concern," Thea blurted into the phone, "Meredith Dean is missing." Then she hung up. Let them chew on that for a while, she thought. If they're hiding Malcolm he'll get the message.

She picked up the phone again, this time dialing the number of the Canine Corps. Though she could hear muffled barking in the background, it was a relief to finally talk with someone.

"Juneau is working out wonderfully," said Thea. "I just can't thank you enough."

"I'm glad you like each other," said Hal with a chuckle. "I'd been saving her for someone who could appreciate her."

"You don't have to worry, I'll take good care of her," said Thea. "If you like, we'll come back for a visit someday."

Hal said he'd be looking forward to that, then the background noise became too disruptive and they had to end the conversation. Thea felt better already but she'd have felt even better if she could have reached Meredith.

Then she considered the possibility that in addition to the phone call, she could send an email to Andree at The Sea Hag outlining her concerns, and have her forward it to either Malcolm or Meredith. She had The Sea Hag's website with contact information email, but not Meredith's email address (assuming she had one). She hastily jotted an email for Meredith, asking that she call Thea when and if she could, and sent it off to Andree at The Sea Hag.

After she sat back down in the kitchen she thought about Andree. Thea knew she hadn't imagined the way Andree had looked at Malcolm and she was certain she'd detected jealousy when it appeared they had spent the night together. Was she just being protective over the Deans or was she somehow romantically involved with Malcolm? Though Andree was married, in today's society it seemed that being married to someone else hardly mattered.

* * * * * *

If Thea were asked to put her feelings for Meredith into perspective it would have been difficult for her to comply. Meredith was more than just a patient's mother or even a nice lady who had treated her with warmth and compassion and friendship. No, to Thea she represented family and motherhood, everything Thea wished she'd had as a child. In her blurred memory, anyone would have been preferable to her real mother, a mother she could recall only meeting twice.

Thea was thirteen the first time she saw her natural mother. The school bus had dropped her off at her regular stop two blocks from her grandparents' house. As she walked home it began to drizzle. Thea held her vinyl binders above her head and started jogging. Then when she got closer to the house she noticed a woman sitting on the third and last sequence of stone steps on the path up to the mansion.

At first Thea thought the woman was a vagrant. When she'd gone downtown with her grandmother she had seen similar women hanging around Drake Street and near the older hotels. But this woman, who wasn't really that much older than Thea, was smiling at her in a sly way that made Thea uncomfortable, almost as if she knew her. Then Thea realized that she must, for she called out her name.

Thea's steps slowed. She glanced up at the house. A curtain moved. It was her grandmother, who watched her journey to and from the bus religiously every day. But this time her grandmother's pinched, tear-streaked face disappeared from the window when she caught Thea's eye. Puzzled, Thea turned to the young woman who had been following the mini drama with amusement.

"What a bitch!" the woman said, laughing. She dried her hands on the sides of a canvas drawstring purse, reached into the depths of it and brought out a pack of cigarettes. She lit one and inhaled deeply, blowing a smoke ring. She held out the pack to Thea. Shocked, Thea shook her head. Her eyes traveled back to her grandmother's window. But she could see no one there. She took a long look at the woman before her.

The woman was very pretty in a hard, frenzied way. Her long brown hair fell loosely over a tight pink sleeveless sweater with a low V-neck and pearl buttons down the front. She wore a black leather mini-skirt with a side-slit that came almost to her hip. But her high-heeled black patent shoes were scuffed and peeling, like her hot pink nail polish. Then Thea noticed the strange scars and pin pricks that covered her bare arms. She glanced quickly away.

The woman took a long drag on her cigarette and coughed.

"So you're Thea," she said. "Well, what do you think of me?" She reeled back and burped. An unfamiliar sour smell filled the air. Suddenly Thea realized the woman was drunk. Disgusted, she marched up the path toward the door. The woman grabbed her arm.

"Hey," she slurred. "Don't walk away from me!" She frowned. "Don't you know who I am?"

Thea shook her head, but an unpleasant thought had begun to nag at her and she did not want to acknowledge it just yet.

"No. I don't. I don't care, either."

The woman snorted with laughter. "You sound just like your old lady, you know that? Just like your old lady."

"Don't talk about my grandmother like that," Thea shouted. "You have no right calling her names, you don't even know her." The woman laughed even harder.

"Oh my poor baby," she said, wiping the streaming heavy mascara at the corners of her eyes. "What have they done to you?" She held out her arms toward Thea. "I'm talking about me. I'm your mother."

Thea stared at the woman with such pain and disbelief in her eyes that it washed the laughter from the woman's face.

"Hey," she began. "I'm sorry." It was too late.

Thea turned and bolted to the door of the house that seemed to open and close for her as if by magic, and she was entering a fairytale castle that shut her away from the evil creature on the steps. A few moments later, Thea took her grandmother's former position at the window and watched as the woman shrugged and ground her cigarette butt into the step. Then she disappeared from Thea's view and from her life. Almost as if it had never happened, Thea and her grandmother never once spoke of that day.

Now Thea thought long and hard about what steps she should take to discover Meredith's whereabouts. It was impossible to contact Malcolm unless he wanted to be found, which apparently he did not. She tried phoning Meredith's number one more time, again got the answering machine and left another message saying she had found Malcolm. And this time she was certain that someone was listening on her line.

TWENTY-ONE

"What brings you here?" Stan Peltzer blurted out as Thea strode into his office and sat in the chair in front of his desk.

"Two things. One: there's been a strange vehicle following me almost everywhere I go. It tailgated me so close coming back from Cannon Beach yesterday that I missed a curve and ran into a ditch."

"Did you file a police report or contact your insurance company?" said Peltzer.

Thea shook her head. "Apart from scratches on me and the car, there's no real damage, other than the ordeal I went though. I think I'm being stalked."

Peltzer appeared puzzled. "Do you want to file a report now? I can take down the make and license plate and run a search on it."

Thea took a deep breath. "Unfortunately, I haven't been able to identify the driver, the car, or even get the plate."

"So what do you want me to do?"

"I don't know; make a note of it, or something. Until I get more details there's not much else I can do."

"Okay," Peltzer replied. "You said there were a couple of things. What else?"

"I'd like to file a Missing Person report. Malcolm Dean's mother is missing."

Peltzer stared at her, raising his eyebrows in disbelief. "What?"

Good grief, wasn't he even listening? she thought. "I've been in contact with Meredith Dean ever since the surgery," she said. "We've become close. Anyway, she hasn't been home in days and her mail is still there. She's not the kind of person to leave without letting anyone know."

Stan Peltzer cocked his head to one side and studied Thea. "Maybe her son has contacted her. Have you thought about that?"

Thea swallowed hard, deliberating before she spoke. "She might not call the police if she'd heard from him. But I feel certain she would have called me." She didn't like the look on Stan Peltzer's face.

"Dr. Donovan, when did you last talk to Mrs. Dean?"

When had she last talked to her? Not since before Sheldon Steiner's funeral. Or before she got Juneau. Or before she'd gone to Cannon Beach. Or the fight with Erik. It had been days, maybe even weeks, since she'd last spoken to Meredith. But then she remembered she'd left Meredith a message that Malcolm was fine and would be calling her. But had he?

Before she could answer, he said, "I've been looking at the results from the autopsy on a recent murder victim. Either the killer's changed his MO or it's just an unrelated killing. This time the victim is an older woman." He took a few steps toward the door.

"Are you up to looking at a corpse?"

Thea stared at him feeling the color vanish from her face. An unspoken question hung between them.

He shook his head and shrugged. "I don't know. The police have only seen Mrs. Dean once when they were looking for Malcolm. It might not be her." He led her down the long cold corridor to the stainless steel coldness of the morgue.

While Peltzer spoke to the attendant, Thea fidgeted, first feeling hot and sweaty, then cold and clammy. What's wrong with me, she thought, it's not the first time I've been to the morgue. She'd seen lots of bodies before, worked on them in medical school, then later in her Reflesh research. But it was different with someone you knew. She leaned against a pale green wall for support. Peltzer noticed her face changing color, chameleon-like, beside the wall.

"Are you okay?" Thea nodded, unable to speak. Peltzer turned to the attendant.

"Make it quick."

The heavy drawer slid out. Thea took a couple of halting steps toward the body, almost afraid to look.

"Thank God," she exhaled. "I'd psyched myself up to seeing Meredith. It's almost more of a shock to find it was someone else."

Peltzer nodded, understanding. "I hate this place. Let's get the hell out of here." He took Thea's arm and they made their way back to his office. For a moment they sat in silence.

"You know, there is a way we could use this to our advantage," he said. He shuffled some papers around on his desk and didn't look up, almost as if he were avoiding eye contact.

"What do you mean?" Thea asked. "How and why would we take advantage of some poor dead woman?"

"We might be able to flush Malcolm Dean out. We could ask for the media's help in locating a missing person. Meredith."

Thea gnawed at her lip. "You've overlooked the possibility she may be with him."

"I already thought of that, but if she's as decent a person as you seem to think, she'll come forward when she realizes we have a 10-65 out on her." He observed Thea carefully as she thought about what he had just said.

Thea sat quiet for several moments, knowing he suspected her of withholding information. But when the time was right she'd show her cards. It just wasn't the right time yet.

"I'll get the paperwork started on Mrs. Dean," he said. "You go home and get some rest. It would be unprofessional for you to . . . ," he paused as if searching for the right words, "faint when you're operating on someone." To Thea it sounded like a veiled threat.

She left Peltzer's office feeling pulled in several directions all at once. As a physician, she felt morally obligated to protect Malcolm. But that did not preclude her from her responsibility as a law abiding citizen to help the police in apprehending a suspected murderer. And then there was Meredith. Was she protecting her or potentially hurting her by her silence?

Out of recent habit she checked her rear view mirror as she pulled out of the police station. Since the incident with the foreign car she'd been an overly cautious driver. It was nerve wracking having to be so cognizant of every car on the road. She noticed that an unmarked police car pulled out of the parking lot just after she did. When she turned onto the freeway the ghost car stayed a perfect three car lengths behind her, as if synchronizing her movements.

So that's the game we're playing, she thought, Peltzer's having me followed. Then she recalled the strange sounds she'd heard on her telephone and she wondered why she hadn't thought of it before now. The police had tapped her phone! Whether they considered her a key figure or just an accomplice, it helped to explain a few of the events over the last few days. Maybe it had something to do with the foreign car as well.

TWENTY-TWO

Thea arrived home to be greeted by a jubilant Juneau. She felt a twinge of remorse as she stroked the soft fur—it had not been her intent to neglect the dog. Although her life had become much more complicated over the past few weeks than previously, the dog didn't know that. She still needed attention. Grabbing Juneau's leash, she slipped it over the dog's head, an impulsive move because now it would be impossible to put off a walk. But she had one thing to do that would not wait.

Lifting the receiver of the telephone she unscrewed the cap on the speaker. If there was a listening device inside, would she recognize it, or would she just mess up the workings of the telephone? She removed the contents of the receiver, swathed it within a Kleenex tissue and placed it in her sweatshirt pocket. Then she headed into the den and took out the Portland yellow pages, scanning the thirty or so pages of attorney listings. Thousands of potential names jumped out at her, making it impossible to know where to begin. When she came upon the name of Anderson, Forbes & Weinstein she hesitated. Was it possible that another member of the Forbes family practiced law? More likely it was just another coincidence, she reasoned, Forbes was a common enough name.

Thinking there was no point in providing the police with free information if they should have the house bugged as well, she took Juneau for a perfunctory jog around the block then stopped to rest at a local park. She located a park bench, tying Juneau to the leg while she took out her cell phone. On a whim, she dialed the number for Anderson, Forbes & Weinstein and asked if she could make an appointment with Reg Forbes. There was a sudden silence at the other end.

"There is no one by that name in this office," explained the receptionist. "The partner's name is Jonathan Forbes. Would you like me to set up an appointment with him?"

"As soon as possible," said Thea. "Could we make it this afternoon?"

Juneau barked at a jogger passing by, tugging so hard on the leash she almost moved the park bench with Thea sitting on it. She grasped the dog's collar and held her close, though it made it difficult to continue holding the cell phone. She passed the leash from one hand to another.

"Hmmm," said the receptionist. "Yes, it looks like we've had a cancellation. Can you make it in an hour?"

"I'll be there," said Thea, popping the cell phone closed. She turned to Juneau. "Okay girl, let's make tracks." They ran all the way home.

Fifty-seven minutes later Thea sat reading a tattered financial magazine in the lawyer's office, sixteen floors up in a trendy downtown high rise. Someone called her name. She glanced up to see a friendly looking woman in her mid-forties.

"I'm Elaine, Mr. Forbes's Administrative Assistant," she said.

She led Thea through the wainscotted labyrinth of hallways and opened the door to a large office decorated in oak paneling and dusty-pink striped wallpaper. An enormous floor to ceiling window provided a panoramic view of the ships on the Columbia River. While Elaine took notes, Thea gave a brief explanation of the events of the past few weeks, including Steiner's murder, the pursuit of the foreign car and her belief that the police were keeping her under surveillance. She did not mention Malcolm. Elaine closed her steno pad and stood.

"Mr. Forbes will be with you in a few minutes," she said, closing the door behind her.

As Thea waited, she examined the contents of the room. There were few personal articles that disclosed the personality of the occupant. A pitcher of water and several glasses sat on a credenza behind the lawyer's chair. Slightly obscured behind the glasses was a photograph of a man and woman in wedding clothes.

She was just about to walk over and take a closer look when a dark-haired young man entered the room. She stifled a gasp. The man was gorgeous! He smiled and held out his hand in greeting.

"I'm Jonathan Forbes," he said. "Please have a seat."

He dropped into an expensive brass-studded leather recliner, leaned back in his chair and crossed his legs. While he scrutinized her with stunning azul blue eyes, Thea found it nearly impossible to stop staring at him.

"Elaine filled me in on your case. You really think you're under police surveillance?"

Thea opened her purse and removed the object wrapped in tissue. She passed it across the desk to Jonathan Forbes. "Is that a listening device?" she asked. He opened the Kleenex and stared at the contents.

"Looks like normal telephone parts," he said. "What makes you suspect your conversations are being monitored?" He rewrapped the piece and handed it back to her.

"I've noticed interference on the line for a few days."

Jonathan laughed. "Probably just a poor connection. That's your phone company's problem. What do you want me to do?"

Thea thought for a moment.

"For starters, I'd like to know who owns that dark foreign car that's been following me. I haven't been able to get the license and I have no information on it except that it's black or dark blue, fast and looks kind of like a Corvette. If the police are watching me, I want to know why. I also received a threatening note in my mailbox that the police haven't been able to trace."

Jonathan had been jotting down information while she spoke. When she finished speaking he glanced up. He dropped his pen upon the desk.

"I don't think you need a lawyer. At least not yet. You need a private investigator. There's a fellow who does some occasional investigative work for us whom I'd highly recommended. He retired from the police department a few years ago. I could assign him to your case, if you'd like. But I must warn you, he's not cheap."

Who is? thought Thea, but she nodded assent. Jonathan reached into his desk and brought out a couple of business cards. He stood up, walked around the desk and handed them to her. She glanced at the first card and saw the name Joe E. Brown, Private Investigator, Fast and Discreet. Smiling to herself, she followed Jonathan to the door.

"You give Joe Brown a call when you're ready for him to start. I won't do anything until I hear from you again."

"Thank you," said Thea. She looked up into his stunning blue eyes and the thought 'tinted contacts' flashed through her mind.

"By the way," she said. "Are you any relation to Reg Forbes?" She watched Jonathan's face for any change in expression. To her surprise he didn't miss a beat.

"He was my father," he replied.

* * * * * *

Maryann Kowalchuk had not the slightest idea how to change a flat tire. When he was alive, her father had always taken care of that sort of thing for her and then later, her ex-husband. But now that she was without male intervention in vehicle maintenance, one of her car's nearly treadless tires had given out, leaving her stranded on an unlit single-lane road outside Gresham city limits.

In hindsight, she realized she should have taken out emergency vehicle insurance, but it was expensive on her limited budget and too late now. She was at the mercy of strangers. She remembered the advice she had received in her Driver's Ed safety program—if you experience vehicle breakdown, put on your emergency flashers, stay in the vehicle, lock the doors and wait for help to arrive. The only problem was, they hadn't told you how to recognize help when it did come.

At least four cars passed her without even so much as

slowing down. With almost no shoulder to pull over on, it was scary how close they came to sideswiping her. It was just as well she hadn't tried to flag them down, she thought, they'd have run her over as soon as stop.

Near 3:00 a.m. Maryann began to nod off. The outside temperature had plummeted and inside the car the steaming windows had begun to stream with moisture. She shivered and started the engine to warm the interior and the windows became less fogged. After a few minutes she turned it off again because she thought she heard the sound of an approaching car.

Whoever was in the other vehicle thoughtfully turned off his headlights before he coasted slowly to a stop behind her car. She heard the slam of a vehicle door and then the advancing footsteps crunching on the gravel shoulder. Too relieved to be apprehensive, Maryann used her sleeve to wipe away the condensation on her window and waited for her rescuer.

It seemed to take him a long time to appear at her window. When he reached the driver's door and she rolled down the window, all she could tell about him was that he was younger than she. He looked at her with a fixed stare that made him seem inhuman.

"Thank you for stopping," she said. "I've been here for hours. I've got a flat tire."

She stuck her hand out the window and motioned toward the right rear wheel facing the ditch. The man glanced up and down the car, walked over to the right side and disappeared into the shadows of the trees. Maryann slid into the passenger seat, opened the door and stepped down.

Out of the corner of her eye she caught a furtive movement and a glimpse of something metallic. At that moment, instinct told her to turn and run for her life. But the man overtook her with a speed greater than anything she had ever seen before. She had no time to struggle, no time to scream. Within seconds, she was choking on the warmth of her own blood.

TWENTY-THREE

After Thea had driven home and gotten over her initial shock at Jonathan's revelation about his father, she replaced the speaker portion on the phone's receiver and called the number on the business card of Joe E. Brown. As expected, she reached only his voice mail. Though the thought of someone possibly listening in was perturbing, she left a message for him to call her at home instead of at work. She didn't need to provide the hospital with more gossip than usual.

True to the pledge on his card, Mr. Brown returned her call within a half-hour, refused to discuss anything on the phone and insisted on coming to her home. Not only did his forcefulness impress Thea, it gave her a feeling of real security for the first time in ages. When the doorbell rang fifteen minutes later, she realized she was looking forward to meeting Mr. Fast and Discreet. Juneau set to barking and growling until she put her on the leash before Thea opened the door.

Joe E. Brown positively filled the doorway. The neatly pressed pants and jacket he wore must have been hand tailored for his enormous build. He removed a Mariner's baseball cap to reveal a gleaming shaved head. Holding out a hand the size of a baseball glove, it enveloped Thea's in a grasp that made her wince. His face split happily, displaying two beautiful rows of teeth; the top row revealing a wide space in the middle. Then he stepped inside without further invitation.

"I'm Joey," he said unnecessarily, lowering a deep bass voice. "But there's no reason for us to let the neighbors know."

She stared at him in astonishment but motioned for him to follow her into the living room. Juneau, suspicious at first, sniffed Joe Brown's pant leg then licked his hand. Thea took her off the leash and shook her head.

"Some watch dog," she said. "I sure am glad to see you so quickly. Did Jonathan Forbes fill you in?"

"He told me enough that I agree the police probably are watching you."

"There's something I didn't tell Jonathan," Thea said, hesitating. "Knowing what I do now, I'm glad I didn't."

Joe raised his eyebrows in a question.

"Back in the mid-eighties, Jonathan's father died in a murder/suicide with a policeman's wife and was blamed for both deaths. It happened in this house. The case was considered closed, but I think I've uncovered enough evidence to suggest that the policeman himself committed the two murders. If nothing else, it would vindicate the reputation and memory of Reg Forbes."

Joe gave out a low whistle. "It was before I joined the Portland Police," he said, "but I remember the case. It's a fairly common name so it didn't occur to me that the two Forbes were related. You'd need a lot of hard evidence before anyone would take you seriously enough to reopen the case."

Thea snorted in humorless laughter. "No kidding. Anyway, the important thing to me right now is to find out what you can about the driver of the car that's been hounding me."

"I'll do all the usual checking around in records. Maybe even talk to some of my friends who have sharp eyesight," said Joe with a wink. "I'll watch your house for the next few nights and follow you to work in the morning. Maybe we'll get lucky and the guy will show up."

Thea nodded. "Sounds good. What do you drive so I'll know it's you and not panic?"

Joe stood up and Thea noticed, with embarrassment, Juneau's hair all over his slacks. She apologized, offering to get a lint brush. He seemed unperturbed and shook his head. He strode over to the window, pulled back the drapes and pointed to a rusted, gold Dodge Dart parked in front.

"Think you'd recognize that piece of junk?" he asked,

giving a short laugh. Thea laughed with him.

"If it's good enough for DEQ," she said. "It's good enough for me."

* * * * * *

There were two things in the morning paper that set Thea's mood for the day. The first was the plea from the police for assistance in the disappearance of an elderly woman, Meredith Dean. The second was that another young woman, Maryann Kowalchuk, had gone missing overnight, her car found abandoned on the side of the road. It chilled Thea to read of both on the same page.

She was relieved to return to the sanctity of home at the end of the day and find Juneau waiting for her in the back yard. Joe Brown pulled up in his battered Dodge soon after. She wondered if the neighbors were beginning to notice anything unusual with the increase of traffic around her house. But Joe was just checking in, nothing to report, alarming or otherwise.

That night she retired early, the thoughts of the murdered women uppermost in her mind. Joe and Juneau gave her a modicum of security, but could they protect her if someone threatened her life? She forced herself not to allow her imagination to enact such a scenario and drowsed off reading a book, Juneau lying beside her on the bed.

As she lay sleeping a myriad of faceless bodies and driverless cars dominated her subconscious. She moaned and shivered, clasping the sheets close to her. Rolling to the other side of the bed she bumped into a warm male body lying next to her. In the throes of sleep it neither shocked nor surprised her. He enclosed her in his arms, pulling her against him. Reveling in his warmth and strength, she opened her eyes to the face of Malcolm Dean.

He lowered his head and kissed her eyes closed again, stroking the length of her body underneath her nightgown, warming her throughout. She answered his kiss with the passionate heat of long repression and they merged as if they had become one person. In ecstasy, Thea murmured his name, abandoning all coherent thoughts. Suddenly the sound of shattering glass fragmented the dream into a nightmare.

She awoke to the commotion of Juneau barking and glanced quickly at the rumpled blankets beside her. But Malcolm was not there; had never been there. In another part of the house someone shouted and swore amidst the crash of fracturing furniture. Then came the dull thud of a fist meeting flesh. Near the front door Joe Brown shouted her name.

Thea leaped out of bed, ran to the door and threw it open. Joe dangled a struggling man by the neck of his shirt. With barely restrained force he sent him sprawling across the living room floor.

"Excuse me for waking you, Doctor. Do you know this piece of shit?"

Thea glanced down at the fellow who lay moaning in pain. It wasn't just the throttling he'd received from Joe that caused him to writhe in agony upon the floor. Despite her medical training, she found herself gagging at the sight and smell. The man's face was a mass of swelling and putrefaction, unclean wounds weeping with infection. And then she got another shock. It was Malcolm Dean.

"Oh my God!" she gasped. She knelt down beside Malcolm and glanced up at Joe.

"Shut the door," she whispered. "Then come and give me a hand with him."

Joe stared at her for a moment, then ran and closed the door and drapes. He turned out all the lights except one bright lamp nearby.

"You know this guy?" he asked in disbelief.

"Yes," Thea said, exasperated. "He's a patient of mine and it looks like he's going to die unless I get some antibiotics into him."

She ran off toward the bedroom and returned with a blanket and her doctor's bag. After she covered the now convulsing Malcolm with the blanket, she took a rapid inventory of the bag's contents, spilling them out onto the carpet in her haste.

"Damn!" She did not usually keep many medications with her and what she needed was not in the bag. She removed a disposable syringe and a vial of Penicillin, drawing out as much as she dared give him without knowing the etiology of the infection.

She wondered what on earth she should do with him. If she took him to the hospital now the police would place him under arrest until he was well enough that they could take him into custody. On the other hand, if she kept him here without proper medical facilities available he could die.

She glanced back down at the patient, inserted the needle and emptied its contents. Malcolm, drifting in and out of delirium, did not even notice. She had to make a decision and she had to make it fast. As if hearing her thoughts telepathically, Malcolm opened his eyes and fixed a glazed, feverish stare upon her.

"Please don't take me to the hospital," he begged her, voice cracking. "Don't take me." Then he lapsed into unconsciousness again.

Thea's mind raced. She would have to make a surreptitious trip to the hospital to get more antibiotics, dressings and whatever else she needed without actually admitting him to the hospital, all without being discovered. She looked up at Joe.

"You heard the man," she said. "I'm not doing him or myself any favors by not taking him in, but he saved my life so I guess I owe him that." She stood up and straightened her back. "The medication should keep him for a little while but I'm leaving you to babysit. If he says anything in his sleep, for God's sake, write it down. It might be important."

Then Thea retrieved a sealed sterile scalpel and a tiny plastic pouch from the floor. Taking a small scraping of the infected area on Malcolm's face, she placed it inside the pouch. She caught a glimpse of Joe's face, now looking like he was about to be sick, and made a point of ignoring him. She held up the bag and waved it.

"If I'm lucky one of the lab people will be working late

and help me with this," she said. She glanced at her watch. It was 1:15 a.m. "I'll be back as soon as I can."

Thea grabbed a jacket from the hall closet and was just about to reach for the door handle when the doorbell rang. She and Joe stared at each other.

"Who the hell else are you expecting at this time of night?"

"Don't answer it," she whispered. "Give me your car keys and I'll go out the back way."

Joe nodded, reached into his pocket and tossed the keys in her direction. She caught them in her right hand. Then she turned and, scrunching down, tiptoed to the back, all the while praying that the visitor would not also think of trying the back door.

TWENTY-FOUR

Thea made it out the back door without seeing anyone, crawling around the shrubbery as furtively as an autumn slug before she located Joe's battered Dodge in the alley. In his haste to stop Malcolm from entering her house, or maybe just because it was a worthless pile of garbage, Joe had left it unlocked. Thea let out a grateful sigh when it started on her first try. Then it backfired, ripping through the still night like a shotgun blast.

"Shit!" said Thea. She lowered her head to prevent being seen, deciding against turning on the headlights until she was out of sight of the house. She drove cautiously. In this neighborhood it was important to not attract any more attention than the car's broken muffler had already. Fortunately, the rest of the trip to the hospital passed without incident. Then she realized she had left her hospital I.D. at home.

As luck would have it, the Security Supervisor met her at the automatic doors and asked for identification. She gave him a withering, *'you know who the hell I am'* look that intimidated and outranked him enough that he let her pass. Thea made a mental note to mention the wisdom of that decision to him some time in the future, a time when she did not have to break the rules herself.

She slipped unnoticed past the doctors' lounge and into the locker room. After entering the lock combination, she retrieved the white hospital coat with her name tag clipped to the breast pocket. She strode down the deserted corridor, and after making certain no one was watching, stepped inside the medical supplies closet. Most of the items she needed to cleanse and disinfect the wounds were readily available.

She took no more than was necessary for the next few days—there would be ample time during normal hours to secure additional supplies. Not only was there the danger of being caught with bulging pockets, which Administration frowned heavily upon in these budget-cutting times, there was also the possibility that Malcolm would have to be admitted to hospital or die.

Now there came the challenge of obtaining antibiotics from the Pharmacy. She took a deep breath, eased the door open a few inches and moved into the corridor. The Pharmacy Department was halfway between the supply closet and the Emergency Department. She hoped there would be no one walking in the halls to recognize or detain her. Malcolm did not have much time. But just then a small commotion between a couple of drunk teenagers in Emergency temporarily diverted the graveyard shift's attention.

When she reached the Pharmacy Department she slipped her hand into her pocket for her prescription pad. She paused for a moment realizing that if she put Malcolm's name on a prescription it might be recovered by the police. She searched her memory for any recent inpatients that might have legitimate use for such a drug and scribbled out a prescription for antibiotics. She considered for a moment then wrote out a prescription for painkillers, rang the Pharmacy door buzzer and passed the slips of paper through the window slot. The pharmacist on duty opened the window and nodded to her.

"Fifteen minutes," he said, closing the window again.
Thea understood the precautions. It would be easy enough for any drug-crazed individual to come here looking for a quick fix. Now she had time to kill. Suddenly she realized she couldn't remember if Malcolm had any allergies to antibiotics or other medicine. Before blindly giving medications she would have to consult his history chart. But it would be too difficult to access a computer without being seen. She would have to go down to the pre-computerized dungeon called Medical Records.

Instead of using the slow hospital elevator, she took the

stairs to the basement. Removing the hospital keys she always kept in her lab coat pocket, she unlocked the door and stepped into the dank, dustiness of Medical Records. In her research she had spent interminable hours here and fortunately understood the archaic filing system.

She flicked on just one set of lights, glanced at row upon row of dusty file-packed shelves lining the room and headed for the 'D's. But Malcolm's file was not there. Realizing it could be cross-referenced in the khaki steel files, she tried the surgical department. It was not among the surgical files either.

After a few minutes Thea located the Department of Psychiatry cabinet and this time her efforts met with success. She removed the file and sat cross-legged upon the floor to read. With a small pang of regret she reread the last notes that Sheldon Steiner had written while Malcolm was in his care. Then, satisfied that Malcolm would not be in any danger from the medication, she replaced the file.

While it was a long shot, it suddenly occurred to her that Peter Volk might once have been a patient. Knowing she still had about ten minutes to kill before the prescription was ready to be picked up she searched through the 'V's. To her unbridled delight, found a thin, yellowed folder labeled with Peter's name. She opened the folder in anticipation, but there was not much more information than what she already knew.

He had been under psychiatric evaluation in the Emergency Department after the murder of his wife. Acute catatonic schizophrenia was the official diagnosis, with a recommendation for admission to a psychiatric hospital, to be kept under strict supervision. Thea shuddered when she recognized the distinctive backhand slant writing on Peter's chart. Sheldon Steiner had been the admitting psychiatrist.

Just then she heard footsteps outside the door. She stood up to put Peter's file back into place. But as she thumbed through them alphabetically, just before the slot for Peter's file, she stopped. There was a file with Derek Volk's name on it. Her stomach did a quick flip. As she started to reach for it she stopped. Was that the sound of the doorknob turning? To her horror she realized she'd forgotten to relock it when she came in. She took three long strides to the light switch and flicked it off, crouching in the darkness. Then she heard the Medical Records door creak open.

Thea held her breath lest she make a sound. Her eyes and throat tickled from the dust and she felt her nose tingling as if she were about to sneeze. A male figure stepped into the room, casting the beam of a flashlight back and forth across the unlit depths. Thea's sinuses began to water and her body tensed itself to break into a sneeze. Though she stifled it as hard as humanly possible, she inadvertently let out a tiny squeak. The man stopped abruptly, flashlight poised several feet from where Thea cowered.

"Who's there?" he growled. He waited a few seconds as though not really expecting an answer, then began his shadowy walk again. Suddenly he stopped, let out a yell and leapt backward. A large rat ran squealing across his feet into the blackness. Thea pursed her lips so she wouldn't scream.

"Fucking rats!" the guard shouted. He turned and almost ran from the room, slamming the door behind him.

Thea left out her breath in a long sigh and coughed softly. That was too close. She waited for a couple of moments to be certain he was not coming back then slipped Peter's file back into place. Then she let herself out of the room. As she passed by the lab she wrote out instructions and the name James Doe on an adhesive label, marked it 'Stat' and stuck it to the bag containing the specimen she had taken from Malcolm's face. Then she slid it into a cubicle for retrieval.

She wondered how Joe was doing at the house. She picked up the prescription from Pharmacy, took a little-used exit from the hospital to the doctors' parking lot, got back into Joe's Dodge and headed for home. It wasn't until she pulled into the back alley behind her house that she remembered the file marked Derek Volk. Someday she'd have to go back and see what was in it.

TWENTY-FIVE

There was no doubt in Thea's mind that Joe was overjoyed at her return. He helped her unload the contents of her lab coat pockets onto the kitchen counter, then sat back to watch as she prepared to dress Malcolm's wounds. But he averted his eyes when Thea jerked down the back of Malcolm's pants and undershorts, exposing his buttocks.

"Anything happen while I was gone?" Tearing the cellophane off a clean syringe, she drew out a large dose of Demerol from one of the bottles, jabbed the needle into Malcolm's flesh, and injected the contents. Then she placed a towel under his head and before disinfecting the scratches, began removing the necrotic tissue from his face.

Joe snorted in disgust from the chair behind her.

"Perhaps you didn't notice that this place reeks like an abandoned slaughterhouse. He puked on me, he lashed out and swore at me, he stinks and quite honestly, I don't know why you don't just turn him over to the police."

Thea glanced up from her work for a moment to look at Joe and had to laugh at his expression.

"Poor baby," she sneered. "This guy has been through a hell of a lot and yes, he may be a murderer, but that might be because I screwed up his surgery. I owe him at least this much. Do me a favor and get that pink hazards-material disposal container from under the bathroom sink."

Joe returned with the hazards container and placed it on the kitchen counter before backing hastily away. She gathered the contaminated gauze pads, cotton balls and scalpel blades, stood up and dropped them into the container.

"We'll have to carry him to the spare bedroom," she said,

squatting beside Malcolm's feet. "You take the heavy end."

Joe jumped up from his chair, slipped his arms underneath Malcolm's and lifted. With Joe's strength taking over, Thea held the feet for balance only. Together they carried him into the bedroom and lowered him to the bed. Thea covered him with a blanket, glanced at her watch and yawned. No wonder she could barely keep her eyes open. It was almost 4:00 a.m.

"He'll be out till mid-morning," she said. "Why don't you get some sleep?" Joe nodded and hesitated. Then Thea remembered she still had his car keys. She reached into her pocket and handed them to Joe.

"It's fast enough," she said, smiling, "but you'd better do something about that muffler."

Instead of heading back to her bedroom, Thea decided it would be easier to monitor Malcolm if she slept in the same room. She wheeled a folding cot from the spare bedroom closet and opened it to an already made bed. She flopped down upon it, scarcely having time to close her eyes before she fell asleep.

Several hours later she awoke to the sound of someone chanting, a sound so bizarre yet so familiar that when she discovered the source, she couldn't believe it came from Malcolm. It sounded as if he was repeating 'jigsaw' over and over, just as she had heard Peter say it.

Thea reared up. Watching him, it became apparent he was emerging from the euphoria of the painkillers and regaining consciousness. As his eyelids began to flutter his rapid chanting slowed and Thea realized that he wasn't saying jigsaw at all.

"The kid saw," said Malcolm, staring at her with eyes still clouded from the effects of the drugs. "The kid saw the whole thing." From the way he was looking at her, he obviously thought she knew what he was talking about. He was wrong. She picked up his wrist and took his pulse. When she was satisfied with the results she gently laid his arm back upon the bed.

"What do you mean, the *kid saw*?"

Malcolm struggled to sit up but was still too weak. He fell

back upon the bed in frustration. Thea cringed at the obscenity his face had become. But the scratches were scabbing over and with the infection abating, it appeared to be healing. Soon it would be ready for an insertion of Reflesh to smooth over and fill the wounds.

"Peter Volk's kid was the only one apart from Peter himself who knew what happened the night of the murders."

"Everyone knew *that*," said Thea, "but the coroner's report stated Alicia died of a single gunshot wound, just as Reg did. I read the report in the file you keep in your room. Why did you have it anyway?"

"So much for privacy." Malcolm shook his head in exasperation. "It was my father's. He had been the first on the scene, allegedly after Peter, that is. Once he'd interrogated Peter, something told him that Peter was lying and that Alicia hadn't been killed by Reg. For whatever reason the coroner's report was a work of art in errors and omissions; maybe because the coroner was a friend of Peter's, or maybe just because Peter was a detective with the Portland Police. There was mention of a puncture wound that wasn't life threatening, so it didn't kill Alicia. She was still alive until she was shot. But the fact remains: there was an unexplained wound. It was a murder all right, but not a murder/suicide. My father tried to prove a cover-up."

Thea frowned. "That's the one part I could never figure out," she said. "Wouldn't the bullet wound have obliterated the knife wound?"

"If the caliber of the bullet was lined up perfectly and large enough to obliterate the knife wound, maybe," Malcolm said. "The bullets found in both bodies were from a .357 Magnum. My father must have had reason to suspect that Peter stabbed Alicia and would have done the same to Reg, but somehow a gun got involved and he shot Reg. In trying to stage a cover-up, Peter realized it would look like a murder suicide if Alicia and Reg both had gunshot wounds. Alicia's wound probably looked a little like a circle with a line through it."

Thea shuddered, yet was fascinated by his theory. "I think I can figure out how the police attributed the deaths to Reg."

Malcolm nodded. "Most likely Peter found them together. He stabbed Alicia, then when Reg produced his gun in self-defense, Peter managed to get it from him and shoot him with his own gun. After that he shot Alicia and planted the weapon in Reg's hand. It would have worked except I believe that Peter's kid walked in and saw him do it. Fortunately for Peter, the kid was too traumatized by the sight to testify. Or maybe Peter traumatized him later. Only the kid knows."

"But who is the kid? Where is he? I've checked the phone books, directories, everything. There's no one listed by the name of Derek Volk anywhere."

"I've been trying to work that one out for a while too," said Malcolm. "Peter went ballistic after the murders and eventually they committed him to an asylum. Unless the kid had relatives to take him in, he was probably either adopted or put in a foster home. It's more likely than not he changed his name." He studied Thea. "All we know is that he lived in this house for the first five years of his life."

Thea gave him a dark look.

"Thank you," she said. "That makes me feel so much more secure."

Then for a moment her memory flashed back to when she was in Medical Records looking through Malcolm's file. There had been the one on Derek Volk, Peter's son. Other than just the psychological report, it might have contained more information on the child than just being a witness to a killing. The next time she was at the hospital she'd go down to Medical Records and check it out.

Malcolm winced in pain. "Got something for the agony?"

Thea nodded and reached for the bottle of Demerol. While she was drawing the contents into the syringe, Malcolm shifted position and held out his arm for the needle.

"I wonder whatever happened to the knife or whatever it was Peter used to make the puncture wound on Alicia," he mused. "He must have felt it was so incriminating he'd have to get rid of it. Neither my father nor the crime scene investigation team ever found another weapon at the scene."

Thea paused with the needle in midair.

"Sorry, wrong end," she said, flinging back the blankets. Baring his backside again, she thrust the needle in, causing Malcolm to let out a yelp. She apologized again.

"I can help you out with the knife problem," she said. "I don't think it was a knife. Someone had hidden a letter opener behind a false wall in my bedroom."

Malcolm bounced up. "Do you still have it?"

Thea nodded. "I gave it to the police as evidence, but they gave it back to me. They identified the source of the blood as Alicia Volk's. They said the prints on the letter opener's hilt were Peter's."

Malcolm gave a short, rueful laugh. "Of course they were. He hadn't expected it to be discovered."

Thea frowned. "What I don't understand is why the coroner would cover up the cause of death."

"Maybe it was just human error or maybe someone bought him off, who knows. He died a couple of years later, so the explanation died with him. Only two people know what happened."

They stared at each other for several seconds.

"I know what you're thinking," Thea said finally. "I found Peter and tried to talk to him. Oddly enough, all he can do is chant, *'jigsaw'*, although now I know what he's really been saying all these years is *'kid saw'*, just like I heard you do under the anesthetic. He's been riding around on the space shuttle so long, reentry is pretty unlikely."

"I guess we'll never know unless we find his son," said Malcolm. He pulled the covers closer around his neck and his eyelids drooped, suddenly weary from the Demerol. Thea watched him for a few moments until he fell asleep.

"I'll find the kid, or die trying," she said and pulling the door closed, left the room.

TWENTY-SIX

Now that Malcolm was back in the city, Thea knew that eventually he would have to give himself up to the police and provide an alibi as to his whereabouts on the nights in question. For the moment he still needed round the clock nursing care until he was completely out of danger. Though she had to be in the office that morning, afterward it might be worth one last try to attempt communication with Peter. First she needed someone to watch Malcolm. When he awoke she asked the question that had been bothering her for a while.

"Do you know where your mother is?"

Malcolm, still drowsy, muttered, "I had her come to Cannon Beach. I left her with Andree and Steve."

Thea's eyes narrowed. "Are you sure? I called Andree several times without success. I even took out a Missing Persons on Meredith. The police have been looking for her for several days now." She scrutinized his face for any clue that might reveal a lie. Whether he was telling the truth or was just so consummate at deception now, Thea could not say.

Malcolm shrugged. "She was there two days ago and safe. Andree's looking after her. That means not divulging her presence."

For a moment Thea felt a childish pang of jealousy, as if a favored sibling had been given a privilege she had not. She knew it was ridiculous, yet in some ways Meredith had become a surrogate mother to her.

The pain in Malcolm's face had lessened and with it the need for painkillers, although she might have felt more comfortable with him unconscious. Fortunately he had fallen asleep again, but without Meredith or Joe to look after him, she was at a loss as to who she should approach for help. On impulse she dialed Lauren's number.

As it turned out, Lauren had no clients or house showings that day, only a market estimate in the evening.

"What's the big secret?" she asked Thea. "Can't you tell me on the phone why you need to see me?"

"I'll explain when you get here, just please try to make it fast, I've got patients booked in an hour." Thea hoped she didn't sound too abrupt; after all, it was Lauren doing the favor. And friend that she was becoming, Lauren arrived within fifteen minutes of Thea's phone call.

"What is . . .?" Lauren started to say when Thea opened the front door, but she stopped when Thea held a warning finger to her lips. She grabbed Lauren's arm and was about to pull her inside the house when she saw Erik walking up the path toward them.

"Oh, shit!" Thea muttered. Lauren whirled around, puzzled. Thea caught the look in her eyes and shook her head. "Never mind, I'll explain in a minute." She forced herself to smile a welcome for Erik and raised her lips to his for a quick kiss. He glanced at Lauren, smiled and nodded, then turned back to Thea.

"Did I catch you at a bad time?" he said. "I just stopped by to see if you wanted a lift to work."

Thea hesitated. "Erik, this is my friend, Lauren. I think I've mentioned her to you before. She has some papers for me to sign. We were just going out for a quick coffee before I leave for the office. I'll see you there a bit later."

She felt a small twinge of regret at his crestfallen look, realizing she'd been neglecting their relationship, if they still had one. But there was no way to predict his reaction if he discovered Malcolm at her house.

Erik shrugged and his mouth twisted in either resignation or hurt feelings. He turned and walked down the sidewalk toward his car, never looking back. Thea turned to Lauren and let out a heavy sigh.

"So *that's* Erik," said Lauren with a low voice. "Not bad."

Thea waited until Erik's car was out of sight until she opened the front door for them again.

She turned to Lauren and smiled ruefully. "Yes, he's quite a catch. I'm just not sure if he's the right fish for me." She led Lauren into the house and locked the door behind them. Lauren gazed around the room in appreciation.

"You know, I haven't been in here since I showed it to you. You've got the old place looking great. Are you going to show me the moving panel in the bedroom?"

"Maybe later," said Thea. "Right now I want you to meet Malcolm Dean. I should warn you, I hope you have a strong stomach because his face is a mess." She headed for the guest bedroom and knocked before she entered.

"Malcolm," she called out.

When she heard a faint, 'come in', she opened the door and she and Lauren stepped inside. Behind her she heard Lauren's sharp intake of breath, no doubt from shock at the sight of Malcolm's face. But when she turned to look at Lauren, she saw with surprise that Lauren was staring at Malcolm not with repulsion as she had thought but total rapture.

With her Realtor's ability to look beyond the tacky wallpaper and peeling paint of old houses, she could see past the hideous mutilation of Malcolm's face, revealing the man behind it. Thea realized that she may as well not have been there. They only had eyes for each other.

Thea glanced at her watch. "Lauren, Malcolm. Malcolm, Lauren. Now that's taken care of, I've got to go." Lauren glanced up from the bedside, taking notice of Thea for the first time since she'd entered the room.

"The instructions for his antibiotics are beside the bed. Here is my number at the office," said Thea. She handed Lauren her business card. "Call me if you need anything."

Lauren smiled wanly, turned and passed the smile on to Malcolm. "Don't worry, we'll be fine," she said. Malcolm raised his eyebrows in anticipation and waved from the bed. Thea rolled her eyes and left the room shaking her head.

* * * * * *

After the last of the day's patients had disappeared from the waiting room, Thea left the office and headed toward the sanitarium to interview Peter Volk. This time she vowed to go through proper channels and talk with the staff psychiatrist first before seeing Peter. Together they might be able to work on piercing the barrier Peter had built around himself.

She parked her car in the visitor's parking lot, started walking toward the clinic and stopped at the entrance door. For a moment she had a strange premonition and she glanced back to her car. Then she saw a sight that turned her knees to water. The dark foreign car was leaving the parking lot! She rushed into the building and up to the reception desk.

"Can you tell me who just left?" she demanded. "Someone just drove out of the parking lot in a foreign car. Who was it?" The receptionist looked up, perplexed.

"No one passed me. It could have been anyone leaving from any number of exits in the building." She stared at Thea.

Suddenly Thea realized how the girl must see her, watching her for any telltale signs of violence, maybe even wondering if she were a patient. She took a deep breath, regaining her composure.

"It's all right," she said. "I'm Dr. Thea Donovan. I'd like to speak to a staff psychiatrist about seeing Peter Volk." The receptionist's expression changed.

"Oh, I'm sorry," she said. "Did someone call you? Are you family?"

Thea shook her head, confused.

"I'm sorry," the receptionist said again, her face becoming wrinkled in consternation. "Mr. Volk passed away last night." Dazed, Thea shook her head.

"Maybe that's who you saw," the girl went on. "You just missed him."

"Who?" demanded Thea. "Who did I miss?"

The receptionist gave her a long, curious stare. "It was Mr. Volk's son. He just picked up Peter's personal effects."

"You must have his name," Thea insisted. "Could I have a look at the signature on the visitor's log?"

The receptionist slowly reached under the desk, never taking her eyes off Thea. She stood up, placing a clipboard between them. Thea read over the names on the release forms, staring hard at the signatures as if closer scrutiny might render her capable of deciphering the mostly illegible scrawls. But she neither recognized the signatures nor was able to read any familiar names. She let out a loud sigh of frustration.

"Aren't there any forwarding numbers, even the person taking care of funeral arrangements?"

The girl shook her head. "He didn't want to claim the body and left us cash to look after disposal of the remains." She stopped, gazing off down the corridor, lost in thought. She glanced up, meeting Thea's eyes.

"I just remembered," she said. "There's one thing we forgot to pack. Mr. Volk's jigsaw puzzle is still in the Recreation area. We can go and get it, if you'd like."

Thea was just about to decline, recalling her last visit. Then she realized that this was all she had to go on. She nodded, following the girl down the hallway to the locked room. There were only a few patients inside, none of whom appeared interested in their presence.

The receptionist led Thea over to the chair where she had last seen Peter. The puzzle lay in the same position as before but this time it appeared to be assembled. Then Thea noticed that several pieces were missing. She turned to the receptionist.

"Did Peter do this?"

"No. He really wasn't capable of doing anything. Whenever the doctors or other patients would stop by and talk to him they'd occasionally fit in a piece to pass the time. No one ever saw Peter do it, though. It's a mystery why anyone would give him a gift he wasn't capable of working on."

"You don't know who gave it to him?"

The girl shook her head. "One day it wasn't there, the next day it was. Too bad about the missing pieces, though. It's a nice picture."

Surprised at not having noticed the subject matter of the puzzle before, Thea glanced down. Though roughly a half dozen pieces were lost, the picture was unmistakable. It was a photograph of an erupting volcano, lava and rocks spilling down the sides of the mountain like blood and bones.

* * * * * *

The house was quiet when Thea got back. As she remembered the way Malcolm and Lauren had been looking at each other, she wondered if she should knock before she entered. She unlocked the front door and let it swing open, banging against the wall. An anxious Juneau, obviously kept inside the whole day, raced past her legs and out the door. So instead of removing her shoes as she customarily did, Thea stomped, deliberately loud, across the kitchen floor.

But when she reached Malcolm's room, she saw that he was sound asleep and Lauren was nowhere to be seen. She tiptoed over, took his pulse and placed her palm on his forehead. His face felt damp and feverish to her touch. She took out the vials of drugs and filled a syringe. She was considering increasing the dosage of antibiotics when Malcolm stirred and opened his eyes. There were smears of blood on his face and hands.

"Lauren?" he asked, blinking.

"No, it's me, Thea," she said. "Where did the blood come from?"

Malcolm glanced at his hands. "I scratched the scab on my face and it started bleeding. Where's Lauren?"

"Well, she's not in the house," Thea said, a little annoyed. "I wanted her to look after you until I got back. Any idea as to where she could be?" She reached for an alcohol swab, tore off the wrapper and cleansed a site on his arm, then injected the syringe of antibiotics.

Malcolm glanced over toward a clock on the wall, concern washing over his face. "She left a couple of hours ago. I was feeling sick to my stomach so she went out to buy some 7-

Up."

Thea finished with the medications, tossed the needle into the hazards container and sat on a chair beside him.

"I've got 7-Up in the fridge, didn't she find it?"

He shrugged. "I guess not." He paused for a moment, remembering. "Joe phoned. He said to call him back, something about finding that car you were looking for." He looked interested. "You buying a new car?"

Thea shook her head. "Not hardly." Her mind raced. It didn't seem like a good idea to talk to Joe about the foreign car with Malcolm in the room. On the other hand, until Lauren got back she couldn't leave the house. Malcolm interrupted her thoughts.

"Any luck with Peter Volk?"

"I was too late. He died last night. Not only that. His son picked up his things just before I got there. How's that for lousy timing?" She was just about to say something about the car then instinctively stopped herself. It was strange for Lauren to leave like that. The more she thought about it, the more she felt something was wrong. Then the landline phone rang. Excusing herself, she ran and answered it in her bedroom.

"Dr. Donovan?"

"Yes?"

"This is Lauren Benton's office. She had an appointment to show a house an hour ago but didn't arrive. She gave me your number in case I had to reach her. Is she still there?"

Thea felt an icy chill run up and down the length of her body. She forced herself to speak in a normal voice.

"She left here a few hours ago but she may have had car trouble. I'll try to reach her at home." She hung up the phone, her hand shaking. Scarcely comprehending her actions, she pulled open the night table drawer and glanced inside. The paper packet containing Peter Volk's letter opener was missing.

She stood up, straightened her shoulders and tiptoed into Malcolm's room. She could only see the wounded side of his face, and for the life of her she couldn't fathom the expression on it. Was it smugness or was he masking worry? Sensing her presence, he shifted around to face her.

"No sign of her yet?" he asked.

Thea was just about to answer when she heard a low, deep growl from Juneau, a sound that frightened her because she'd only heard the dog growl in anger once before. She ran to the back door and threw it open but Juneau wasn't at the door. She was snarling at a pile of rags tossed under the tall rhododendrons where they grew thickest in the yard.

Filled with foreboding, Thea crept over to the bundle, hating to look but unable to tear her eyes away from it. And as she got closer she saw a pair of legs. She allowed her eyes to travel slowly up the body and past the darkening red pool until she reached another unmistakable red, the curls she knew were Lauren's. When the world around her stopped revolving, she lurched toward the house and dropped to the floor, sobbing.

From the guest bedroom she heard the sound of rustling bedcovers and then Malcolm's voice.

"Did you find her yet?" he called out.

It was then that Thea made the decision to turn him over to the police.

TWENTY-SEVEN

"I'd say we have an awful lot to talk about, wouldn't you?" Stan Peltzer leaned forward, placed his elbows on the desk and rested his chin in his hands. "How about you start by filling me in as to your whereabouts the past few days?"

Thea couldn't tell if he was furious with her or just profoundly disappointed. It didn't really matter what he thought of her. She knew that in his opinion, she had broken the law many times and many ways, and what she divulged to him in the next few minutes would determine her immediate future. She decided for the benefit of everyone, including herself, to reveal everything she knew.

"If you'd turned Malcolm in when you found him in Cannon Beach, you might have saved the lives of at least two women."

Thea winced, knowing she deserved that, but she let him continue.

"The Volk murders were considered a closed case. I guess now we'll have to send someone out to try and question Peter."

Thea shook her head. "It's too late, he died last night. And there's something else. I'm sure it was his son that drove away in the foreign car."

Peltzer didn't appear surprised. "If Peter committed the murders, he served a life sentence of his own making. At least this time he saved the taxpayers some money. Did you ever file a complaint against the car's driver?"

"I still haven't been able to identify the make or get the license plate number. There were no witnesses to any of the events, so it would be difficult to go after anyone. And if it's his son, at this point, I have no idea who he is."

Thea hesitated. "Not to mention, so much of what happened bordered on protecting Malcolm. If I told you one thing, I'd have to explain another. It was just too complicated. My main concern was Malcolm's health. I believed that, despite Dr. Steiner's warnings, Malcolm was innocent and it was my responsibility to prove that innocence."

"Your responsibility was to come forward with any information pertinent to our investigation in Dr. Steiner's death. Taking the hypocritic oath doesn't permit you to aid and abet a suspected killer."

"Hippocratic," corrected Thea, though she knew the bad pun was intentional.

Peltzer shrugged. "Whatever." He slipped a sheet of paper out of a file on his desk and passed it to Thea. She glanced at it, noticing it was a list of dates during the past year.

"I want you to think carefully about this," he said. "And see if you can remember if you were with Malcolm Dean on any of those dates, and if so, approximately what time." He leaned back in his chair, watching her.

It was nearly impossible to remember exactly what she'd been doing on any given day, but she felt certain that on the dates in question she had not been with Malcolm. Just in case, it was worth double-checking.

"I don't think I can give him an alibi for any of these days," she said, handing the paper back to Peltzer. "But if you give me a copy, I'll have a look at my calendar at home just to make sure. What charges are you filing against Malcolm?"

"We have enough evidence to charge him with the murder of Sheldon Steiner. It will be a while before conclusive DNA testing on Malcolm will link him to several female murder victims, including your friend Lauren."

A sudden rush of anguish washed over Thea. It wasn't that she had forgotten about Lauren, she had just forced herself to banish the vision of Lauren's broken body out of her mind. After calling the police she had waited outside on the front step, unable to confront or look at Malcolm. A short time later the ambulance with its police escort arrived to take him into custody. And despite his angry protests, the police arrested him without incident.

Thea, standing with Stan Peltzer, had averted her eyes as they took Lauren away and tried to avoid watching Malcolm as they lifted him into the ambulance. But at the wrong moment she turned and their eyes met. Then Thea saw a pain so intense it rivalled any physical suffering she had ever witnessed, a pain of loss and betrayal. And she knew that she was the cause of it all.

Interrupting her thoughts, Detective Peltzer pulled a package out of his desk drawer and held it out on his open palm for her to look at. It appeared to be a standard Ziploc plastic bag containing several flat objects.

"Ever seen these before?" he asked. She leaned closer and noticed that the objects were two small pieces from a jigsaw puzzle. Her eyes narrowed in contemplation.

"If you'd asked me that a week ago, I'd have said no. But they are the same size and color as the jigsaw puzzle in Peter Volk's hospital room. If you're lucky, the hospital staff might not have thrown it out yet. How did you get them?"

"We've found a piece at each murder scene. Because it was considered crucial evidence in an ongoing investigation, it wasn't made public. The first one was found under the woman who had Reflesh under her fingernails. The second one was discovered under Lauren Benton's body. Unfortunately there are no prints on them."

Thea covered her face with her hands and moaned as if she were in pain. She lifted her eyes to Stan Peltzer's.

"I've answered all your questions," she said. "Now you answer one of mine. Has my phone been tapped and am I being followed?"

Peltzer had the grace to look embarrassed. "Some of my superiors felt you knew more than you were letting on," he said. "Now you've proved them right. We're not charging you yet, but I warn you, if there's anything else you want to tell me, now is the time."

Thea shook her head. "Nothing, other than Malcolm told me his mother is staying in Cannon Beach. If you need to talk to her I can get you the number. But now that you have Malcolm, she'll probably return to Portland on her own." She stood up. "Am I free to go?"

Peltzer nodded and began sorting through the paperwork on his desk. Just as Thea was halfway out the door he called out her name.

"I almost forgot," he said. "After we read Malcolm Dean his rights he asked to see you. He's under armed police guard at St. Augustus Hospital until he recuperates. If you want to talk to him, you'll have to have an officer present."

Thea shook her head. "I don't think I can see him for a while." The image of Lauren lying crumpled and cold flashed across her brain like an evidence photo from the scene of the crime. She turned and walked out of Peltzer's office.

"Maybe never," she whispered to herself, ignoring the stares as she walked down the long corridor of the police station.

* * * * * *

Knowing the police had sealed off her house as a crime scene, Thea could not return until they were finished with their investigation. Instead she headed for her office at the hospital where Malcolm was now under the same roof. But she drove that thought from her mind because now she remembered that before her discovery of Lauren's body, Malcolm had told her that Joe had called.

When Thea disclosed the tragic details of the day, Joe made all the appropriate noises expected of him, because after all, he had not met Lauren. But he refused to divulge any of his information on the phone. Twenty minutes later he appeared at Thea's office. Reaching into his shirt pocket he drew out a snapshot and dropped it onto Thea's desk.

"Recognize it?"

Thea raised the photograph into the light of her desk

lamp and examined it. It was a photograph of a man and woman, with a vehicle in the background. When she finally met Joe's eyes, she looked bewildered.

"Where did you get it? Who are those people? They look familiar."

"I got it from your lawyer's office. Amazing the things you'll find hidden in the back of someone's desk," said Joe, innocently examining his nails. "I know who the man and woman are, but I'd like to hear what you think first."

Thea stared harder at the photograph. There was no doubt that the car in it was, if not her pursuer, the identical model. As for the two people, a woman perched on the hood and a man standing beside her, she could not say, but they made a handsome couple. The man had the full head of wavy hair of the eighties and wore a broad shouldered, loud checked suit with stove-pipe legged pants. The woman was drop dead gorgeous in a strapless sundress, with deep golden blonde hair that flowed over her shoulders and down her back. Thea stared at Joe in disbelief.

"You stole it from Jonathan Forbes's office? Isn't that biting the hand that feeds you?" she asked.

"If he was feeding me I'd only weigh 95 pounds," said Joe, laughing.

"What made you think to look there?"

"After you told me that the Forbes men were father and son, I thought I'd snoop around a bit, but I came across it by accident when I was looking for a pen. I showed it to him and to his credit I don't think it crossed his mind that it might have been the car you were talking about. He told me it's a picture of his father. He didn't know the woman."

"I think it is Alicia Volk," Thea declared. "What did he say about the car?"

"You're correct. It is Alicia Volk. Jonathan said it's a Maserati Ghibli his dad got back in the mid-eighties. He mentioned that collectors will pay six figures for them today. It would be an understatement to say he seemed irritated that he hadn't inherited it."

Thea raised her eyebrows. "What happened to it after Reg died?"

Joe shrugged. "Jonathan says he doesn't know. His mother was eight months pregnant with him when Reg was murdered. Unfortunately his mother died a few years ago, so who knows what became of it. I doubt if there are many around, so I probably can trace it and the registered owner through the local DMV."

Thea became quiet, sorting through the myriad possibilities crossing her mind. Finally Joe broke the long silence.

"I've been worrying about you since your friend died," he said, looking a bit embarrassed. "Do you carry a cell phone so we can keep in touch?"

Thea nodded. "I'm not really good about keeping it with me if I don't have pockets, but given the circumstances, I'll try harder to make sure I have it, and turned on."

Joe reached into his enormous jacket and produced a cell phone. He clicked it on and handed it to her.

"Here's my home number and my cell number. Take them down. I work out of my house and even when I'm gone, I check for messages frequently. It would make me feel better if you have all my numbers, just in case you need to get hold of me at any time."

Thea nodded, jotted the numbers in her own cell then handed back his phone. "I feel safer already," she said, meaning every word. "Every little piece of information you find brings us one step closer to solving this nightmare."

* * * * * *

Shortly after Joe left, the office phone rang. Thea jumped. She hadn't told anyone where she was going. It was a colleague, another plastic and reconstructive surgeon on staff at the hospital. Her relief was short-lived. He wanted to discuss a mutual patient.

"Dr. Donovan," came the hesitant voice of Dr. Herb Kaplan. "There is a patient here by the name of Malcolm

Dean. As you know, he's going to need reconstructive surgery. The police told me a bit about your history with him and that you're no longer acting as his physician, so the Emergency Physician on call asked me to perform his surgery. Unfortunately, I have no experience with Reflesh. Not to mention, the patient refuses to let me do anything other than evaluate his condition and insists on you doing the work."

Thea would have been no more shocked or surprised than if Elvis had entered the room. Could Malcolm really expect her to be impartial after everything that had happened, or even have enough faith in her to recreate his face again? Not only could it have drastic emotional ramifications, with everything that had happened it was probably unethical as well.

"It's impossible!" Thea said flatly. "Give him some other options, but I'm not one of them."

Dr. Kaplan sighed. "If you know the patient, you'll realize that he's intractable once he's fixed his mind on something."

Thea hesitated.

"It would be better if you talked to him," snapped Dr. Kaplan. "I'm all talked out." She winced as the sound of his phone being hung up slammed in her ear.

Thea took a deep breath and replaced the receiver on the phone. Then she stood, stepped into the tiny private bathroom adjoining her office, combed her hair and put on some lipstick. She wasn't a child any longer. She had created something defective and now it was time to correct the mistake.

TWENTY-EIGHT

The first person Thea saw when she stepped out of the eighth floor elevator was not the armed guard placed outside Malcolm's room, but Meredith Dean herself. For a few moments the two women stood there in awkward silence while Thea juggled the weight of emotional burden and guilt. It was Meredith who made the first move, holding out her arms to Thea in motherly welcome. And Thea responded.

After a few moments they pulled apart, facing each other with tears in their eyes and hundreds of unanswered questions jumbling their thoughts. Meredith looked like she had aged at least ten years and there was a crestfallen expression that had never been there before. Thea took a deep breath.

"How is he?" she whispered. Meredith rolled her eyes and gave a short, rueful laugh.

"He's the same as he was when they first brought him in. He's ranting and raving about being here, about being kept prisoner and about being innocent." She gave Thea a long, scrutinizing stare.

"You do believe he's innocent, don't you?"

Thea shook her head sadly. "Meredith, I just don't know anymore. Two days ago I would have unequivocally agreed with you, but after the last couple of days, things have become too complicated." She stared at Meredith for a moment, feeling a little hurt.

"Why didn't you return any of my calls?" she said. "With everything that's been going on, I was so worried about you I filed a Missing Person report."

Meredith appeared contrite. "I know. I'm sorry. Malcolm thought it was best if no one knew my whereabouts, especially you. He felt the police were watching you. Looks like he was right."

Thea sighed in resignation. She walked toward the door of Malcolm's room and held up her I.D. for the policeman to see.

Just before opening the door she turned to Meredith and said, "It's my responsibility to help him recover in any way I can, but this time I'll have to distance myself." Then she walked into Malcolm's room.

He looked much better than the last time she had seen him. Despite the misshapen, healing scars on his face he had good color and appeared healthy and rested. When he saw Thea he gave no outward expression suggesting his thoughts, just watched as she sat on a chair beside his bed.

"Deja vu," he said softly, raising his eyebrows in irony.

Thea tried to force a smile but could not. The image of Lauren's broken body seemed to hover above Malcolm's head like a banner and whether he was responsible for that or not, it was the way Thea would remember her for the rest of her life.

"Dr. Kaplan told me you refused to let him do your surgery."

Malcolm nodded. "You broke it, you fix it."

Thea's face wrinkled in sudden resentment, but she held back any angry words she had been thinking.

She was silent for a moment then said, "I'll check with the hospital Board to make certain it meets with their approval. If you truly want me to try again, I'll do it. After that, I'll get Dr. Kaplan to look after your postoperative care. The less we see of each other, the better." She stood up and started to leave the room but instead turned and half-closed the door.

"If you want me to try to return you to the way you looked before your initial injuries, I'll have to rebreak and rebuild the facial bones again. The trauma could be fatal."

Malcolm reached over to the hospital night table, picked up a hand mirror and gazed into it. He smiled and looked up at Thea.

"I've grown accustomed to my face," he said, with mock humor. "Seriously, I don't want a completely new face again.

Just repair the Reflesh."

At Thea's uncertainty, he made a comment probably intended to reassure her, but instead brought a numbed horror.

"This new face has enabled me to pick up girls like I never could before."

* * * * * *

The surgery took less than an hour and involved only one side of Malcolm's face, the insertion of Reflesh and laser leaving a thin, red scar that would disappear in a few days. Everything considered, thought Thea, it could have been much worse. Despite what he'd become, this time there would be no major readjustment. At least, not for Malcolm.

After dictating her postoperative reports, Thea sat contemplating recent events over a cup of bitter hospital coffee. Yesterday she had made a short call to Lauren's only family, a sister living in California. Lauren's ashes were to be scattered over Monterey Bay and a memorial service held shortly after.

Thea had offered her condolences but gave her regrets for not attending the service. Though she hadn't known Lauren very well at all, she preferred to remember those she loved as they were in life, not lying artificially painted in a coffin or blown like dust upon the water. She still carried the memory of her grandparents' funeral around with her like a snapshot, thinking that, side by side in their matching caskets, they looked like aged dolls, inert in their packaging. And it was at their funeral that she had last seen her mother.

Her grandparents had died, like many couples who have spent more of their life together than apart, within a few days of each other. With the help of their church's priest, Thea was left to make funeral arrangements. Distraught and languid from sorrow, she had taken a couple of prescribed Valium to survive the interminable Catholic send-off for the dead.

After several hours, in her euphoric haze it seemed as if the priest would himself drop dead from exhaustion. Then a high-pitched giggle erupted from the back of the cathedral.

Shocked into silence, the priest stopped his diatribe and the entire congregation turned to discover the source.

A filthy bag lady reeled down the aisle, laughing and cursing as she ricocheted off the pews. Two men jumped from their seats and escorted the woman from the church. A red-faced Thea recognized the woman as her mother, paying her last disrespects. Then the priest resumed the eulogy, and Thea realized with profound relief that it was only she who knew.

She shook the cobwebs of ancient pain from her mind and concentrated on another problem. She had thought that by now Jonathan Forbes would have called her with more information. Impatient, she took the initiative and dialed his number. The receptionist asked if she would like to make an appointment. She hesitated, then Jonathan himself came on the line.

"Thea," he gushed, "how are you? I've been meaning to call you."

Sure you have, thought Thea, but she accepted his explanation as overwork, in truth a believable explanation. Then she asked if he had come up with any new leads.

"Some," said Jonathan. "Why don't we meet for dinner and pool our information."

They agreed that he would pick her up at 7:00 that evening. Thea forced herself to sound enthusiastic, but instead was filled with apprehension about the evening and their motives for dinner. She left the hospital without performing a postoperative check on Malcolm. Now he was Dr. Kaplan's responsibility.

At her house for the first time since Lauren's death, Thea found herself looking at it in a new way. It now seemed to her as if the house itself was possessed by an intangible evil, something that lurked within its walls, possessing and corrupting with every creak of the floor and rattle of a window. She imagined she could smell the stench of death in the rooms. She knew the house was not malevolent, it was human depravity that made it seem that way. But for the first time, she considered selling and moving out.

She forced herself to think only of the evening to come and chose a sleek, black Diesel designer dress, shorter than anything she usually wore. Brushing out her thick, light brown hair, she coiled it up into a French roll and smiled at the sophisticated image reflected in the mirror. Maybe with a confident new look she could pry more information from Jonathan.

In the kitchen she fixed herself a martini to bolster her courage—it had been a while since she'd had a date of any kind—and drank it faster than she knew she should. And when the doorbell rang a few minutes later, her face had a glow. But it was not Jonathan at the door. It was Erik.

Thea squeezed her eyes shut and grimaced in frustration, then tried to make it appear as a cheerful grin. She so rarely saw Erik these days, yet he always managed to turn up whenever she was about to leave with someone else. It was almost as if he kept watch on her somehow, though she knew that was unlikely. But it would be an awkward situation for everyone if Jonathan were to arrive now.

"Aren't you going to invite me in?" Erik sounded a little peeved. He stared at her for a moment, as if he were seeing her for the first time. Then without waiting for an invitation, he brushed past her into the house and sat on the sofa. Thea closed the door behind him, glancing at her watch. If Jonathan arrived exactly on time she still had fifteen minutes to get rid of Erik.

"Don't you ever call first?" she asked in annoyance. "It is possible for me to have other plans."

Erik, who had not taken his eyes off her since he entered the room, studied her face.

"Are you seeing someone else?" he asked softly, a pained look coming into his eyes.

Thea tried to hide her frustration. "Look, we've never agreed not to date other people. The only relationship we ever committed to was a professional one. We hardly ever see each other and when we do it's in some sort of confrontation. If we're meant to be together, it will work out eventually. Right now we need to give each other some space."

"Like letting Malcolm Dean sleep here?"

Thea's stomach did a quick flip and she felt herself grow cold all over.

"How did you know he was here?"

Erik shrugged and gave a short, humorless laugh.

"You must think I'm pretty stupid and naive. I know more than you think I do. If you don't want to see me anymore, let's break it off honestly, not sneaking around and making excuses the way you're doing." He stood up, walked toward the door and placed his hand on the doorknob. He turned to her one last time.

"I've never cared for a woman the way I did for you," he said, his voice quavering. "But I don't see how we can continue to work together after this. I'll email my resignation to the hospital Board in the morning." He closed the door quietly behind him and left before she could utter a protest. For a moment Thea felt a strange mixture of regret and relief. But did she really want Erik out of her life?

She reached into the closet and took out her long raincoat. Remembering Joe's advice, she thrust her cell phone into a deep pocket. Though Jonathan Forbes arrived ten minutes late, she was grateful for having the extra time to compose herself after Erik's bombshell. And though she was not romantically interested in him, Jonathan was so delectable in a suit he erased all recent memory of Erik.

Jonathan had made reservations in the restaurant at the top of the Hilton, providing a panoramic view of the city, Mt. Hood and Mt. St. Helen's. Off in one corner a pianist played romantic tunes on a gleaming grand piano. Jonathan ordered an expensive bottle of champagne and held up his glass in a toast.

"To tonight," he said, "and sharing." Lightly tapping his glass to Thea's, he gazed into her eyes. Thea took a sip of the champagne and mentally cautioned herself not to have more than one drink. In her present state of mind it would be easy to get caught up in the moment.

"Cheers," she said. She cocked her head to one side and

studied him above the rim of her glass. "Tell me about your father." Jonathan nearly choked on his champagne.

"What's there to tell? He died before I was born."

Thea smiled in an engaging way. "You must have been curious about the murders, about him being branded a killer, and then his alleged suicide. Did you ever suspect he was innocent?" Jonathan stared at his plate.

"It's true, I thought he'd been framed," he said, slowly looking up at her. "It was hard growing up without a father and my mother refused to discuss him with me. Do you know how I finally found out about him?"

Thea shook her head.

"One of my professors in law school used the case as a precedent, not realizing the accused's son was sitting in the classroom. In the impartiality of university lectures, I don't think anyone else made the connection, but it tore me apart wondering if I'd somehow turn out the same. According to Joe I have you to thank for potentially clearing his name of murder charges."

Thea shrugged. "It will take the District Attorney a while to close the case, but it all just fell into place after I discovered the letter opener. You said we should pool our information. Is there something I should know?"

Jonathan reached into his inside jacket pocket and produced a long envelope. He slid out some papers, unfolded them on the table and passed them to Thea. It was the Last Will and Testament of Reginald Forbes. Thea scanned the pages then handed it back to Jonathan.

"Summarize it for me."

Jonathan clasped his hands together and leaned forward on the table in a conspiratorial way.

"Well, first some back story. From what I was able to find out, Alicia grew up in a wealthy family, in the house you now own. She was always a bit wild and dropped out of college against her parents' wishes. Later she began supporting herself with exotic dancing in local nightclubs.

"She and Peter met when he was off duty one night at the

club she was dancing in and a couple of drunks started to harass her. He stepped in and rescued her. She was a single mom with an eight-year-old son. They got married for all the wrong reasons and as a match were polar opposites. They had a child together, although it was mostly Peter who raised the two boys. Before too long she was hanging around in nightclubs again while Peter was working. No doubt she was unfaithful, as well."

"This is the first time I've heard there were two kids," Thea exclaimed. "How did your father happen to get involved with her?"

"Alicia met my father when she and Peter came into his office to file a legal separation. Although my father was Peter's attorney, he must have become attracted to Alicia. Shortly after, she and my father began their affair. It was only learned after the killings that the Maserati was in her name. My father had purchased it as a gift to her, though he kept it with him so their affair wouldn't be discovered. Who knows, they may have even been planning to divorce each of their spouses so they could be together."

Thea's eyes opened wide in undisguised astonishment. Jonathan shrugged. "Extravagant, I know. Anyway, when both died, uh, simultaneously, it went to the heirs to her estate. Guess who that was?"

"Peter?"

"No. She left him nada, zip, absolutely nothing, not even the title to the house. She willed everything to her sons, to be held in trust until they reached legal adult status."

Thea stared at him. "Someone must know if there is a little Peter or two running around."

"Someone must have. The estate was settled back in 1987, but all the paperwork has since been destroyed. I got this much information because my father's partner had kept the file for me."

Thea was just about to ask if there was anything else his father's partner might know when her cell phone rang. She gave Jonathan an apologetic smile as she answered it. It was only Joe, checking on her to make certain everything was all right. Jonathan made no comment as she refastened the Velcro cover on the phone and slipped it back into her clutch bag. There was an obvious, uncomfortable silence.

Thea let her gaze wander around the room, taking in the laughing couples at each table. Then she noticed something that distorted the room into a surreal painting, setting her nerves vibrating like piano wires. Erik sat alone at the restaurant bar. When he caught her eye he raised his glass to her in a mocking toast. Thea turned back to Jonathan, who looked bewildered.

"Do you know that man?" he asked. Thea nodded, wondering what to do next. But she refused to give Erik the satisfaction of seeing her leave. The pianist had moved from playing popular Broadway tunes to classic waltzes. She gave Jonathan a warm smile and placed her hand over his.

"Let's dance," she whispered. They stood up and melded together on the dance floor under Erik's burning, watchful gaze.

They danced to three songs and when they finally sat, Thea noticed Erik had gone. It bothered her that he had seen her with another man, even someone she wasn't involved with, but the sooner he accepted that their relationship was over, the better. Even so, his presence had taken the steam out of the evening. So pleading a headache, Thea asked Jonathan to take her home early.

TWENTY-NINE

When Thea and Jonathan got back to her house it was dark and quiet as death. Juneau was nowhere to be seen. Jonathan waited outside the door until Thea switched on the lights and after giving her a peck on the cheek, said goodnight. Part of Thea wanted him to stay, but another part of her acknowledged that it was best if he didn't. Still wondering why Juneau had not barked to be let in, Thea stepped into the back yard to look for her.

She glanced around, trying not to look at the corner of the yard where she'd discovered Lauren's body. There was no sign of the dog in the back yard either. Perhaps she had been too trusting in leaving her to run free. It would be her fault if Juneau turned up in a Shelter. Then out of the corner of her eye, she noticed a slight movement. But when she went to check, she saw that it was only a small square of paper, a sugar wrapper blown in by the wind.

A memory long-hidden by her subconscious tried to surface. But her tired brain was too overstressed to recall the significance of the wrapper. She headed back into the house and after double-checking the door locks, tossed her evening clothes onto the floor and scrambled into bed.

The next morning she called the local animal Shelter and asked if they had brought in a dog matching Juneau's description. It disheartened Thea to learn that Juneau was not there. Then she spent several hours placing Lost Dog ads on internet sites and at the Shelter, her stomach in knots without her beloved fur child at her side. Praying that the dog would return on her own, Thea took a shower and was dressing for the office when the phone rang. It was Detective Stan Peltzer.

"Dr. Donovan, I thought you should know we've got enough evidence to charge Malcolm Dean with the murder of Lauren Benton."

Thea felt a wave of weary resignation pass over her. Until that moment she had still held out hope for Malcolm's innocence, if not for his sake, for Meredith's.

"The blood on his hands matched Lauren's?"

"No. The blood on Miss Benton was hers just as the blood on Malcolm Dean was his, like he said. It was the Re-flesh again. She must have put up a pretty good fight. We found it under her nails."

Thea shivered in horror, trying not to imagine what Lauren had gone through in the last moments of life.

"So he was telling the truth."

Stan Peltzer gave a laugh of incredulity.

"He was lying like road kill," he said. "According to his primary care physician he's healthy enough now to transfer out of the hospital. Day after tomorrow we'll put him into maximum security. You'll probably be subpoenaed to testify at his trial. I'm sure you'll be relieved that this should be the end of your involvement."

Thea was silent. There was nothing left to say. Until the trial, Malcolm was out of her life. Her testimony at it would cause further irreparable damage to her relationship with Meredith, probably severing it completely. She did not want to think about that.

"There's no chance of error?" she asked, with an ache in her heart not totally attributable to her affection for Meredith.

"I'm sorry," said Peltzer, sounding sincere. "I know how you must feel. But if there was any doubt in our minds it's overshadowed by the opinion of the District Attorney . . ."

He left the rest unsaid because they both knew the evidence against Malcolm was formidable. But there was no way he could know how Thea felt. She had lost so much in such a short time. Despite what she had told Malcolm about not seeing him again, she knew she had to, if only to apologize for what she had done to him.

After she arrived at the hospital, Thea realized that if she didn't make an effort to see Malcolm first, she would be kept busy with scheduled surgery and making rounds on postoperative patients. In addition, it was possible that he would be moved to another ward before she had a chance to talk to him. With that in mind, she headed straight for his room, producing her I.D. for the guard at the door.

She felt a tiny twinge of uncertainty before she entered. But as she swung open the door she saw with relief that at this early hour he was still asleep and Meredith was nowhere to be seen. As she gazed down at his perfect profile in repose, a thousand emotions assailed her. Could this man really be a ruthless killer?

She stared down at Malcolm, tears filling her eyes. It seemed as if she had seen him this way more often than not, prone and helpless in a hospital bed. What would it have been like if they had met under normal circumstances, gotten to know each other as a man and a woman, or as friends, not as doctor and patient? His eyes opened and stared into hers.

"I'm sorry," she said. "So unbelievably sorry." Then she turned and ran out of the room.

* * * * * *

After leaving Malcolm's room she found herself at a loss at what to do next. Erik's brother, Drew, had told her that the Reflesh machine would be ready in a day or so, in plenty of time for her next operation. Not wanting to rely on anyone else to verify that the machine was now usable and free from damage, which would ultimately affect the surgery, she hastened down to the lab to check things out for herself.

She was pleased to see that the door to the lab was locked as it should be. Perhaps things would finally start to work in her favor. Maybe she had been wrong all along in believing Malcolm was innocent. Time would tell. If the killings stopped, perhaps the police had found their man after all.

Stepping into the darkened room of the lab, she pulled

the door closed behind her and locked it for safety. She flicked on the light switch and the brilliant fluorescent lighting flooded the room, temporarily blinding her. When she was able to see she noted that everything appeared to be in place, readied for her next surgery. She sighed with gratitude. Things really were going better.

Making her way over to the Reflesh machine, she paused for a moment. Drew certainly knew what he was doing. The machine looked just as it had before the sabotage. She didn't know if the police were going to also charge Malcolm with the damage to the hospital equipment, but when faced with multiple first degree murder charges it was hardly relevant.

There was just one thing left to do before she could be certain the machine was indeed ready for surgery, and that was to test it by making a Reflesh mask. She wished she'd thought of it before she'd left home or she would have brought a photograph with her. Still, there had to be something in the lab that would suffice; a magazine photo perhaps.

She scanned the room, looking for anything that might work, and noticed a magazine lying beside the coffee machine. It was nothing more than a multi-paged advertising flyer, but there were pictures of people in it. The majority of the photos were of Realtors listing their agency's services, and she noted with an enormous surge of remorse that Lauren's photo was among them. Flipping quickly through she found a full face photo of an older man and folded the magazine back to flatten it.

She moved back to the Reflesh machine and lifted the lid of the scanner. To her surprise there was a photo already inside the machine, face down. Then she realized that either Erik or Drew must have tested the machine to see if it was functioning properly. She removed the photo and turned it over. It was of a beautiful young woman with long blonde hair. And Thea knew she had seen this woman somewhere before.

She thought back. Feeling a small pang of jealousy, she considered whether it could be the woman in the foreign car that she'd thought she'd seen Erik driving. Then she realized that it could not be her. This woman was older than the one in the car. The face was oh, so familiar, yet she still couldn't place her.

She set the photo aside, laid the magazine face down on the machine scanner glass and lowered the lid. Then she moved to the refrigerator and took out a container of the generic Reflesh that they used for experimentation. Carefully she poured the Reflesh into the machine hopper then turned on the switch, waiting for the material and the machine to warm up before the final mask would be formed.

While she was waiting, she looked at the photo again. And then it came to her. This looked like the woman she had seen in the photo Joe had taken from Jonathan Forbes office; the photo they believed was that of Alicia Volk. But why would Alicia's photo be in the scanner? And more importantly, who would have placed it there for scanning?

Then came the light bell sound that told her the Reflesh machine had finished the mask. She opened the container at the base that held saline solution and saw the mask of the male realtor floating there. She pulled it from the solution and examined it closely. Drew was obviously good at his job. The mask was perfect. Hopefully next week's surgery should be equally as uneventful.

After cleaning the machine and tossing away the mask, she slipped the photo of the blonde woman into her purse. She'd take it to Detective Peltzer the next moment she had free and find out for certain if it was Alicia Volk. And if it turned out to be her then the next step would be to find who wanted to bring her back to life.

THIRTY

Thea went through the rest of the day performing her duties as if she'd been preprogrammed. She thought about consulting a professional to help her cope with the stress she was under, but the stigma of that seemed worse than the vulnerability she was feeling. Then late in the afternoon she had a moment to herself. For the first time she remembered the file she had seen behind Peter Volk's—the file that had shocked her when she read the label marked 'Derek Volk'. Fortunately, at this time of day it would be unnecessary to use furtive measures to retrieve it.

In the Medical Records department she asked for the file on Derek Volk. The secretary signed it over to her without question. Thea did not take time to inspect it then. Because of its bulk she wanted a quiet, private place where she could analyze the contents at her leisure. If it occurred to her that it might be inappropriate or even unethical of her to peruse a medical file of a deceased child, she no longer cared.

Before she left the hospital she decided to check on Malcolm's progress one more time. When she stepped out of the elevator she was dismayed to see the police guard sleeping outside the door he was supposed to be watching. She went over and shook him awake. Together they entered Malcolm's ward. Malcolm was no longer there.

For a moment they stared at one another, digesting what the implications of Malcolm's freedom would mean to each of them. But as the shamefaced policeman radioed the bad news to his commander, Thea began to tremble. She knew how difficult it was to find Malcolm if he chose to hide. Would she be in danger from him? Just then she heard herself paged for a telephone call. She took the call in her office and sure enough, it was Stan Peltzer.

This time she had nothing to hide but she did have more information to relay to him: the photo of Alicia Volk and the file on her son, Derek, once she'd had a chance to go through the contents. For once he seemed to believe her and did not waste time keeping her on the line. Grateful, Thea hung up the phone and turned to Gwen, who was holding out a sheet of paper.

"Should I pay this out of the hospital account or out of your personal account?"

Thea took it from her and scanned it quickly. It was an invoice from the law offices of Anderson, Forbes & Weinstein. Itemized in detail and billed every fifteen minutes at the rate of $500 per hour was her office visit to Jonathan Forbes several weeks ago, a three hour dinner meeting last night and a bill for the dinner itself. Thea shook her head in wonderment.

"I don't believe it," she said. "I wonder what the bill would have been if I'd slept with him." She glanced over to a shocked Gwen and started to laugh, but in reality she wanted to cry. "Pay it from my personal account."

When Thea reached home she saw that Juneau still had not returned and there were no messages in her email that suggested anyone had seen her. Near tears, she decided to walk around the neighborhood to look for the dog. Donning a bulky cardigan sweater, she made certain she stuck her cell phone in the pocket. But when it became obvious that Juneau was not to be found anywhere in the neighborhood she returned home and made a pot of coffee. Then she proceeded to read over the contents of the file on the child, Derek Volk.

Because it was in chronological order, she removed the contents, flipped them over and began reading through the papers on the top. The earliest record was from 1986 when the five-year-old boy by the name of Derek Volk had been admitted for psychiatric evaluation after witnessing the murder of his mother and her male friend. There were pages and pages, letters to police, lawyers, Children's Services, professional testimony to the boy's lack of memory of the incident, his mental fragility, and recommendations against him testifying in court. And on all the records there was a cross reference to another file: Andrew Carter.

Silently, Thea cursed, wishing she'd taken a quick look at the file before she'd left Medical Records so she could have requested both. But maybe it was possible to discern the story from this file alone and she'd retrieve the one on Andrew Carter later.

Then the paperwork moved forward with the majority of it being correspondence between Children's Services and the psychiatric department, as CSD sought to place Derek Volk and his older half-brother, Andrew Carter, in foster care. She stopped, bewildered, and thumbed rapidly through the papers. After being placed in foster care with a family named Sorenson, the family decided to adopt both boys, changing Derek's first name to Erik to avoid media attention.

She looked at the name upon the file again. Erik was Peter's son! It had been Erik who witnessed the murders. But how much, if anything, did he remember of the murders? She realized that Sheldon Steiner, who would have had access to all psychiatric records, may have seen this file. Was that the key to their early hostility? She read on. When Erik was thirteen his new family had brought him in for counseling. She glanced at the notes Erik's psychiatrist had made back in 1992.

'Very troubled young man, repressed anger and latent dislike of women. Past medical history includes depression and mood swings. I recommended psychiatric counseling several times a week, but he resisted and his adoptive family agreed with him. He has no memory of witnessing the murder of his mother when he was five, so I felt it wise not to discuss this with the patient. However, I can't help but be concerned.' That was the last entry. Erik had never returned as a patient.

Stunned, Thea closed the file. The file explained everything. Steiner must have found out about Erik's past, either inadvertently or through consulting with another doctor. Because of doctor/patient confidentiality he had kept it to himself. Yet in subtle, cryptic ways, he had warned Thea about Erik. But there had been no way to know what to warn her about.

'Latent dislike of women' was the phrase that haunted her. Erik had told her he loved her, cared for her more than any other woman. But he had seen his adulterous mother brutally murdered, though he had grown up with no memory of it. Yet maybe deep down in his psyche, he *did* remember, or had found out somehow, and that would be enough to send anyone over the edge. Yet Erik had seemed so normal and in control.

In control. Yes, that was the cliché that described Erik as it had described his father. Domineering and controlling. Erik's work had not suffered. He was considered brilliant, above reproach in his professional life. But he had not been able to control her and how had that affected him emotionally? Thea shuddered at the thought, wishing that Juneau was here to comfort her.

She set the file aside to take back to the hospital in the morning. Then she'd get the file on Andrew Carter and see what secrets it held. She wondered if she should call Stan Peltzer and inform him of her discovery. But what difference would it make? It was Malcolm they were after; Malcolm who was charged with the murder of three women. In truth, all Erik was guilty of was withholding information on his father, who was dead. Even a very tenacious District Attorney would have trouble prosecuting Peter for murder now.

Thea sighed, feeling desperately alone and needing something stronger to drink than coffee. She stood up, walked to the liquor cabinet and poured herself a brandy. Without the dog for company, the silence was beginning to unnerve her. She took a long swallow of the brandy and carried it over to the television. Just as she was about to turn it on, there was a soft scraping upon the back door.

For a moment the nerves in her stomach convulsed in terror. Then just as suddenly, her terror turned to jubilation. Juneau must have come home! Even with the thought of seeing her dog again, she tiptoed to the door with trepidation in every step. If it were Juneau at the door, by now she would have been whining to get in.

"Juneau?" whispered Thea. "Is that you, girl?"

She bent low near the back door and got down on her knees, listening as hard as she could for any scratch or snuffling sound that would tell her it was a dog outside and not something horrible. But there were no other sounds. Deciding to investigate, she buttoned her sweater to keep out the cold. As she pulled the sweater close, she felt a bulky object and realized she still had her cell phone in there, but she left it in the pocket anyway. Then she grabbed a flashlight from a kitchen drawer. When she got to the door she hesitated. The gentle tap came again.

"Juneau?" Thea said louder, hesitantly turning the door-knob.

Then someone kicked the door open with savage force. It crashed into her forehead, sending her spinning backward across the room. She lay on her back unable to focus as she watched the room spin and turn black, not knowing if it were pain or panic that switched out the lights.

THIRTY-ONE

In the complete darkness of her surroundings, Thea could not immediately comprehend what had just taken place. Her stomach ached with monotonous agony and she was aware of an overwhelming feeling of weakness. A burning tingling in her arms and legs forced her to shift position but she nearly screamed from the pain in her stomach. She discovered she was unable to move in any direction. It took several minutes before she could determine what immobilized her.

Bumping in vain against whatever was confining her, she let her mind go back to recall the last few minutes before she had blacked out. Who could have done this? More important, why would anyone want to hurt her? She felt her heart begin to flutter from rising anxiety and she forced herself to take slow, deep breaths to regain calm.

As she attempted to move again, a searing stab shot up her arm and she realized that she had just gotten a large splinter. From the cramped location and inability to move, she became convinced that she was trapped in a large wooden box.

She pressed her hands against the enclosure surrounding her. There was enough space above her head to stand, but she could only do it for a moment. As she clutched her hands to the dull aching of her stomach, she flinched in horror and pain. A warm stickiness covered her fingers. Afraid to analyze the true extent of her injuries, she pressed her hand tightly on her stomach to stop the bleeding. Then she began to explore her prison.

It must be a very large box, she thought, wincing with every movement. Forcing her arms up to chest level, she began pounding the sides with her fists, yelling out as loud as she could. But there was no other sound to suggest that anyone had heard. After a few minutes she decided to rest and save her strength. Just then a tickling sensation crawled up her cheek toward her forehead. Realizing it was a spider, she pressed head against the wall to kill it, almost laughing at the absurdity of what she was doing.

Suddenly weak, she dropped to her knees and lapsed into unconsciousness again. A ringing sound in the distance awakened her. At first she thought it was just her ears ringing from her bruised head then she realized it was a telephone. It rang several times and stopped. Then she heard her own voice, sounding tinny and far away.

For a moment it puzzled her then she realized she had forgotten to turn off the answering machine when she returned from her walk. She strained to hear the voice leaving the message. It was Stan Peltzer.

"Dr. Donovan, we just wanted to check in to see if you've had any contact with Malcolm Dean. We've put out an APB on him and listed him as dangerous, so don't take any chances this time." He hesitated for so long Thea thought he was going to run out of time for his message. Then he continued, "Call me, even if it's just to let me know you're all right."

A tremendous sense of relief flooded over her. She was still in her house! Then she realized with growing horror that not only was she in her house, she was trapped behind the sliding wall in her bedroom. No one would ever think to look for her here.

Angrily, Thea kicked the board in front of her but managed to bang her knee instead. For once she would have loved to call the police, if only she could. She felt a hard lump forming in her throat, threatening to make her cry. Then she heard a tiny beep. Her cell phone! Whoever had put her in this box had not taken the time to search her. She had forgotten she'd left it in her cardigan pocket.

She slid her cramped arm up along her side, then into her pocket. Pulling out the phone, she unfastened the Velcro flap and squinted at the dimly glowing buttons. She had another problem. The phone had beeped because the battery was dying.

Fighting down her intensifying fear at the possibility of losing the battery life, she considered who to call first. With limited time available she did not have much choice. Joe would be easiest because his home number was programmed into the memory. But when she called Joe's number, the line was busy.

"Damn," Thea hissed. "Damn, damn, damn."

She thought again and it hurt her head trying to recall Stan Pelter's number, which was not on auto dial. But with the pounding in her head, 911 or 0 was all that came to her. Choosing the latter, she closed her eyes and concentrated as she pushed the button. Then she nearly cried from relief when she heard the operator's voice on the other end.

"I'm hurt. Please get help," she said into the speaker. Her voice began to rise in panic. "Someone has me trapped in my house."

"Can you give me your location, please?" Thea began to recite her address but was interrupted by the operator.

"I'm sorry," she said, sounding fainter. "You'll have to speak louder, we have a bad connection. Name and address, please."

But as Thea began again she realized she could no longer hear the hum on the line. What she feared most had happened. The phone had gone dead. She switched it off, hoping the battery might rejuvenate enough to try Joe later; even just a text might go through. She tried to kicking the wall out again, but it held fast and when her toes began to hurt she stopped.

Suddenly she announced in a loud voice, "No more of this quality woodwork for me. If I ever get out of here I'm going to buy a new house with sheet rock that will crumble like soggy crackers when you kick it." Tears slid down her dusty cheeks.

What seemed like hours later, the house phone rang again. She immediately recognized the distinctive clip of the Englishman, Hal Goodfellow, who had given her Juneau.

"Dr. Donovan, just wanted to let ya know that yer dog's

come back to me. Give us a call, will ya, to let me know if ya want me to bring 'er back?"

Thea felt an enormous swell of relief. At least Juneau was alive and well. For a moment she wondered how she would be discovered—dead or alive? Without light to see, the pain in her stomach was not a reliable way to determine the severity of her wounds. This time she not only wondered who had done this to her, but how many other people knew about the sliding wall.

She remembered telling Stan Peltzer about it when she had turned in Peter's letter opener. She had told Lauren, but Lauren was dead. Might Lauren have told Malcolm? Then again, Peter had known, but he was dead, too. When he was five, Erik had known, but did he remember? And her lawyer, Jonathan Forbes, knew. It was possible that he might be the key to the whole mystery. In her present state, with her mind scrambled from pain and trauma, it was all too puzzling.

Then the phone rang once more and the voice that spoke to the answering machine was Erik's. When she thought of how she'd tried to avoid him these last few weeks, it tore her apart. Despite what she'd read on his psychiatric file, she still had difficulty believing Erik ever had anything but her best interests at heart. How she would love to see him now. She ached to feel his protective arms around her.

"Thea, I just can't leave it like this. We have to talk. I don't want to live without you." She heard him hesitate for several seconds. Then in a barely audible voice, he whispered, "I love you."

Weak from fear, exhaustion and loss of blood, Thea slid to the floor. She landed hard upon her backside but with the distracting pain of her other injuries, scarcely noticed the discomfort. Leaning back, she tried to lie flat, but felt a foreign object pressing into her back. Inching to one side, she placed her palm on top of the object and ran her fingers over it. Searing heat shot up her finger, sending a warm stickiness onto the floor. It was a knife and a sharp one at that.

She closed her fingers over it cautiously, feeling for the blade gingerly so as not to cut herself again. It appeared to be the scrimshaw letter opener that she had placed in her night table drawer. Her assailant had used it to stab her. The letter opener had come full circle, back into its hiding place in the wall. Who could have found it? But for the moment who had done it no longer mattered, because Thea now had something to help set her free.

She grasped the hilt of the letter opener and with excruciating, painstaking effort, began chipping at the wall. The wood was thick and solid, and even in the dark she could tell it was splintering in pieces the size of toothpicks each time she attacked it. She persisted, poking with the pointed end until she had opened a slit in the wood that was the size of a knife blade. She paused to rest for a moment then held her breath in anticipation. Someone was walking around in her bedroom.

Her first instinct was to shout for help, but then she realized that perhaps the person in the bedroom was not a friend. If that person wanted her dead and she called out, they would open the wall and finish the job. She bent down and leaned against the wall, pressed her face to the slit in the wood and peeked out into the bedroom. But whoever had been walking around had gone.

Too cautious now to make a noise, she began moving within the framework of the walls, crawling along the narrow floor. As she moved forward she began to notice a strange, sickly-sweet smell that in her earlier distress had not been aware of before. She stopped, unable to move any further because the weight-bearing studs made it too narrow for her to pass through. And the smell was stronger here.

Tentatively she thrust out her hand, groping in the darkness. When she made contact with fabric, then something softer that felt like hair, she choked back a scream. She cursed herself for her stupidity. Encountering the stench of rotting flesh once in a lifetime is enough to render it infinitely unforgettable. How long had the body been stored there and why hadn't she smelled it in her bedroom? But even as she asked herself these questions, she already knew the answers.

Though she had no way of knowing the state of the

body's decomposition, the mahogany wall was as tight as if hermetically sealed. Then there was Malcolm who had been in her bedroom recuperating from his facial wounds, himself no bouquet of roses with his pustulent wounds and persistent vomiting. She remembered now that Joe had remarked on the smell, but long accustomed to unpleasant odors, she had scarcely noticed. Since Lauren's death, she hadn't been home much. Could Malcolm have had an opportunity to place a body in the house?

Thea shuddered at the thought of having slept while that abomination melted in the same room. But the fact remained that someone else had been in her house more than she had over the last week. Whoever was in the house now was not there to help her, or he would have called her name. And she knew that he did not intend to leave a witness.

She crawled back to her former spot. A shaft of light glinted through the opening she had carved. The air was fresher here. Occasionally she could hear the person moving from room to room. Once she caught a glimpse of a shirt and trousers, which only confirmed her suspicions that her attacker was male. But he never spoke or came closer to the wall.

Despite her injuries, Thea realized she was hungry. Chipping at the wall had exhausted her and she yearned for something to keep up her strength. She searched her pockets for the candy that she sometimes carried around but found only an empty paper sugar packet.

A sudden flash of memory of her initial encounter with Erik flooded back, of his passion for sugar. And then she recalled that it had been Erik who approached her the day they met at the seminar, inexplicably knowing about her and her research. Had he been setting her up all along? Could Erik be her attacker?

Wearily she lay back down on the floor and drifted into a sleep fraught with images of the past. She dreamed it was Christmas morning and she was a child again, cavorting under the Christmas tree. Beaming at her as she unwrapped gift after gift, were Grandpa and Grandma, standing before the crackling fireplace with glasses of spiked eggnog in their hands. She stared at the burning wood, mesmerized by the warmth of the flames. Then the smoke began to billow out, blurring the dream and choking it from her subconscious.

Suddenly it seemed as though her grandmother let out a high-pitched scream of warning. She awoke with a jolt of fear. It wasn't her grandmother who had screamed, it was the squeal from the smoke detector. Peering through the slit in the wall she saw smoke filling the room.

"Help!" she shouted, pounding at the wall. If anyone were still in the room, they chose not to hear.

Thea struggled out of her sweater and with the help of the sharp letter opener began cutting it into strips. She stuffed the torn wool along the base of the wall, sealing any cracks she could find. Then she removed her pink silk panties. Poking them with the knife, she forced them through the slit so that they dangled on the other side of the wall. If the Fire Department arrived before the entire house was in flames, pink panties hanging on a wall might attract their attention.

Though the air in the wall was still breathable, Thea cowered low on the floor trying to avoid the smoke. The unmistakable crackle of flame upon ancient wood grew louder, closer. Far off in the distance, the whine of sirens pierced the terrifying snap of the flames. Then she heard another sound. Outside a dog was barking.

She forced herself to remain calm, not to hyperventilate. Timing was everything. She must reserve her strength to create enough noise so she would be heard above the roar of the fire. Then she heard the crash of an axe upon her wooden door, the rush of water from the pressurized hoses, the relentless barking of the dog.

Using every ounce of stamina left, she began shouting and banging until a male voice yelled in response. Then the panties disappeared from the hole in the wall and a bewildered quiet followed.

"I'm trapped behind the wall," Thea yelled. "Pull the cord of the swag lamp that hangs on the right." What seemed like hours later, the wood panel slid noisily into the wall framework and Thea crumpled forward in a heap at the feet of a firefighter.

THIRTY-TWO

It felt strange being a patient instead of the doctor. Though she'd undergone emergency abdominal surgery and was still heavily anesthetized, Thea was aware of the police presence outside her room and their need to question her. That could wait another day. After everything she had been through the last few weeks, she wasn't going to complain about the opportunity to rest. No matter how hard she tried to stay awake and aware of her surroundings, the painkillers whisked her away from the troubles of the past.

Early the next morning after the surgeon and his nurse had made their rounds, Stan Peltzer poked his head through the doorway.

"Are you awake?" he said, sotto voce.

Thea struggled to sit up and grimaced in pain. "I am now."

"I need to ask you a few questions, get a statement."

Thea nodded. "Did you get him?"

"Who?" asked Detective Peltzer, in much the same voice as he might have answered, 'yes'.

Anger flared in Thea. "The man who tried to kill me. Malcolm Dean."

Stan Peltzer looked embarrassed. "That's why we need to talk. We've got somebody in the burn unit, but honest to God, until the DNA results come back, it's impossible to tell who the hell he is. About all we know right now is that it's a man. We're waiting for dental records. Tell me what happened after you left work."

Being as thorough as she could, Thea related the events of the past day since Malcolm had gone AWOL from his hospital room and she'd left shortly after. If Detective Peltzer seemed frustrated that she couldn't get a positive I.D. on her assailant, he was diplomatic enough not to let on. When he finished his interrogation, he stood up, pausing at the door.

"There's someone who is anxious to see you. Do you feel up to it?"

Thea nodded, wondering who knew she was here. First there were some questions she needed answered.

"Have you identified the body in the wall?"

"She was a woman whose car was found abandoned on a deserted road near Gresham. Her name was Maryann Kowalchuk. I don't know why he brought her to your house. Maybe he thought we were getting close to identifying him and he needed to put her somewhere no one would think to look and link her to him."

"What is the condition of my house?"

Stan Peltzer cleared his throat. He had a difficult time meeting her eyes.

"You know what tinderboxes these old houses are. They couldn't save it," he said. "It was a miracle they got the two of you out alive."

Thea fell back upon the pillows in shock. Peltzer gave her a sympathetic smile and tiptoed out. After he left there was a soft, tentative knock upon her door.

"Come in," she called out. Thea could hear a staccato clicking just before the door opened. Then Juneau came bounding in, her body shaking as she began ecstatically licking Thea's exposed hand. Hal Goodfellow followed her into the room.

"How on earth did you get her into the hospital?" whispered Thea, stroking the dog's head.

"I asked for directions to the Ophthalmology Department and told them she was a seeing-eye guide dog." He laughed then suddenly became serious.

"Juneau turned up at my place last night. I figured for her to be that far from home, someone must have dumped her. I left a message on your machine but the damn dog wouldn't leave me alone. She kept yapping and trying to drag me out of the house. I tried feeding her, but she wouldn't eat. Eventually I thought I'd better bring her to you meself. When we got to your house she ran right up and starting scratching on the door. Then I saw the smoke and called the Fire Department."

Thea smiled rather sadly. "The two of you probably saved my life," she said. "But I don't have a place to live and won't be able to give her a home for a while."

He winked. "No problem. Now she knows you're all right I'll look after her until you're mended." He leaned over and patted her hand, then led Juneau out of the room.

Shortly afterward, a nurse came in to check on Thea, inserted another needle of painkillers into her pincushioned bottom and left her to sleep.

When she awoke the room was dark with fragments of fluorescent light shining under the door. With the I.V. providing her nutrition, the staff had let her sleep through the supper hour. Every few minutes she could hear the busy hospital staff hurrying up and down the corridor. The sound made her nostalgic to be back among the healthy and working.

She sat up slowly, tentatively testing the stitches in her abdomen. Either the painkillers were doing their job or she was already healing. It made her feel strong and vital again. She looked down and saw that some optimistic person had placed a pair of hospital slippers beside the bed. Sliding her feet into them she stood up and waited to see if she would become lightheaded. After a few moments, she felt strong enough to take a few steps.

She peeled off the adhesive tape that secured the I.V. needle into the port site on her hand, flinching as she jerked it out. Then she retaped the site to prevent it from bleeding. She opened the room's metal locker. Inside she found a canvas-like hospital robe. She slipped it on over her nightgown. Then she walked over to the door and pulled it open a couple of inches. The guard that had been outside her door earlier had gone. She opened the door a bit further to get a view of the nursing unit where a solitary ward clerk was engaged on the telephone.

Thea smiled to herself and walked past unnoticed.

As she waited for the elevator, she glanced at the clock in the corridor and saw that it was 7:38 p.m. With visiting hours ending soon there would be enough people in the hallways to make her seem like just another patient. She boarded the empty elevator and pressed the button for the basement.

The Medical Records secretary glanced up at her with alarm in her eyes as she approached.

"Dr. Donovan," she whispered, "are you sure you should be out of bed so soon?"

Thea smiled, though she was certain from the ache that had started up in her stomach it came off as more of a grimace.

"I'm okay," she said between gritted teeth. "I need to take out another file. Can you get me the records on a person named Andrew Carter? You'll find it in the Psychiatry Department files."

The secretary's eyes narrowed, but she nodded, scrambling quickly to her feet and heading to the file cabinets as if afraid Thea was about to pass out. When she returned she handed it to Thea without speaking. Then she immediately went back to work, as if she was aware that the less she knew about Thea's motive for wanting the information, the better.

With slow, painful, halting steps, Thea made her way back to her private ward, noting with dismay that her police guard was back on duty. She met his questioning look with a smile.

"I got bored so I'm catching up on some patient notes," she explained as he opened the door for her. He shrugged with disinterest. She was back in her room. That was the important thing.

Once in her bed, Thea reinserted the IV into the port site on her hand and took several long, calming breaths as the painkillers surged through her bloodstream. Feeling better, she leaned back upon the pillows, opened the file marked Andrew Carter, and began to read what seemed like a duplication of Erik's file.

'Thirteen-year-old Andrew Carter was brought in for psychiatric evaluation after witnessing the murder of his mother and her male friend. His younger, half-brother, Derek, aged five, who was also present at the crime scene, is himself under evaluation (see file marked Derek Volk). Andrew's presence at the scene of the murders was strictly circumstantial. He was supposed to have been in school but unbeknownst to his parents had skipped class that morning to return home.'

The notes and paperwork that followed were again, almost duplicates of those in Erik's file, except for the mention that Andrew was not Peter's natural son, hence the different last name. But the final notation, which was dated 1987, stated: 'The boy has had an exceptionally difficult childhood. His biological father is not known and before his mother married Detective Peter Volk, she had been investigated several times for child endangerment and neglect. It's heartening to see how devoted and protective Drew, as he prefers to be called, is to his younger brother, Erik. Case in point, Drew has stated that there is nothing he wouldn't do to protect his little brother. Nothing at all. We applaud his heartwarming sentiments and hope these two boys will be able to live a normal, carefree life.'

Thea closed the file slowly, a growing sense of unease settling over her. The drugs were beginning to cloud her mind, she thought, as images of Erik, Malcolm, Jonathan, and Drew emerged. The police believed that the person in the Intensive Care Unit was the man who had murdered three women, Dr. Steiner, and had come very close to killing her. But who was he? And were they aware of his identity, or were they deliberately hiding it to draw out the real killer? There was only one way to find out.

She unhooked the I.V. from the port again and repeated her earlier measures to leave the room, opening her door cautiously. The police guard was in place and didn't seem alarmed to see her. She held up the file.

"I need to take this back to my office," she said, "I'll only be a few minutes." The officer nodded and went back to reading a copy of *Field and Stream* someone had left behind.

Thankful for the recent boost of pain medication she made her way to the elevator and hit the button to the fifth floor, the location of the Intensive Care Unit. The first person she saw when she stepped out was a uniformed policewoman outside one of the wards. She hesitated a moment, then walked up to her.

"I'm Dr. Donovan," she said. The officer nodded, smiling a gentle recognition.

"Who's the patient in this ward?" she asked, pointing to the door. The policewoman started to tell her but she could see for herself. 'John Doe' was written in large block letters upon the card in the name slot.

"I'd like to go in for a few minutes."

The policewoman shook her head. "I'm sorry, Dr. Donovan. I'm under strict orders not to let him have any visitors, not even you."

"Did Detective Peltzer say that?" Thea demanded. She decided to appeal to the cop's sense of fairness.

"Detective Peltzer was quite upset that I couldn't identify the man who attacked me," she continued. "I'm a doctor; I won't let anything happen to him. Even though he's severely burned, I still might be able to recognize him now. Let me try, please?"

The officer looked uneasy. She glanced around as if fearful they were being watched. Finally she said, "Okay, but just for a few minutes." Thea squeezed her arm in gratitude, leaving the officer muttering to herself.

Steeling her nerves for the sight that would greet her, she walked into the room. She froze before the patient's bed, watching for any movement with the attentiveness of a bird of prey. An intermittent positive-pressure apparatus artificially inflated his lungs with compressed air causing the rhythmic upward/downward deflections on the electrocardiogram that indicated there was life beneath the Spandex bandages. And the electroencephalogram monitor portrayed brain activity.

It was difficult to imagine that the mummified object lying there was responsible for the murders of two women, her friend Lauren and nearly herself. And it was almost impossible to hate what was now little more than an elastic-swathed mannequin. Yet hate him she did, but because she could not identify him it was an impotent, unfocused hate.

She stared at the person, anger heating up inside her. If it were Malcolm, he had gotten what he deserved. Before any of this happened, she would not have wished the anguish of burn pain upon her worst enemy. And he was definitely her worst. She would not rehabilitate him again. If he recovered, he could face the death penalty or at the least, life in prison, scarred and mutilated. Some might say he was better off dead.

It was strange she had not seen Meredith anywhere. Perhaps, she too, had finally given up hope and now knowing the truth about her son could not bear to be near him. Thea stared at the monitor measuring his degree of life; at the machine that temporarily kept his lungs inflated and heart beating. Her eyes traveled down the machine to the electrical cord, stopping at the plug stuck in the socket. A tiny, terrifying, little voice inside her head seemed to speak to her.

"Pull it," the voice suggested. Thea's stomach did a quick flip and she almost knocked over a chair. She swallowed the lump of guilt that formed in her throat, humiliated that she could have allowed herself to sink to the depths of a killer. But still, the voice made a reasonable argument. Would it not be more humane to end his life now rather than put him to death later?

Her heart pounded so hard it drowned out the persistent beep of the monitors. She stepped forward to stare down upon the motionless body, her hand hovering like a hummingbird near the cord of the life support machine. For a moment she imagined the mouth slit in the bandage moved. She passed it off as imagination. Then she heard a soft moan and a word emerged from the tortured lips. One word.

"Daddy?" said the man. Then she knew. And the horror of the knowledge was far greater than the terror she had known as a prisoner in the wall. The man in the Spandex was the man with whom she had spent innumerable hours. Hours spent working, laughing, making love. A man with whom she once thought she wanted a future. It was Erik.

She glanced at the cord and at her trembling hand hovering in judgment, and came to a decision. Then she turned and ran from the room, past the astonished policewoman, past the evening nursing staff of the Intensive Care Unit to the sanctity of her room. As if in a dream she heard the thunder of feet in the corridor, the roar of the crash cart wheels bearing down on her. Far in the distance she heard someone shouting, "Code Blue."

THIRTY-THREE

"We've got to stop meeting like this," Stan Peltzer joked, dragging a chair to sit beside Thea's hospital bed. She glanced up from her magazine but could not bring herself to smile. There was nothing left to be happy about and now the immediate future didn't look too promising, either. Had the policewoman on duty told Peltzer about her visit to Erik's room? Thank God she'd decided not to pull the plug and instead let him die on his own.

"I guess I have to make a statement, now that you know who was in ICU."

Detective Peltzer looked rather sad and gave a listless shrug. "Whenever you feel up to it."

Thea hesitated, reluctant to face what had been at the back of her mind for some time. "Will I be charged with anything?"

"We could have charged you with obstructing an investigation or withholding evidence but eventually you helped rather than hindered the investigation. It wouldn't benefit anyone to bring charges against you and it would only make more paperwork for me." He grinned. "We'll let you off on your own recognizance." But then the moment of levity was over and he quickly became serious, speaking so low she had to lean closer to hear.

"Erik went into respiratory failure, probably attributable to the amount of smoke he inhaled in the fire, but the autopsy should tell us for certain. Malcolm Dean's been released and we expect him to be acquitted of all charges once we get more information on Erik."

Thea gazed sadly across the room, trying not to let Peltzer

see her eyes filling with tears. But he'd had enough experience to understand what she was feeling.

"Were you lovers?" When she didn't immediately respond, he added quickly, "I'm sorry. I'm out of line. It's none of my business."

But Thea nodded, hot tears spilling down her cheeks. Peltzer handed her a box of tissues from the nightstand. She dried her eyes and blew her nose.

"I'd broken our relationship off a few weeks ago for several reasons. His behavior had become bizarre. I didn't understand it then, but I do now. Sheldon Steiner saw it coming. I think Malcolm Dean's father saw it coming." She looked down at the sheets covering her. "Why can't we recognize these people before we allow them to become destructive?"

Stan shook his head. "I wish I had the answer to that."

Thea frowned, remembering. "Maybe it was his way of getting back at me. Did he set Malcolm up?"

"Yes, although some evidence against Malcolm might have just been coincidence, like the Reflesh under the fingernails. It didn't occur to us that Erik might have used it on his hands to cover his fingerprints."

Thea sighed and pulled the blankets closer around her neck as if she were cold. She was suddenly reminded of Erik's occasional inability to complete their lovemaking. Was there a relationship between his impotence and the subsequent murders? Or could his childhood trauma at witnessing the death of his mother have contributed to a loss of conscious morals in which case he might not, legally speaking, have been responsible for his actions? She glanced at Stan who appeared lost in thought.

"I heard Erik's voice on my answering machine, telling me he loved me. Perhaps he was trying to provide himself with an alibi by making it appear he was phoning from somewhere else. He didn't know I was still alive and could hear him."

She paused, hesitant about asking questions or volunteering information which might hurt more than help.

"I have the files from Medical Records for both Erik and

his half-brother, Drew. Given the circumstances, I can probably get permission to turn them over to you. They might help you finalize the case." She paused, "In spite of not remembering the murders, Erik must have begun having psychological issues years ago."

"We've already looked at Erik's medical file. We think his break from reality began around 1992. According to his psychiatric records, Erik had already experienced several mental breakdowns. When Erik and his brother inherited the Maserati from their mother after Drew turned twenty-one it could have sent him over the edge. He might have even begun to recall some of the repressed memories of the night his mother was murdered, taking on an alter ego. The only release he experienced was when he killed."

"Now you're beginning to sound like a psychiatrist."

Stan Peltzer reached over and patted her hand.

"To catch these guys you have to understand the way they think," he said. "The only problem is each time you do you lose a piece of yourself. By the way, we traced that note you found back to a hospital printer here, but it was impossible to know who had made it. We've located a witness who claims they saw someone fitting Erik's description breaking into the Dean's garage, which is where he got the explosives to rig Steiner's car. And when we showed his photo to a local bookstore clerk they remembered selling a copy of *Historical Oregon Homes* to him."

"Then everything he did to me was premeditated." Thea shook her head. "Do you think it's true that most murderers really want to be stopped?"

"I think they're like children crying out for attention. In Erik's case he left a piece of his father's jigsaw puzzle at the scene of the two murders. By leading a trail to his father, he was also leaving a trail to himself."

Thea was just about to reply that from what she'd read Erik had no memory of his father, when they were interrupted by a knock. Thea glanced at Peltzer. He got up and opened the door, then gave a short wave goodbye and held the door open for the next person to enter. With a sudden jolt of shock, Thea saw that it was Malcolm and close behind him, Meredith. Peltzer and Malcolm exchanged cold, appraising stares, but said nothing. Meredith gave Thea a shy smile and sort of tiptoed over.

"Hi," Thea whispered. Meredith stroked her cheek. Malcolm sat on a chair near the bed.

"I've heard about everything you've gone through lately and that your house burned down," she said. "Malcolm has found his own place now, so I want you to come and stay with me until you're better. You can even bring your dog."

Thea began to protest but Meredith squeezed her hand.

"Please say yes," she pleaded. "I've always wanted a daughter, even a temporary one."

Thea smiled and reached out to hug Meredith but recoiled from the rejuvenated pain in her abdomen.

"Thank you," she said, gritting her teeth against the discomfort. "But just until I can get resettled. If I stay with you too long I have a feeling my next home might be a fat farm."

Meredith laughed, then glanced back at Malcolm and nodded to him.

"I'll leave the two of you alone for a minute," she said, vacating the room before Thea could protest. Then, for what seemed like forever, they stared into each other's eyes. Finally, it was Malcolm who spoke.

"You thought I was a killer." It came out as a statement, not a question.

Thea sighed. "My judgment was clouded by hypothetical evidence. There were so many variables after the surgery, after you disappeared. The longer you stayed away, the guiltier you looked." She cringed at the hurt in his eyes.

"I thought you'd gotten to know me better than that. I trusted you. I thought you felt the same about me. At different times, we saved each other's lives; that's got to count for something."

"I'm sorry," Thea murmured. "Please try and forgive me. You seem to forget you once told me not to trust anyone."

Malcolm smiled at that.

"Maybe you did the right thing, after all. Once you're staying with my mother I hope you'll get to know the real Malcolm Dean."

He stood up just as the door opened. Jonathan Forbes walked in carrying a brandy snifter with a single red rose floating inside. Malcolm glanced from Jonathan to Thea.

"I guess I should go now," he said.

Thea gave a short, humorless laugh.

"Why?" she said. "It's just my *ex*-lawyer."

Malcolm grinned at her, but didn't move from beside the bed. Jonathan shot him a cursory glance then placed the glass on the stand beside Thea.

"How much is that going to cost me?" Thea asked caustically, indicating the rose. She winked at Malcolm who looked uncomfortable.

Jonathan's forehead wrinkled in consternation, not knowing what she meant. In his defense, Thea had to admit that he was probably incapable of separating a genuine act of kindness from a business transaction.

"Never mind," she said in resignation. "What are you doing here?"

"I heard on the news about the attack and the fire, and that you were in hospital," he said, "I just wanted to make certain you're all right."

There was a heavy, awkward pause during which Thea and Jonathan locked eyes in a long stare fraught with significance and for reasons she couldn't fathom, simmering resentment. Finally it was Thea who broke the silence.

"As you can see, I'm getting better," she said, watching him, wondering at his true motive for the visit. She'd come to realize he wasn't interested in her as a woman, not that she had any interest in him romantically, either. Not her type at all.

To her annoyance he continued to hang around for a few minutes, moving this, straightening that, until she couldn't stand it anymore.

"Was there something else you wanted to ask me?"

Without waiting for an invitation, he sat upon the chair beside the bed.

"There's a rumor going around that Erik had a visitor last night. I'm not interested in that, though, I'm actually looking for his brother."

At that moment he seemed unable to look at Thea and glanced down at the floor, poking at something with the toe of his shoe that she couldn't see. Thea showed no emotion at his veiled threat. She was thankful she'd overcome her urge to pull the plug. And if the autopsy couldn't implicate her, neither could Jonathan.

"I don't have any contact information for him," she replied. "He did some work for us here in the lab but it was all done through Erik's company, of which he is a partner. Why do you want to see him?"

Jonathan had the grace to look embarrassed. Thea's eyes slid over to look at Malcolm who was watching him with the sort of interest that a cat shows with a moving object.

Jonathan reached inside his pocket and pulled out a legal document. He placed it upon the blanket covering Thea. "I was hoping to make him an offer on the Maserati."

Thea's pulse rate sped up until her heart pounded so hard she could feel it in her temples. He'd known all along who had the car, and therefore, he also knew that it was Erik who had been pursuing her. But there was a piece of information missing from the picture. Why? Why would he want to chase her down, frighten her, threaten her life? She was no threat to anyone. Hadn't even been a threat to Steiner, for that matter. But now the foreign car had come back into life in a bizarre fashion.

Though she had come to understand that the true value of the car would be determined by a collector, to Jonathan the value was intrinsic and there could be no replacement cost. The only tie he had to the father he had never known was a car that had been willed to someone else. If it didn't come back to him this time, to what lengths would he go to secure it for himself?

He stared back at her, unflinching. "So you have no idea where he lives?"

Thea shook her head. "Nope. Sorry. Can't help you there."

Jonathan looked directly at Malcolm for the first time since he'd entered the room, then back at Thea. "Okay," he said, patting her blanket absently as he retrieved the document. "I hope you get well soon." Then he left the room.

Malcolm broke the silence that followed Jonathan's exit. "That was quite a revelation. The vehicle's worth a small fortune. Do you think he'll try going through legal channels to gain ownership, or use a more nefarious method?"

"He's an attorney who wants something; who knows how far he'd go," said Thea. Malcolm gave her a supportive hug, planted a kiss on her forehead and left her to rest.

But after Malcolm had gone, Thea gazed at the space he had vacated, not really seeing anything. Then she noticed the rose Jonathan had brought and decided it would look better adorning the inside of a garbage can. She struggled to her feet, grasped the bowl in both hands and took a step toward the sink.

But on her second step a hard object on the floor embedded itself into the soft pad of her bare foot. She stopped, lifted her foot and peeled the object from her instep. For a moment she stared at the thing in her palm, unable to shake the surrealism of finding it in her hospital room. It was another piece of Peter's jigsaw puzzle. Jonathan must have been the one who left it, a warning of sorts that he could play rough.

She watched the water from the bowl swirl down the drain, then dropped the rose and bowl into the wastebasket, and hobbled back to bed. She reached for her cell phone on the nightstand and dialed Stan Peltzer's number to tell him about the puzzle piece. It probably had no relevance, but it didn't hurt to tell him about it, just in case they needed it to close the files.

Lying back upon the pillows, she stretched leisurely and yawned. If she was well enough in the morning she'd ask to be discharged. Then she'd head over to Erik's apartment and see what secrets might still be there waiting to be discovered.

228

THIRTY-FOUR

As Thea had hoped, the Admitting Physician signed her discharge papers the next day and she was allowed to leave the hospital at noon. Despite Malcolm and Meredith's protestations, she declined their offer for a ride to Meredith's house where she would be staying until she found a new place to live with Juneau. She needed time to herself and to see what was left of her home and her belongings. Then, if she had enough strength, she would go to Erik's apartment to retrieve a few items she'd left with him in the past. If she found Drew's contact information she'd call him to find out about funeral arrangements, but if Jonathan wanted to know his whereabouts he'd have to do the legwork himself.

After getting picked up from the hospital by the rental car agency she headed over to her former neighborhood. There is no good way to prepare yourself for viewing your home after it's been burned to the ground, Thea mused as she stared at the charred, sodden shell of her house. A yellow 'Caution, Crime Scene' tape had been placed around the perimeter, essentially blocking her passageway if she chose to abide by it. She didn't. Ducking underneath it, still holding her aching stomach, she roamed aimlessly for several minutes, looking for anything salvageable. But there was nothing left. Only decent homeowner's insurance, she thought wryly. And vehicle insurance. Even her Mercedes had been destroyed. A fresh start. Again.

She got back into the rental car and made her way to Erik's apartment, thankful she'd held on to the set of keys he'd given her. It was an equally strange sensation entering his apartment alone. She'd never been comfortable in this place and even less so now.

She headed to the bedroom and found the few changes of clothes she'd left there, tossing them, along with her personal items from the bathroom, into a grocery sack she found in the kitchen. She glanced around the stark chrome and white kitchen, so clean in its European design. Then she noticed an address book lying beside the landline phone near the doorway. She picked it up and stuffed it in her purse. A quick glance around told her there was nothing left for her here. That part of her life was over.

She returned to the rental car and sat there, trying to decide whether to go straight to Meredith's house, head down to Wilsonville to pick up Juneau or just kill time alone. Instead she pulled Erik's address book out of her purse and scanned the contents. There were a lot of contacts listed, none of whom she knew, but then they'd shared very little other than what went on with the Reflesh project.

But under the 'Ds' she saw Drew's address and number listed and thought about it for a few minutes. The address was out in the country, east of the city, and not somewhere she was familiar with. Still, it might be good to touch bases with him and discuss whatever arrangements he was making for Erik's funeral.

She programmed the rental car's GPS with Drew's address then took a moment to send a text to Meredith and Malcolm, telling them that she wouldn't be at their place until later in the afternoon. She'd pick Juneau up the next day when she had the energy to deal with a dog. Or two dogs, she thought, realizing that Sport would likely be at Meredith's house as well.

As she drove off through Portland's main streets the GPS informed her to access Highway I-205. Fifteen minutes later it guided her to take Exit 224. Beginning to wonder if she should have brought someone with her to watch the directions, Thea pulled off to the side of the road and took a closer look at the GPS map. It showed she still had a half-hour of driving before she'd reach her destination.

Sighing, she pulled back onto the road, following the intoned directions from the GPS until she found herself maneuvering the car along a twisting dirt road, shrouded by over-hanging trees and hidden driveways. Finally she located the number listed as Drew's address and pulled down a long gravel driveway that led her to a secluded wood cabin and a series of haphazard outbuildings.

She pulled the car to a stop and sat inside, surveying the surroundings. There was no indication that anyone was here. Feeling a little vulnerable sitting there with no one aware of her presence, she was just about to turn around and go home when she noticed a car parked under a prefabricated steel carport. Curious, she emerged from the rental car and locked it. Then she headed toward the car.

There was no mistaking it, she thought, having had so many close calls with this vehicle over the past few months. It was a 1980's vintage Maserati Ghibli, in mint condition, and most assuredly the one that Jonathan Forbes lusted after. She glanced around to see if anyone had noticed her presence, but found she was still alone. She tried opening the driver's side door and found it unlocked.

Not quite knowing what possessed her, she slipped into the driver's seat and sat there with her hands on the steering wheel of the luxurious auto. As beautiful as it was, there was something sinister to it, a definite feeling that she should not be there. She glanced to the passenger side and a frown crossed her face. Pieces of Reflesh clung to the leather seat.

A wave of nausea surged up through Thea's esophagus. With it came a moment of panic. Then she remembered that Drew had been working on the Reflesh machine and if this car was what he drove to work then it was entirely possible for there to be the occasional scrap of Reflesh lying around. But it had unsettled her to the point that she realized it was time to leave. Drew was nowhere to be found.

She slid out of the Maserati and softly closed the door, hoping she'd never see the car again. Then she stopped. For a second she thought she heard a voice. It might have come from a neighboring acreage, she told herself as she made her way toward the rental car. She clicked the unlock button on the key fob and was just about to get back in her car when she heard the voice again. To her active imagination it sounded like a cry for help.

Thea turned. There was no one around and the other outbuildings were nothing more than lean-to wooden shacks, possibly once used for raising chickens or rabbits. She made her way to the cabin, carefully skirting piles of garbage and cans that had been tossed on the ground rather than in a landfill. When she came to the cabin she found the front door was locked.

She moved to the window and peered inside. But the windows were so filthy that she couldn't make anything out other than a couple of scattered chairs and a sofa that looked as if the springs were broken. Trash littered the kitchen counters, with the leftover contents of cans spilling onto the floor.

Disgusted, she turned away and started back for her car. Then the sound came again. A faint cry, so quiet it was difficult to tell if it was human or animal. A warning bell went off in her head. *Get the hell out of here, Thea. This is not a place you should be.* But she couldn't ignore the cry, even if it was a rabbit in a trap.

She moved around to the back of the cabin but found there was no door other than the one in front. There was another window, though, and this one, despite being as dirty as the others, was open a few inches. She thrust her hand in the opening and forced it to one side. Then she stopped to listen.

"Is anyone in there?" she called out softly.

The cry came again, not discernible words, just a sob. Heart pounding, Thea glanced around for something to stand on and saw a large section of a log used as a chopping block with a hatchet stuck in the center of it. She rushed over to the hatchet and began jerking it back and forth to loosen it. As it wrenched free the razor-sharp metal head smacked her in the thigh, ripping open her pants and slicing a three inch gash into her leg.

"Damn, damn, shit!" she hissed as pain seared through her leg. She dropped the hatchet and rapidly assessed the damage. Though blood trickled down her thigh and pain coursed red-hot through her body, she found she was still able to move her leg to walk. She took a deep breath and left the hatchet laying it on its side on the ground. Then she rolled the chopping block beneath the window and stepped up.

The room at the back of the cabin was in just as terrible a disarray as the front room had been. Blankets and sleeping bags were tangled together on the floor. Suddenly she realized this place, as isolated as it was, was probably a meth house. And it was a very dangerous place for her to be. But the person inside might be overdosing and in need of medical care, she told herself. As a doctor she couldn't ignore it.

The cry came again.

Knowing she was taking an enormous risk, Thea hoisted herself up to the window and crawled through the opening, dropping heavily to the floor below. Searing pain shot through her cut leg as she landed. A variety of fast food garbage and used hypodermic needles had cushioned her fall. Thankful that none poked her, she shuddered, and glanced about. The place appeared to be as deserted as the outside and she really didn't feel like exploring any more than was necessary. It was time to go.

Then a voice said very quietly, "Help me. Please help me." It was coming from one of the two bedrooms.

She froze, unable to decide whether to run and get help or follow her instincts and the voice. She made her decision and entered the bedroom. The smell nearly knocked her over.

There, tied to a steel bed frame, was a young woman with long blonde hair. There was something wrong with her face, but Thea couldn't quite figure it out. Then she realized that the woman was wearing a sort of mask. It sat askew, half sliding down her face and neck. And then Thea realized what it was. Someone had tried to replace her face with Reflesh. But they didn't have the skill or the knowledge to complete the process. And to her horror she saw that the mask was an attempted replica of Alicia Volk's face. That was where the resemblance ended.

She hurried forward, knowing that she needed to get this

woman free and to the safety of her car. Though the odor of decay was overpowering, she knew she had to work fast.

"Help me," the girl pleaded, struggling to free her wrists.

"Don't move," Thea urged, "I'll get you out of here but you have to stay still." Her fingers worked at the knots holding the woman to the bed, but her recent hospital stay had weakened her. Finally she had one hand free, then the other. The woman fell to the floor in a dead faint.

"Shit," Thea whispered, "come on, sweetheart, we've got to get away from here." With all the strength she could muster she lifted the girl's arm over her shoulder, and slung her arm around her waist, ignoring the rotting Reflesh that slid across her arm. Half lifting, half dragging, she got to the front door of the cabin and flung it open.

"Where the fuck do you think you're going?" Drew said, holding the hatchet lying sideways across his chest like a bandolier.

THIRTY-FIVE

"I'm taking her to the hospital," Thea retorted. "Don't you try to stop me." She kept moving toward her car, ignoring Drew and his hatchet, all the while praying that if this girl was his handiwork he still had a rational side to him.

"You're not taking her anywhere," he said calmly. He raised the hatchet above his head. "Turn around and go back into the cabin."

Thea eyed him cautiously. The girl was dead weight on her shoulder, threating to drag her down. She knew that if she let her fall and tried to run, he'd be on her before she could reach the car. And she knew the girl was close to death, so rampant was the infection on her face.

Drew nodded toward the cabin, herding them as if they were cattle. Thea turned and obediently began walking, half dragging the girl with her until they were inside the room. She let her slip gently to the broken sofa, then sat beside her, holding her close.

"So," Drew said. "This was unexpected. I thought you'd still be in hospital." He sat on a chair on the other side of the cluttered tiny room and cradled the weapon across his lap. Sitting there, he looked so much like Erik it was unnerving. But he resembled him in a deranged, muscle bound way that gave her the creeps.

"They discharged me this morning."

"How did you find this place?" he said in a conversational tone.

Thea glanced down at the girl who had passed out from weakness. "I went to Erik's apartment to pick up a few of my things and found his address book."

"Ah, my brother. My poor dead brother that you discarded like an empty syringe after you were done using him for your beloved Reflesh project."

"It wasn't like that," Thea protested. "We had some issues but I always had feelings for him."

"Like the feelings you had for your patient, no doubt," he sneered. He tilted his head. "You remind me of my mother, in ways. She used men, too. It cost her in the end, though."

Thea stared at him. With his build and strength, there was no way she could overpower him, even if she were in top condition. The only way she could get away with the girl was if she managed to outwit him.

"The police say that Erik was the one who killed those two women, and my friend Lauren. They also believe he killed Dr. Steiner, and tried to kill me. But it was you, wasn't it? Why would you set your brother up as a murderer?"

Drew jumped to his feet. "That's not how it was," he shouted. "You stupid bitch. Don't you see? All these years I've been looking after Erik. I was there when his father killed our mother and her boyfriend. It was like a gift when he couldn't remember anything. Can you imagine being a kid, going through life with the image of your father stabbing your mother, then shooting her to make it look like someone else did it?"

To Thea's relief he sat down again, sliding the hatchet back across his lap. The woman moved slightly beside her, causing Thea to shift her weight, pressing the hardness of the cell phone in her pocket against her thigh.

"But he wasn't my father so I didn't give a damn if he went to jail. I told him that I would tell the police everything if he didn't let Erik and me go. He could do whatever he wanted as long as we didn't have to stay with him. But instead of confessing to the murder he had himself committed to an insane asylum, so I guess that was as good as prison."

"Why did you kill those women?" Thea asked. "Why did you put that woman in the wall in my bedroom?"

"Jeez, Thea," Drew said, frowning. "You sure ask a lot of questions for someone in no position to do so. All his life, all

Erik wanted was his mom. He was five when she died. He missed her. After he met you I thought maybe you'd be the woman to take her place. I mean, he was an adult man, after all, he shouldn't need his mommy. But then you let him down, too.

"Erik and I shared everything. When he told me what he'd learned about the Reflesh Procedure it seemed like the perfect way to bring his mother back. Find a girl with blonde hair and graft mom's face on her. Voila!"

Thea suppressed a shudder. "And Steiner?"

"He got in Erik's way. Tried to ruin his career. Meeting you boosted Erik's career exponentially, but without you, it would be taken away. If you were gone Erik knew enough to still go on and do surgeries. He didn't need you."

"He didn't need you, either," Thea retorted. "You needed him but he was his own man." She watched as Drew's face changed from casual scorn to a barely repressed anger. Then he smiled in a way that made her blood run cold.

"Unfortunately, Erik's dead now, thanks to you. So neither of us need you anymore. Now pick that worthless hag up and both of you get to the bedroom."

Thea started to rise, lifting the woman as best she could from her slouched position on the sofa. Drew watched with grim amusement at their effort.

"Come on," he urged, "you can do better than that. You managed to get out of your bedroom wall, didn't you?"

At Thea's startled look he chortled, "Yep! Me again!"

She chose to ignore his glee, instead concentrating on moving the young woman into the bedroom where she prayed she could form a plan for escape. Then without warning the girl projectile vomited, splashing both her and Drew with blood spattered bile.

"Stupid fucking bitch!" Drew shouted, glancing down at his clothes. He grabbed a grimy dish towel from the kitchen and ran it under the tap, the hatchet balanced precariously under one arm. He began to mop at the front of his shirt while the weapon began to slide just a little. Thea seized the moment.

In one movement she dropped the girl at her side and leapt behind Drew, grabbing the hatchet's handle from behind and jerking it away from him. Then she stood between Drew and the girl, the hatchet raised in a defensive position. He glared at her.

"Okay, the tables are turned just a bit," Thea said. "Get outside." Drew glowered, but obeyed, moving through the front door.

Thea did not dare to take her eyes off him but as she passed the girl on the floor she whispered, "Don't worry. I'll get you out of here."

When they were both outside the house, Thea said, "Get in the back seat of my car."

At first Drew looked as if he didn't understand what she meant. She repeated her words. He stumbled toward the rental car, glancing back every couple of seconds, but she kept behind him a safe distance. When he'd gotten into the car she clicked the locks, which also set the alarm. It wouldn't stop him but it would give her enough time to react if he were to try to escape.

With her eyes still glued to him she pulled her cell phone from her pocket with one hand, the hatchet safely ensconced in the other. She glanced down and quickly pressed 911.

"I'd like to report a murder," she said, staring at Drew as she gave them the address. Then she hung up. That should get them here in a hurry, she thought. Drew glared at her from the back seat of the car, leaning forward as if he was about to open the door. She saluted him with the hatchet, swinging it around her head a few times like an enraged Viking. He fell back against the seat cushions.

Then a whimpering came from the direction of the cabin. Thea half-turned and saw the young woman crawling across the front steps of the cabin toward her, one hand outstretched in a silent plea. Thea took several running steps to help her when without warning she was hit from behind. Her cell phone flew from her hands and she was thrown, face-first into the dirt, the phone trapped beneath her. Winded and terrified, she glanced toward the car and Drew. But he wasn't in the car anymore. *And where on earth was the hatchet?*

Then she saw it. In his rush to attack her, Drew had stumbled and fallen on the sharp edge of the blade. As he lay spread-eagled and prone, the hatchet, embedded in his chest as it had been on the chopping block, elevated his body inches above the rough dirt. Only now it was soaking in his blood.

Thea rolled over to one side and grabbed her cell phone. She saw Joe's name on the speed dial and pressed the button, praying that she'd reach him on the first ring. When he answered she sighed with relief as she gave him the address.

"Joe," she said, her voice shaking, "I've got another job for you. Call Jonathan and tell him I know where he can get a great deal on a used car."

Far off in the distance, the approaching crescendo of sirens was the sweetest music she'd ever heard.

ABOUT THE AUTHOR

Leigh Goodison is the author of *Wild Ones*, a coming of age/young adult novel, the nonfiction handbook *The Horse Trailer Owner's Manual,* and *Goodies from the Great White North*, a recipe book/cooking memoir.

Leigh grew up in the Lower Mainland, Okanagan, and Shuswap regions of British Columbia, Canada. Before she turned to writing and editing full-time, she spent many years working in the medical and legal professions.

Leigh's articles, short stories, essays, and poetry have appeared in literary magazines and newspapers across North America.

Currently she lives in Washington state.

www.leighgoodison.com